Soul Lost
by
Beth Warstadt

Soul Lost

Cover Photo by
Tereshchenko Dmitry
through Shutterstock

Beth Warstadt

Dedication
To Bonnie who first believed in me
To Michelle who made it better than it was

To Steve, Kevin and Brian who give everything meaning

Soul Lost

Inscription on the statue of Alfred the Great in his birthplace, Wantage, England:

Alfred found learning dead
And he restored it.
Education neglected,
And he revived it.
The laws powerless,
And he gave them force.
The Church debased,
And he raised it.
The land ravaged by a fearful enemy,
From which he delivered it.

Alfred's name will live as long
As mankind shall respect the past.

From Asser's <u>Life of King Alfred</u>:

Then the aforesaid revered king, Alfred, but at that time occupying a subordinate station, asked and obtained in marriage a noble Mercian lady...

Beth Warstadt

The Beginning

January 840 AD
Wessex, southern Britain

Merlin leaned back on the bench, stretching his long legs and using the wall of the house as a backrest. Even in this coldest winter month, the bright sunlight warmed his cheeks and glowed through his closed eyes. No matter what time or place he visited on Earth, he always chose this same appearance. He liked to appear old enough to look wise, allowing his dark brown hair to be streaked handsomely with gray. His body was always tall and virile, and he always moved with strength and confidence.

Contentment warmed his spirit as the sun warmed his body. He looked down at two-year-old Alfred playing near his feet in a puddle. The child was slapping his hands in the mud and laughing at the patterns the spatters made on his clothes. So bundled in his clothing that he could hardly move, the young prince was managing nonetheless to make quite a mess of himself. Merlin was glad to see it. Children need to be messy, he thought philosophically. It connects them to their Earth.

This part of the Earth is particularly beautiful, Merlin continued to muse, drinking in the landscape before him. He loathed Sir Hugh, the lord this manor, but he had to give him credit for choosing the perfect site for his house. It was set on a small hill nestled at the edge of the New Forest and blessed with a panoramic view of broad meadows and distant water. The setting not only gave them a magnificent view, but it also made their defenses almost impenetrable as they could see any attack coming for many leagues. True, the forest offered cover to any who sought to steal upon them from the rear, but an attack from this vantage was extremely unlikely. The woods carried the aura of magic, and they were widely feared to be home to a legion of mischievous creatures and malicious spirits. The people of this time were so superstitious that even the marauding Danes would not brave its dark mysteries. The forest offered the manor more security than any amount of fortification ever could.

Merlin had adopted this dark forest as his home. Rumors whispered behind closed doors and secret-shielding hands speculated wildly about where he had come from and what he did in those woods. In fact, people knew him by two different names: Merlin Emrys when he walked among them as a wise, mystical sage; and Merlin Wylde when he disappeared into the enigmatic shadows. He was greatly amused by the 'shocking' stories he had heard of wild orgies with wood nymphs, spells cast to make inanimate objects walk and talk, and potions brewed to make simple folk throw off their clothing and run naked through the market. The people of this time would never understand that he was not human; he was not even from this universe. Almost all of them believed the Earth dropped off at the edge of the great sea, and the sky existed like a rainbow from point to point on a flat earth. It would be pointless to try to describe a different universe to them when they had no concept of 'universe' at all.

Although he liked humans very much, he relished his mysterious reputation. It was useful to have them be wary of what he might do. That fearful respect gave extra weight to his opinions and counsel.

Merlin smiled fondly at little Alfred. A child so young could not understand that the event taking place inside this house would be the most important of his life. In his time travels Merlin had discovered that Alfred would be a great king. He would be a groundbreaking law maker and a stunning defender of justice for all of his citizens, not only the rich and not just the men. His reign would be a model for governments into the 21st century. But of all the magnificent moments he would experience, of all of the remarkable things he would achieve, this day was the most significant one of his entire life. Many people achieve greatness in their lives, but far fewer find a soul mate with whom to share it. When Merlin had met Alfred the king in a future time, he had also met Alfred's queen; the queen being born as Alfred sat there making a mess in the mud. He had observed them as adults long enough to see how often they bowed their heads together in private conversation, brushed hands, or leaned toward one another in affectionate unity. That kind of love was a rare find indeed. Merlin was filled with joy for him that the child was too young to feel for himself.

From the corner of his eye, Merlin caught a mist rising in the nearby woods. A mist on such a cold, clear day? It was too late for the sun to be burning off the morning frost. As he watched, it grew in size and began to move away from the forest. It moved as though it was alive, as though it had intelligence, as though it had intent.

Merlin moved futilely into its path, hoping his body would block it, but knowing that it would not. As its first fingers touched his face, dread grabbed his insides and squeezed every breath from his body. He had been touched by an evil that was all too familiar. That mist was unmistakably Malcolm, enraged and consumed with revenge.

Merlin grabbed Alfred and ran into the house. Inside everything appeared as it should, and the bustle of activity in the room deterred him from sounding any sort of alarm. When he saw how Kathryn was straining in her labor, he knew that there was nothing that could be done. She couldn't be moved, and no one was about to leave her. Merlin stayed out of the way, holding his breath and trying to stem the danger by the sheer force of his will.

It was plenty hot enough to make the body sweat, in spite of the cold, clear January day. Half dozen women moved with purpose from one task to the next preparing to care for the newborn baby and her mother. A fire roared in the huge fireplace making shadows jump and dance on the stone walls and their beautifully embroidered tapestries.

The woman lying on the bed, Kathryn, wife of Sir Hugh of Eastlea and lady of this manor, was sweating most of all, straining to deliver a baby none too eager to leave her womb. It seemed as if the child knew some reason she did not want to come out that the adults could not guess.

Kathryn was so tired from her long labor that she was hardly aware of anything going on around her. Queen Osbera sat by the bed and held Kathryn's hand, wiping the exhausted mother's brow with a cool cloth. The queen's serene expression gave no indication that Kathryn was squeezing hard enough to crush the bones in her hand.

Mildred, the midwife, checked for signs of the baby. "I can feel her head, mi'lady. It won't be long now." Her calm words set off a frenzy of activity among the other serving women who gathered the hot water and hot towels from the fire. They put rags and blankets within easy reach and brought close the basket that would serve as the baby's bed.

'Her' head. Mildred spoke confidently of the baby as a girl because it was widely known that the wizard Merlin had predicted with confidence that the child would be female. Though she had not yet drawn her first breath, she was already betrothed to the youngest son of her mother's closest friend, the woman now holding her hand and wiping her brow. When Kathryn's daughter came of age she would be marrying Prince Alfred, fourth in line to be king of Wessex, son of King Ethelwulf and Queen Osbera.

Alfred was perfectly still in Merlin's arms, mesmerized by the activity and the moaning woman on the bed. He tightened his little arms around Merlin's neck, and Merlin held him tight to protect him against the impending catastrophe.

"Push, mi'lady," Mildred commanded. In this venue the old serving woman was in charge, and Kathryn tried hard to comply with the instructions that she barked with authority. Mildred had brought too many babies too count into this world, and she knew exactly what she needed to do. "Take a deep breath," she said in a soothing voice, "and push again."

Kathryn squeezed Queen Osbera's hand and pushed until her face was red and swollen like a balloon, blood vessels blue and bulging in her temple. This was not her first delivery, but it had been her longest and most difficult. This girl-child, so different from her boys, refused to be separated from her. She strained against the contraction, took a breath, and pushed again. "Here she comes. Here comes her head." Encouraged, Kathryn pushed with renewed vigor.

"Kathryn," said the Queen with encouragement and compassion, "you are almost done."

Finally, they heard the gargled cry of the first breath of life. Kathryn's whole body relaxed and for the first time since her labor began a whole day before, she smiled. "It is a girl?"

"Yes, mi'lady." Mildred said joyfully. "She is beautiful. She is perfect."

Kathryn looked up at Osbera to see her eyes filled with tears. "She is perfect, Kathryn," she said. "Absolutely perfect."

Mildred began to bundle up the red-faced, squalling infant. "She's eager to be with her mother. She wants none of me," she laughed.

Without warning, the mist began to seep into the room. It came through the very walls, needing no more than the tiny chinks between the wood and stone. Merlin watched helplessly as it grew in size and began swirling around like a ferocious storm. Slowly one and then another of the busy women shuddered at the sudden chill in the hot, steamy room. The mist broke its shape and sent tendrils to steal the breath from each of them in turn as it searched for its prey. There were no open windows and no open doors for such a thing to enter, but enter it had.

The mist found its quarry, momentarily creating a spinning vortex around the bawling newborn. As quickly as it had blown in it blew out through the apparently solid wall.

There was deafening silence.

Immediately Kathryn's body tensed. "Why did the baby stop crying?"

Everyone was frozen in place like statues. The horrible silence was replaced with soul-chilling wails. Mildred moved to look at her with tear-filled eyes. "The baby is dead, mi'lady."

"What!" Kathryn screamed searching frantically for her precious, long-awaited daughter. "No! It cannot be!"

"There was evil in that vapor, mi'lady. It sucked the life right out of her little body," Mildred choked out.

The Queen's face reflected Kathryn's horror like a mirror. "Oh my God… Oh Kathryn…"

The drama before him sent shudders through Merlin's body. Everyone but Kathryn was wailing. Even the Queen, whose reserve he had never seen breached, was shaking with the power of her sobs, her face buried in her hands. Kathryn had fallen back into her bed as though struck dead, vacant eyes staring unblinking into the fathomless void of her despair.

Merlin knelt by Kathryn's lifeless body, taking her limp hand and bringing it up to his face. A terrified Alfred clambered onto his mother's lap, and she clutched him to her, spilling her sorrow onto his little neck.

In the center of it all was the heartbreakingly still body of a perfect baby girl.

Chapter 1

September 868 AD
Wessex, Southern Britain

Alfred pounded across the earthen courtyard between his private chambers and the great hall of the castle. He hated it when Ethelbald summoned him, as though he was some underling, some servant, instead of the brother of the king. Whenever Ethelbald wanted him it was never for anything good, and so Alfred was working up some serious anger to be prepared. He hated being interrupted, he hated being summoned, and he hated his brother.

He pushed open the heavy oak door and strode into the enormous hall. He carried himself with the bearing of a king, even though his chance at the throne behind three brothers was poor. Although the youngest, he was the most regal of the four and stood several inches taller than the other three. The Spartan life he had chosen contrasted sharply with the excesses of his older brothers. His body was lean and muscular, his complexion clear. He had a full head of thick, dark brown hair that he kept short for the sake of ease. His eyes were sometimes blue and sometimes gray, but few saw any warmth of spirit there. The monks with whom he had spent most of his days since childhood had taught him chastity and piety, but they had no luck teaching him humility. Perhaps they would have had more success if Alfred had not been anointed as the spiritual son of the Pope by the Pope himself on a trip to Rome with his father. The Pope had been impressed with Alfred, and Alfred was impressed with himself.

Alfred paused briefly inside the door. The hall was of size to hold a small army. The floor of packed dirt was covered with straw that was swept away and replaced every few days. The rough stone walls were cold but solid. Only the right wall had windows, and those were at eye level and small so that they could be easily covered with a shutter in case of attack.

The distant wall was covered floor to ceiling with rich red velvet drapes ordered by the queen from her Frankish home. The drapes covered a hidden door behind which was the staircase up to the sleeping quarters of the king and queen.

The left wall had two large doors at either end, one leading out toward the kitchen, the other leading to the private quarters of the other residents of the castle: menservants and ladies-in-waiting on the ground floor; and members of the royal family up the stairs. Large, beautifully embroidered tapestries hung between and on either side of the doors. There were also tapestries on the back wall through which Alfred had entered. The women of their country were known as far away as Rome for their beautiful needlework. Their tapestries depicted the stories of legend and history with more artistry than even the best painters of their time.

Tables and benches were carried in and out according to their need. Currently there were two long rows of tables lined up and pushed together with benches down either side. It was a quiet time, and the hall was empty of most of the court and its serving people. The few girls who were serving the head table curtsied and twittered when they saw Alfred. He paid them no mind. He knew he was handsome, but it was a trivial matter, and he had no time for silly girls or romantic games.

The large round table at the far end sat permanently to serve the needs of the king. Instead of the usual benches, this table was surrounded by chairs, the two largest of which were reserved for the king and queen. Every seat was occupied. Ethelbald sat in his customary chair, and Alfred cringed to see his brother's wife, Judith, seated next to him. Formerly his step-mother, now his sister-in-law, always, it seemed, destined to be his queen, much had passed between them to create animosity on both sides, and whenever Alfred was called into her presence, it did not bode well for him. Judith and Ethelbald together only meant one thing: life-ruining devastation.

His two other brothers, Ethelbert and Ethelred, and several of the noblemen who had estates nearby occupied the other chairs. As always, except for mealtimes, they were pouring over the maps that covered the table, discussing strategies for defense against the ferocious invading Danes from the north.

Alfred could have predicted that this was what they were doing. He guessed that Ethelbald was about to send him off to Mercia again, to review the state of affairs up there. Mercia was the country immediately to the north of Wessex, and its security was the key to Wessex's defense. The Mercian king, Burhred, repeatedly sent requests for help, but Ethelbald didn't want to commit more soldiers until he had no choice. Their battles against invasion on every front had been long and hard these last years, seriously depleting the population of its youngest and strongest men. There were very few left to work the farms and produce necessary goods for both battle and everyday living. He did not want to waste the remaining men unnecessarily.

As a result of this situation, Ethelbald had been plaguing Alfred with frequent trips to the Mercian court and Mercia's northern border with Northumbria. Northumbria had fallen several months before, and its pious king had been brutally murdered as a threat of things to come. It was unusual to send a prince for such surveillance, risking a member of the royal family unnecessarily. These tasks were usually accomplished by trusted agents of the king, ambassadors who had served well in battle and had the experience to size up the situation and offer good advice to both sides. Ethelbald never sent Ethelbert or Ethelred. He sent Alfred because it showed that he was held in low regard. Though Mercia had once been the premier kingdom of Britannia, it had been weakened by years of poor leadership, and its court was now crude, barbaric and vulgar. This particularly offended Alfred, who was obsessively devoted to his own piety. As a result, it gave Ethelbald great joy to send him there.

When Ethelbald saw Alfred standing by the door, he got up from his chair. "Ah, Alfie," the king greeted him with insincere enthusiasm, his booming voice filling the hall and reverberating off the stone walls, "I am glad to see you." His face looked pleasant enough, but his eyes were cold blue steel.

Nearly two decades separated the two brothers. Two decades and a world of ideas. The king had explored all of the pleasures he felt life had to offer——the pleasures of food and drink and sport, the company of willing women, the companionship of rowdy men——and he neither understood nor respected Alfred's love of books and study. He kept him close because of Alfred's gift for strategy and his prowess on the battlefield. When they were at war, the two men were of one mind. Alfred was sure on a horse, quick on foot and matchless with a sword. In-between battles, however, the king's best use of his little brother was as entertainment, offending his righteous sensibilities and trying to humiliate him before the court.

"What do you want? I was in the middle of something." Alfred did not pretend a pleasant demeanor. There was no point. He and his brother had everything out in the open, without pretense of esteem or affection. Some thought it would have served Alfred's interests better had his attitude been more agreeable, but he did not care what anyone else thought.

"Good news, little brother," Ethelbald said with affected cheerfulness.

Alfred detected the menace underlying the words and was put on his guard. "Good news for you or good news for me?" he asked suspiciously.

"Why, good news for all, of course." Ethelbald swept his arms about as if he was the most beneficent of rulers, but he was smirking with a mischievous grin.

Damn, Alfred thought, this is going to be bad. "And that is…?"

"You're getting married," the king answered with great glee.

"Married to whom?" The nice head of steam Alfred had worked up had been a drop in the bucket that was now filled to overflowing with his rage.

"To the daughter of the Mercian king, you lucky dog," Ethelbald laughed. He had rendered a masterful blow to Alfred, and he knew it.

"Elswith? You are not serious?" Alfred growled, knowing that he was. "Elswith is crude and vulgar," he said haughtily, "and the very thought of her makes me sick. When I was there last she hardly ate at all but drank mead and apple wine until she could not even stand." He did not add that the last time he had seen her she was having her way with some young serving man on the table in the dining hall and looking brazenly at Alfred to see how he would react. "I will not marry her, Baldy," Alfred said with derision. "She will not bring Wessex honor or esteem." Or me, he thought. She will not bring honor or esteem to me.

The king's expression darkened and the mock joviality fell away from his face. "I believe that you will, Alfie. No matter what you call me," he spat, "I am your king. And I command you to marry the Mercian princess."

"You and the boys," Alfred replied indicating his other two brothers, "play the political game and play it well, God help you. Do not bring me into it. I have other things to do, more important things than to attach myself to that wench."

"Northumbria is fallen, and Mercia is all that stands between us and invasion by the Danes," replied Ethelbald. "You have been there. You have seen for yourself the sorry state of affairs."

"If you need Mercia's resources in the family, marry her to Rupert. They are perfect for each other." Rupert was their cousin, the son of their father's sister. He had no interest in anything but drinking and wenching, and princess or not, Elswith was a wench.

"Burhred doesn't want Rupert," Ethelbald said firmly. "He has seen that you are a capable manager and leader of men. He feels that you could change things up there and save them from the same fate that befell Northumbria. Much as I hate to admit it, I believe he is right."

"Then pick another bride," Alfred said trying to keep the pleading tone from his voice. "What about her cousin, Grace? She is a pious woman who spends her days in prayer and meditation, cloistered from the excesses of the court."

"Elswith is his daughter. Burhred insists that she be married first." Ethelbald chuckled and exchanged a knowing glance with his wife. "And rightly so, for how else will he find her a husband? Besides, Grace has taken her vows and joined the order of sisters at the abbey there."

"And so I too have taken a vow. I do not join the order only because I cannot forsake killing." Alfred's eyes flashed. "That I do for you, and for our people. You need me to fight. You need me to lead." Alfred tried to hold on to his haughty attitude. "Ethelbald, no matter what our differences, I have served you well. Do not do this."

"Alfred, the good of the kingdom must prevail," Ethelbald replied, unyielding. "Mercia needs us. They need our troops, and they need our resources to fortify themselves and fend off these attacks. In return they are willing to be subjugated to us and pay us tribute." Ethelbald's eyes flashed. "We also need their resources. We also need their men. We need them as a buffer between us and devastation. All this we get for one reasonable price. You." Ethelbald's tone allowed no room for argument.

Elswith, My God! Alfred groaned inwardly. How could he stand it? He tried to imagine himself having to look at her thin face with its leering grin and puffy eyes every day. He could stay away, of course, stay out with the men as much as possible, and even sleep with them in their encampments. Perhaps he could hide out in the monastery with the monks. He could give orders for those brothers to take up his literary cause and continue his work, in the same way that he had the brothers here working day and night on transcriptions and translations.

He would be expected to make a family with her. Burhred had no sons, and he would most certainly be looking for grandsons to be his heirs. In the time he had spent in Mercia, she had flirted shamelessly with him, but Alfred could barely stand to be in the same room with her. Repulsion gathered in his stomach and threatened to explode through his mouth. How could he allow such a woman to be the mother of his children? Children? Children with Elswith? He could only imagine what little wild beasts they would be. "I have made a vow of chastity, Ethelbald," he repeated. "I cannot marry."

Ethelbald looked darkly amused. "Your responsibility to me overrides any vows you have made to others, brother, even God. Why would a man take such a vow? Can it be that you prefer the company of young men?"

"That would explain a lot, wouldn't it?" Judith teased. She was taking particular pleasure in the situation.

Alfred found this so offensive that he thought his head was going to explode. To suggest that he, who sought always to live a God-like life, would have such impure and unnatural longings! The truth was that Alfred had drives and desires the same as any other man, but he took great pride in the way he had learned to press down those thoughts and divert that energy into God's work. He carefully avoided the company of tempting women and plunged immediately into the closest project at hand whenever such temptations arose.

Looking around the table Alfred could see that everyone present was taking great satisfaction at his discomfort, so he took a deep breath and fought to regain his composure. Ignoring his brother's remark, he replied through gritted teeth, "I have important things to do, Your Highness. I have no time for marriage."

Although Alfred was taller, Ethelbald was more massive. He moved toe-to-toe with Alfred and tried to intimidate him. Alfred would not back down. The two brothers locked eyes as though there was no one else in the room. "You have nothing more important to do than what I tell you to do, little brother," Ethelbald spat. "I am your king. You will marry her."

Without breaking his gaze, Alfred seethed, "I hate you."

"Yes, I know," Ethelbald said glaring, "but I don't care. You will do as I say." Turning around, he walked away, dismissing

Alfred as though he was of no more importance than a stable boy. "The wedding is one month from today."

Anger flashed red in Alfred's eyes as he tried to bore a hole in his brother's back. Finally, he turned on his heel and stormed out of the room.

Chapter 2

It was not easy to slam the heavy oak door of his private chamber, but the power of Alfred's anger strengthened him. He paced like a wild animal in a cage.

Alfred's room was a mirror of the man. It was a large room, with the same rough stone walls and earthen floor that made up the rest of the castle. His walls, however, were not covered by the usual tapestries or draperies. They were bare and stark and cold and made his room seem larger than the others. This impression was further accentuated by the lack of furnishings. In place of the huge beds favored by the rest of the royal family, Alfred had the narrow cot of a monk. He also had a monk's desk with vellum, containers of colored paste and reeds of various lengths with points of various widths. The only decoration was the jeweled sword given to him by the Pope, which hung over the fireplace. His battle-marked chain mail and helmet perched on an unobtrusive chair in the corner as though ready to charge into battle on their own. His real weapons, swords and bows, were kept sharp and ready in a stand next to the chair.

Neither his father nor his brothers had any empathy for Alfred's love of reading and learning. Only his mother had recognized his unusual intellect, gifting him with a small literary volume shortly before her death when he was five years old. His brothers respected only his great prowess as a soldier, never realizing that his gift for strategy and quick thinking on the field was the result of a well-trained mind. King Ethelbald had no understanding of his brother's need to translate great texts into their native tongue, but he tolerated it as long as Alfred was at his beck and call whenever and wherever he wanted him.

Alfred had been twelve when he made the trip to Rome with his father, the trip that changed his life. He saw Britannia for the first time as the world saw it. It was considered an outland, backward and primitive, but important. Very, very important. It was the center of control for the empire's frontier, the last Roman stronghold against invasion from the wild barbarians in the north. Five hundred years after the withdrawal, Rome still felt its loss keenly, and the Pope had been eager to increase his influence there. The Frankish king, only two leagues across the Channel, had pushed to increase his own power and influence by marrying his fourteen year-old daughter, Judith, to Alfred's aging father. When the old man died, Judith had quickly moved to insure that her influence would continue by sinking her claws into her stepson and the next king, Ethelbald.

These experiences created in Alfred an overwhelming desire that Britannia, with Wessex at its head, should become united into a strong power in its own right, independent of all other influences. He felt that one important method for achieving this goal was to make their native language the primary language of all the British Isles. Everyone should speak and read "Anglish." In addition to this he was determined that all the great works of literature, all the important scripture, and all of the history of his people should be written down in their native tongue, raising it to the same level of esteem as Greek and Latin.

Alfred had committed his life to accomplishing this task with an obsession that precluded all but the most essential of other occupations. Except for the commands ordered at his brother's whims, he divided all of his time between making Wessex's troops the most capable, fearsome fighting force in the world and converting all available literature into their native tongue. His "Pope's spiritual son" status had given him a significant amount of authority among the clerics, and he had committed a legion of monks to combing texts in all languages for references to the Angles, the Saxons or the Britons. On his own desk was a copy of the journals of Julius Caesar, from which he was gathering the earliest continental impressions of Britannia. It was the very foundation of his life's mission: to unite all Britannia under one king; to bring her into prominence as a world power; and to secure her place in history.

Marriage certainly did not fit into his plans.

Determined to nurture and relish his anger, he ignored the knock on his door. This intruder was bold, however, and walked in without invitation. It was Merlin.

"Go away, old man."

Merlin was amused. "I heard of Ethelbald's command. Elswith is hardly an appealing bride for you."

Merlin's attitude aggravated Alfred's anger. "I'm so glad my discomfort provides you with entertainment. I do not find this situation funny. I wish I could pound Baldy's face until you couldn't tell his eye holes from his nose holes."

"Not a very Christian sentiment, my pious friend."

"I will seek God's forgiveness when my anger has passed. If this anger passes before I die that is. If not, I will simply have to rely on my good works and God's great mercy."

Merlin's amusement faded. and his expression became serious. "I have something of great importance to discuss with you, Alfred."

"Not now," Alfred said firmly. "I am not in the mind for it."

Merlin raised himself up, giving off an aura of the power he mostly kept hidden. "Yes, now, boy. It pertains to the issue at hand." His tone left no doubt that he would not be denied.

"What then?" Merlin's unusual display had captured Alfred's attention.

"Come with me to Kathryn's. I will explain there."

"Kathryn's? Why?" Kathryn was the only person Alfred truly cared about. She had stepped in to fill the void left by his mother's death, and she had been his only source of love and affection throughout his life. No matter how self-righteous and distant he was with everyone else, he always treated her with love and respect. Currently, however, he was not of a mind to see even her.

"Trust me," replied Merlin. "This is something you will want to know. Even now. Especially now."

Alfred thought of refusing. He had never found Merlin prone to exaggeration, however, and he was unusually emphatic in this matter.

They rode quickly to Kathryn's manor. It was a large house, indicative of the size of the estate. Her two sons had divided the lands when Sir Hugh died, and they had built their own houses, leaving her to amble about the big old manor by herself. It was a lonely life, but she preferred it to the excesses and intrigues of the court. It was no secret that she did not like Judith, and not only because she had taken the place of Alfred's mother and her good friend, Queen Osbera. Judith was conniving and manipulative, and Kathryn did not trust her. She found it more prudent to simply stay home.

Merlin and Alfred found Kathryn sitting between a blazing fire and an open window using the light from both to work diligently on some sewing. "What a pleasant surprise," she said looking up. "To what do I owe this unexpected visit?"

When she saw the expression on Merlin's face, she dropped her work to the floor. "What is it?" she said, her voice filled with concern.

Merlin moved to Kathryn's chair and knelt before her, gently taking her hand and kissing it, disregarding Alfred's presence. Even with his normal lack of sensitivity, Alfred was taken back by the way they looked at each other. Has she always looked at him like that? he wondered. Has he always gazed so at her? How did I miss it? My God, are they? No, surely not. But that look, the power of it. It was as though he was watching them kiss passionately, but only with their eyes. Alfred was stunned. Seeing them together all these years, how had he missed it? Was he stupid or blind or were they merely good at hiding it? They were lovers? But when had this started? Had it been so all along? Kathryn was so pure and so moral. How could this be?

"Kathryn, I have something to tell you, something I have kept from you for a long time," Merlin began. He turned to acknowledge Alfred. "Sit down, Alfred. This is important to you both."

Merlin stood and gathered himself. After a moment, he began, addressing Alfred first. "Long ago Kathryn gave birth to a third child, a baby girl, who died at birth. I had seen the future, one of you and that child, growing up together, intertwined like two roots living strong together as the foundation of a powerful oak tree, ruling a united Britannia. When that baby died immediately after she was born, I knew that something unnatural had intervened. The future had changed. The power of your reign had been compromised."

Kathryn bowed her head. This was obviously a very painful memory for her. She looked up when Merlin addressed her, and Alfred could see tears sparkling in her eyes.

"Kathryn, I never told you that I suspected that she lived. I could still feel her presence. I felt certain that her spirit had been moved but not sent back to God. After all, her body had not actually been killed; her life force, her spirit, had been removed. I searched and searched traveling through time and space looking for the spirit of the girl I had seen. Finally, I have found her."

Suddenly Kathryn's entire demeanor changed. She moved to sit on the edge of her chair, her eyes burning as though with a great fever. "My God, Merlin, how can that be?"

"Her essence was hurled through time, into the distant future, into the body of a child who was supposed to be stillborn. That baby was supposed to have died, and your baby was supposed to have lived."

Kathryn's voice was desperate. "Where is she? Have you seen her?"

"I have..." Merlin shook his head and drifted off.

"What?" Kathryn begged. "What is it? Tell me."

"She has not had a happy life, Kathryn. Her mother there never wanted her and has treated her badly. She has never known a father or any family at all. She has done everything she was supposed to do, but she has no friends to speak of. She is alone and unloved. She needs us as badly as we need her, but she has no idea that we exist."

Tears spilled out of Kathryn's eyes. "Oh, Merlin, my baby. My precious baby girl. Who would do such a thing?"

"Don't you know?"

She spoke her answer so quietly that Alfred could hardly hear her. "Malcolm."

"Yes. As an evil act it was magnificent. It ruined your life," he turned to Alfred, "and your life, and the child's life and her mother's life in the future. Now we are all miserable and the one responsible has congratulated himself with great glee for these twenty-eight years."

Alfred took exception. "I would hardly call my life ruined. Without the distraction of a woman, I have committed my life to God's work. This whole thing started because I did not want to be married, remember?"

Merlin shook his head again. "Alfred, for someone so intelligent, sometimes you are incredibly short-sighted. Not all of God's work requires that you live like a monk. In the not too distant future, you will be king, but now you lack the compassion and passion to lead your people wisely. You are educated but you are not wise. Evil will enjoy great success under your rule as you ignore the needs of your people to pursue that which you mistakenly believe is your mission from God. You need this woman to make you a whole person and a great king."

"How do you know what God has planned for me?" Alfred asked arrogantly.

"Do you think only humans know God, you great fool?" Merlin's tone was imperious and impatient. "Do you suppose you are the only godly being God has created? Just because I am not a monk does not mean I am not a servant of God."

"Fine," Alfred replied, unnerved by Merlin's tone, "God's plan for me was meant to include this woman. She is not here. What do you propose we do about it now?"

Merlin took a deep breath. "We have to go and get her."

Alfred was taken back. "Go and get her how?"

"We'll go to her time and persuade her to come back with us." Merlin paused, "You will have to be a good bit more charming than usual."

Alfred ignored the last remark. "You can do this?"

"How do you think I found her?"

"Yes, but you are…you know…you," Alfred stammered uncomfortably. "You are a wizard. I am a man. How am I supposed to accomplish such a thing?"

"I can make it happen."

Alfred resisted. Although Ethelbald's plans for him were humiliating, the king's apprehension about invasion was well founded. In spite of Alfred's passion for more erudite things, he had to acknowledge that he was a gifted military leader and his brother, his country, needed him. There were legions of men that must be made ready to fight, and their preparation was his most pressing task. His brothers could train them to fight, but only Alfred could teach them to think. The enormity of that mission allowed little enough time for the enormous library of scrolls and books at the monastery library that needed to be read through and translated. And, to be honest, he was uneasy about the prospect of participating in Merlin's magic. "Why can't you do it yourself? Why do you need me?"

"Because she is an adult now, and her free will is fully developed," Merlin said struggling to regain his patience. "Her spirit cannot be moved against her will as it could when she was an infant and so freshly come from God. I don't think she will believe me, but given the chance she will discover her bond with you and be willing to trust us."

"And suppose she agrees," Alfred said skeptically. "Then what? Her spirit no longer has a body here to occupy. She has no place here."

"No," Merlin replied. "You are wrong. She does have a place here. A place that has been empty for twenty-eight years. Her absence has had far more impact than you know. The body she had here would serve no purpose now, as she is not that person. The person she has become is tied to the body she has occupied for the last twenty-eight years. That is the way she will return to us."

Kathryn broke her silence. "Alfred, please. Please go with him. Please try to bring her back."

Although he was never indecisive about anything, Alfred felt indecision now. Merlin's proposal was full of folly. He had no desire to find this woman. He had much better things to do with his time than run off on some wild goose chase. There was no question that he did not want to do this.

On the other hand, Kathryn had rarely asked anything for all of the years of love and devotion she had given to fill the void left by his mother. Her pleading eyes would not bear his refusal.

"All right," he said reluctantly, "I will go. I do not have faith in our success. I do not believe that this woman can make much of a difference in my life that is already so full. But I'll do it," he said quietly, looking at Kathryn."I'll do it for you."

Chapter 3

For Alfred and Merlin on young, strong horses, Stonehenge was not even a day's ride from the castle at Winchester. Each hill was lower than the last, until finally they came to the broad flatness of the Salisbury Plain. It wasn't long before the stones came into view. They appeared small at first because of the distance, growing larger as Merlin and Alfred approached. Finally, the two men were dwarfed by the enormous rocks.

Merlin loved Stonehenge, loved it more than any other place anywhere. Here was the confluence of all things, all times, all places. He could sense the presence of countless other beings, the bridges to countless other universes.

"I don't like this place, Merlin. Never have. Do we have to be here?" Alfred said shortly.

Merlin smiled. "You have nothing to fear here, Alfred. This is a place of great, positive energy. The spirits you feel here mean you no harm."

"Spirits," Alfred snorted with an attempt at derision. His nervousness was not well disguised, particularly to Merlin who knew him so well.

"We should rest tonight," Merlin said. "We need to be rested and alert for tomorrow."

Alfred dismounted and removed his horse's bit and saddle so that it could graze on the plentiful grass around them. He then busied himself building a fire and preparing food.

Merlin also dismounted and freed his horse, but, he was so moved by the aura of the place that he walked from stone to stone touching and stroking them with great reverence. He slipped into a trance-like state, becoming one with the unseen others present there, forgetting his human companion.

When the food was ready, Alfred called Merlin from his reverie. As they sat together, Alfred asked the questions that had been hounding him. "Merlin," he began, "why do we have to be here? What does this place have to do with us?"

"Stonehenge is a bridge, Alfred, a bridge to other worlds. A bridge across which we must pass to travel to the future."

"How?"

Merlin sighed and searched for the right words. Alfred was unusually patient, waiting silently for his answer. Finally Merlin began, "I am from another place, Alfred, a place, not of this world. Surely this does not surprise you."

Alfred nodded uncomfortably.

"We must pass through the place that I am from to reach the place where she is."

"Why?"

"Stonehenge is a bridge from my home to yours, and there are other bridges that lead to other places and other times," Merlin answered. "We will go to the bridge to her time and cross there."

Alfred thought about this. "What is it like there, where you are from?"

"It is nothing like here," said Merlin looking around. "There is nothing to touch, nothing to see, nothing to hear. We have no bodies, no land, no water, no sky."

"Then what is there?" Alfred asked with a mixture of curiosity and anxiety.

"First you will notice the darkness," said Merlin, "not as though you were blind, but as though you had no eyes at all. You will notice that you feel very light as though the substance of your body has been stretched out so that it seems to float. Then you will hear voices, many voices, inside your mind, and you will be able to think of me and hear my voice specifically. Although you have no mouth for speaking, you will think your thoughts and I will hear them."

Alfred tried to follow what Merlin was saying. "With no body, you must have no pain, no hunger, no growing old, and no death."

"It is true that we do not suffer from the myriad of troubles that humans do. But we do have a certain physical presence. We die eventually, but our life spans are extremely long by human standards. Virtually immortal."

"Then why become human?"

Merlin sighed. "Because for all the pain and suffering, human bodies allow for an intensity of experience of which we are otherwise incapable. For some of us, the positive experiences outweigh the negative. Others prefer not to try. But there are many things about this world that I like. I like touching things," his horse came up and nuzzled him. He reached to stroke its nose, "like a horse's nose." He patted it firmly on its neck. "I like the senses of taste and smell, roast beef cooking or chicken stew or apple pie. Or the smell of the forest after rain.

"You do not have these things?"

"It will be hard for you to understand or believe, my friend, but know that God the Creator did not begin or end with your world. There are other beings who live in the stars that you see, and other places which exist beyond your ability to sense them."

Alfred sighed. Though Merlin's explanation made a certain kind of sense, it was still hard for him to grasp. "Fine. How we are going to accomplish this 'travel through time.'"

"We will line up our path through the stones in a certain way using the position of the sun as our guide. Then we will walk through the space between the stones, but instead of coming out on the other side, we will step through into my universe."

Alfred looked perplexed. As Merlin had expected, the concept of a "universe" was difficult for him. "How long will it take?"

"Minutes," Merlin replied. He was trying to make the process sound easy. It was important that Alfred not panic during their trip. "Then we will re-enter the Earth in the girl's time."

"And what time is that?"

"About a thousand years from now."

Alfred thought about this. "Are things the same?"

Merlin laughed and shook his head. "No, no. It is very different. You will find it quite strange."

"How is it different?"

"You'll see. Don't worry. You are clever enough to find your way. There is one thing though," Merlin said as he stood up and stretched. "The language will be familiar because its roots are in yours, but it will not be similar enough for you to speak or understand without help. Close your eyes."

Alfred did as he was told. A serpent slithered in his brain and pushed around the substance of it in a way that made him dizzy. His eyes flew open wide. "What are you doing!"

"Shhhhh," murmured Merlin without breaking his concentration.

Alfred closed his eyes again and tried to focus on what was going on behind his eyes.

"There, now," said Merlin, opening his eyes and exhaling deeply.

What?" asked Alfred, breathlessly, "What did you do?"

"I merely made a minor change in your mind so that you can understand her when she speaks to you."

"How?"

"You'll see. No more questions now. It may be difficult to sleep, but you should at least try." Merlin lay down on his blanket, locked his hands behind his head and looked up at the stars.

Alfred could not even think of sleep. "Merlin, I must know this story. You must tell me more. If I am to believe in our cause I must understand."

Merlin sighed. "It all starts with Malcolm."

"Malcolm?" Alfred said incredulously. He knew that Malcolm was a wizard like Merlin, but not nearly so wise or powerful. He was little more than a mischief-maker, and Alfred had never given him much thought.

"Did you know that Malcolm was born human?" Merlin began. When Alfred shook his head, he continued, "I thought not. He was a person of exceptional gifts born to illiterate, dirt-poor peasants. Malcolm felt always that they were beneath him, and worse, that they were holding him back from achieving the success and wealth that he deserved. Determined to erase his birth identity and forge a new one more to his liking, he set his family's home on fire with them in it when he was thirteen. With no more feeling than a dead man, ignoring their screams and cries for help, he simply walked away. He headed for the nearest seat of government, the home of the king and his court, intent on taking whatever position was necessary to begin his climb to power.

"Somewhere along the way he chanced upon Kathryn. Her beauty, her grace, her kindness…what man could help but fall in love with her?" Merlin's eyes grew misty, his voice distant. Suddenly he recovered himself and resumed his story. "He decided instantly that he had to have her. He hovered around her for days, watching her when she came into town and secretly following her home. He would speak to her from time to time. She always responded kindly, but he could not make his way into her sincerest affections. When word spread that she was to be married to Sir Hugh of Eastlea, Malcolm was distraught. Frantic, he stopped her and begged her to run away with him. She was scared by both the passion of his plea and the danger she saw in his eyes, and so she refused, claiming only that she must do her duty to her father."

"Did you know her then?" asked Alfred.

"I did. She is beautiful now, but you should have seen her then. I couldn't blame Malcolm. No, I couldn't. Her golden hair encircled her face like an angel's halo, and her eyes sparkled as the stars in the heavens. Her sweet spirit was so filled with kindness and light, that wherever she went, her presence pushed away darkness and filled the earth with a vision of heaven."

Again, Alfred was amazed that their passion for each other had eluded him all these years, but he decided it was not the time to discuss that revelation."So she married Hugh," he said.

"Yes, but Malcolm didn't let that deter him. If he couldn't win her by human ways, he would find inhuman ones. He began to explore the dark side of magic, the controlling potions and spells. This is where Cronos comes in. Cronos is a being from my universe who also likes to interact with humans. But unlike me he wants to control and manipulate them like puppets on a stage. He sensed a valuable ally in Malcolm and his arrogant cruelty, and so he made an unusual offer. He offered to restructure Malcolm's body, to go through the long, painful process of turning him into a being from our universe, a "wizard" in human terms.

"Malcolm agreed eagerly, thinking he would simply turn Kathryn's heart and gain her devotion forever. But Cronos left out one little detail. No being can manipulate the heart of another against his or her will. God set up free will as the one thing common to every part of His creation. Every creature, every being has free will. There are ways to enhance certain attractions, certain emotions, but those emotions have to be in place before you do.

"After his return, Malcolm continued to follow Kathryn and speak to her in spite of her marriage. She was always kind and courteous to him, but kept her distance. While he was gone, she and I had become bound by a deep and enduring friendship. He became insanely jealous of us."

"You and Kathryn were only good friends?" Alfred asked slyly.

"Yes, of course. You know that we are still good friends," Merlin said suspiciously.

"Of course," Alfred replied as though he knew a secret that he wasn't telling. "Go on."

"We were two opposing satellites, Malcolm and I, circling Kathryn's beauty and grace. We watched as Hugh became abusive. We each saw the ugly bruises and marks left by his rough handling. We watched as she gave him first one son and then another, then as he lost interest in her and sought the company of other willing women. Let me tell you," Merlin's voice dropped, and he looked at Alfred intently, "that we were both outraged at the injustice. But that was where the similarity ended. I wanted to care for Kathryn, to give her the protection she deserved. Malcolm wanted to own her.

"Kathryn sought safety with me and avoided Malcolm's threatening presence. She and I became inseparable, though it was necessary to be discrete to avoid wagging tongues. Always I watched, often out of the sight of others, and whenever I could be I was by her side. If her husband was full of his cups and struck out at her, I was in the shadows, doing my best to use my powers to save her from harm. When all others seeking the favor of a powerful lord abandoned her as he did, I was her true friend. We shared a love of riding, a love of learning and a love of music, all of which enhanced our time together. I loved her, Alfred. I loved her more truly than I have ever loved anyone. I love her still." His voice overcome with emotion, Merlin paused.

"Seeing her affection for me enraged Malcolm and made him more determined than ever to have her. I offered her friendship, but he was willing to take extreme measures, to worship her, to take her away from all the hardships of her life. But there was nothing he could do to sway her heart. The more forcefully he tried, the more emphatically she resisted.

"Think of our surprise, both of us, when Kathryn became pregnant. Malcolm flew into a rage. How could she let Hugh back into her bed? Hugh abused her, and Malcolm wanted to worship her. Yet she let that great buffoon have his way with her and rejected Malcolm again and again. If he could not have her, he decided, no one could. He determined that child would never see the light of day."

Merlin gave a great sigh. "And that brings us up to right here. He snatched that child from our lives. He left Kathryn distraught and broken. If he wanted her to pay for not loving him, he found the most effective way to strike out at her. We can change that. We can bring her child back and return her to the place where she belongs. Now do you understand?"

Alfred sighed. "I understand that Malcolm is a lot more powerful and dangerous than I thought." He smiled a sly smile, "And now I feel a certain extra motivation to thwart his evil plan."

Merlin smiled back. Alfred didn't often reveal that he had a sense of humor, but it flashed through every now and then. He rolled over and stretched out on his back. "Sleep now, Alfred."

Alfred also rolled over. "Yes," he said unconvincingly.

Soul Lost

But Merlin heard no more from him that night.

Chapter 4

Alfred woke suddenly as the first rays of the rising sun hit his face. He rolled over to see that Merlin was already up and moving around. Sensing his urgency, Alfred was up and ready within minutes. As Merlin moved into position, Alfred asked, "What about the horses?"

"Hmmm?" Merlin replied distractedly. "The horses? They have food and water. They'll be fine. This is not on a common road. I doubt anyone will have the opportunity to steal them before we return."

Suddenly Merlin stopped and turned his full attention to Alfred. "Son, this is very easy and it will not hurt at all. I have told you what to expect, and it will be exactly as I said. Focus on my voice, and you will follow me. Do not try to follow any voice but mine. If you get lost, I will find you, but it will make our journey more difficult."

Alfred nodded without his usual arrogance. He shifted into soldier mode, ready to follow orders to the letter with a focus much admired even by his brothers. He followed Merlin toward the passage between the stones and saw nothing unusual there. He felt certain he would walk through and simply wind up on the other side. The next thing he knew Merlin had disappeared before him. Alfred followed quickly before he lost his resolve.

It took Alfred a few minutes to get oriented. There was darkness as Merlin had warned him, total blackness as though he had no eyes to see with. He could hear a cacophony of voices in his head, too many to tell what any of them were saying. Then he heard one voice loud and clear above the others. It was Merlin. "Focus on my voice, Alfred. I am right here with you."

Alfred tried his own voice. He had no way to speak aloud, so he tried to speak to Merlin with his thoughts. "I feel very strange."

"As you should. This is not your place; you do not belong here. I felt much the same way the first time I came to your world, but I got used to it after a time. You have no need to adjust to being here. Follow me, and let's be done with this."

Alfred was surprised to find that he could move with volition. He felt very light, as though he were a cloud moving through the sky. He sensed that they were passing other "clouds." As they did he picked up some of what was being said.

"Merlin," one said, "you have brought one of them here?"

"It was necessary," Merlin answered. "We must undo a wrong that has been done."

"But you know the laws," said another. "They are not to be in this place. They are not ready. They will not understand."

"He does not need to understand," replied Merlin. "We are merely passing through."

"Odin will not like it," said the first.

"Odin will understand," replied Merlin.

Alfred sensed that he should remain silent, so he simply listened and followed as he had been told. Soon he perceived that they were coming to an opening. He followed Merlin through.

He was immediately blinded by bright light, but as his eyes focused he realized it was only the sun. They had returned to the human world. At least he thought it was the human world. In some ways it was stranger to him than Merlin's world.

There were buildings everywhere, all smooth as though master craftsmen had made them. Merlin pulled him into the shadow of the building nearest them. Alfred's body seemed heavy and awkward as he adjusted once again to being earthbound.

"We must change our clothes," Merlin said in a low voice, speaking once again with his mouth. "Our clothing is so strange to them as to draw attention that we do not want."

"How shall we get these clothes?" Alfred asked copying Merlin's low tone.

"We shall steal them."

Alfred looked at him in alarm. "Steal them?"

Merlin shook this off. "In this case it is justified by the greater good."

Alfred, out of his element, saw no point in arguing. "Shall I grab one of these men as they go by?"

"No," Merlin chided. "There are rooms in the bottoms of these buildings where they wash their clothes. We shall take them from there unseen."

Alfred pictured himself having to render the laundresses unconscious and hoped that he could do it without killing them. When they entered the laundry, however, he saw that he need not have worried. There was no one there. Only a lot of very noisy, very large white boxes that seemed to be possessed by violent spirits.

Merlin walked up to one with a round window on the front through which Alfred could see the clothes tumbling as the inner chamber rolled over. Merlin opened the window and searched through the clothes, finally pulling out two pairs of pants and two shirts. "Lucky," he said. "I think I have gotten it right on the first try." He pulled Alfred into a nearby room with several very small rooms inside. There was much here that was unfamiliar to Alfred, and while he had some uncertainty, he was more curious than anything else.

"Go in there," Merlin pointed to one of the rooms, "and put these on. I will explain the rest when you are done."

The room was uncomfortably small, and its walls did not reach to the ceiling or to the floor. Alfred had some difficulty getting the door shut, but found that once he did he had enough room to move around and change his clothes. He wondered at the large white basin that occupied much of the space. As though reading his mind, Merlin said, "That large white basin is a chamber pot. Relieve yourself into it, and then push the silver handle." Alfred did as he was told and jumped at the loud rushing noise.

When he saw that his refuse had disappeared leaving behind no smell and requiring no one to empty it, he decided that it was a good thing.

The clothing was strange but comfortable. The blue pants were tighter than those Alfred normally wore, but not so tight as the leg wraps he usually wore under them. They allowed him freedom of movement, and they fit over his boots, so he decided he could live with them. He had never seen a zipper, but it did not take brilliance to figure out how it worked. The shirt was much softer than the linen he was used to, and the buttons up the front were familiar, though small. It was a tribute to his intelligence, adaptability and common sense that he dressed quickly and was ready to go without making Merlin wait.

Alfred bundled up his clothes and followed Merlin outside. Merlin returned to the shadow of the building and found a hiding place for their original clothes. "We will need these again when we return," he explained.

That task accomplished, he stood up and rubbed his hands together. "Now," he said with a smile, "to the task at hand."

As they walked down a smooth path that Merlin told him was made of "concrete," Alfred crinkled his nose at the smell. The air seemed stale and wrong. There was too much noise and too many people. These things, these contraptions--Merlin told him they were called cars, and they had replaced horses--he did not care for them one bit. They were loud, they were ugly, and they smelled bad.

He looked up and shaded his eyes against the sun. He had to admit that the buildings were interesting. Their edges were so smooth, and they were so high, and there were so many of them. Some of the architecture was very odd, and yet some brought visions of home.

Merlin stopped so suddenly that Alfred ran into the back of him. They faced a building that was more familiar by far than any of the others. It was made of rough stone, with a broad front entrance and turrets on either end. Alfred guessed that they needed the turrets to see over the closely packed buildings and defend the manor against invaders. The wide stairway leading up to the entryway was unlike those he knew at home, but he had seen some similar in Rome. Many of the windows were of stained glass, and he noted that the owner of this place must be very wealthy to have such things.

Merlin gave Alfred a few minutes to look around and take it all in. Then he explained, "We will find her here, in this library."

Alfred approved. She is in a library. That makes her better than Elswith already. Maybe this wouldn't be so pointless after all.

Chapter 5

September, 2002 AD
Southern United States

Isabel felt like a queen sitting on her high stool behind the circulation desk. It was her favorite time of day. The library was quiet in the afternoon, an unspoken break between the chaotic morning rush of determined, frantic students preparing for their classes, and the siege-type invasion of the after dinner crowd. The setting sun shone through the two huge stained-glass windows beaming a rainbow of light down on the collection of study tables gathered in front of her. The end of the rainbow, she thought, smiling to herself. She felt at home here. She belonged here. She cherished this place and gave thanks everyday for her job.

A lone couple sat at one of the study tables, heads together, oblivious to everything but their books and each other. With no one else manning the desk, and no one else sitting at the tables, Isabel was free to watch their interaction and wonder about them.

They were hardly putting on a public display of affection. Quite the contrary, they seemed totally absorbed in their work. Still, they were "aware" of each other, sitting with their elbows on the table so that their arms were touching, sitting with their chairs pulled so that their legs were touching. He found something to show her and put his hand on her arm to get her attention. Putting his arm across the back of her chair, he leaned into her to point out something in her book. She nestled into him as she listened to what he was saying, perfectly filling the space between his body and his arm. When she looked up at him to reply, her eyes ran over his entire face, focusing finally on his mouth as he spoke. He looked down at her the same way, and Isabel thought they might kiss, but when they looked around to see who would see, they saw Isabel sitting behind the desk and thought better of it. Isabel, of course, had looked away. She sneaked a sideways peek and saw the boy caress the girl's back before pulling his arm away and returning to his books.

Isabel closed her eyes and imagined them walking hand-in-hand across the dark campus after the libraries closed. There would be no need to speak. All of their thoughts would be focused on their entwined fingers. When they passed into the shadow of the Medical Arts building, he would lead her to a hidden bench. Setting their books aside, he would draw her close, and she would mold her body to his with her face at the perfect level, yearning to be kissed. Their eyes would close, and their mouths meet. Isabel imagined that their kisses were slow and passionate, and with her eyes closed she could almost feel what his lips must feel like on hers, full and soft and moist. She could imagine how the muscles in the arms that encircled her would be flexed to hold her close to him. She could feel the masculinity of his flat chest pressed against her soft feminine breast. The pounding of his heart against her side. The staccato drumming of her heart in her chest.

Isabel stirred from her reverie. Lucky girl, she thought. Isabel's mother had told her time after time that she was not the kind of girl that men were attracted to and that she would be a disappointment to anyone who got involved with her. She had nothing of interest to offer. She was too chubby for her short frame and too plain without make-up. She never did anything stylish with her hair that waved in all the wrong places and was an odd auburn color that looked even redder when the sun hit it just right. She got that hair from the father she had never seen, her mother said, and it was a real shame, because her mother's hair had been so lovely and dark before she turned gray. Isabel had long ago given up trying to tame it. She pulled it back in a ponytail which did not quite hold it all so several strands fell forward in her face. She had a habit of pushing them behind her ears to get them out of the way. It wasn't a very pretty way to wear it, but it was practical.

Isabel looked around and saw that the couple was leaving, passing two interesting looking men who had come in. She didn't want to stare at them, but a quick glance told her they were out of place. Somehow their presence unnerved her, even though they didn't look menacing. Her stomach twisted and abdomen seized in a way that nearly doubled her over. She turned away but kept them in the corner of her eye.

She noticed they were coming toward her. Their gaze on her was so intense that it made her even more uncomfortable, and she struggled for a professional demeanor as they arrived at the other side of the desk. She kept her face a blank, disinterested mask as her emotions swung wildly between fear and fascination. "May I help you?"

The older man spoke first. He was tall and handsome, and his demeanor was kind but confident. His medium brown hair was long and flecked with gray, and he had it pulled back in a ponytail much neater than hers. His age was difficult to gauge, but she guessed he was in his late forties or early fifties. His eyes were hazel and very warm, but intense. She could tell he had something important on his mind. "Isabel?" he asked, though he obviously already knew the answer.

She searched her brain for any memories that included this person and found none. "Yes?" she queried back, suspicious.

"We must converse with you about a matter of great importance. Join us, please?"

"Converse about what?" she asked and looked at the other man. Her mid-body seized again, this time like a deer in the headlights. He was so beautiful that she could not look away. He was taller and younger than his companion, probably around thirty. He had short, dark brown hair that seemed determined to fall out of place on his forehead. His gray eyes carried storms, frightening in their intensity, and she felt a little nervous about the thoughts that were coloring those eyes.

"It is of a private nature," the older man replied reclaiming her attention.

"Do I know you?"

"No. We have never met, but it is essential that we talk with you."

"It is, is it? Who are you?" she asked skeptically.

"My name is Merlin, and this is Alfred," the older man said confidentially.

"Merlin? King Arthur's Merlin? Merlin the Wizard?" The wonder she had been feeling was replaced with irritated scorn. "And Alfred? Who is he, Batman's butler? Come on." Isabel had a sense of humor, but she was ready to dismiss these two as she had no desire to be the butt of some practical joke.

The young man looked to the older one in confusion. "Batman?"

The older man shrugged as though it was of no importance. As he spoke again his manner was more urgent. "We must talk with you."

Isabel looked at them and thought about it. What were they up to? Was this a joke? Who would pull such a prank on her? Were these guys dangerous? How much danger could there be in walking around the desk and sitting at a table with them? "Julie," she called to the work-study student in the workroom, "I'm going to help these guys."

"'K," Julie replied absently, her nose stuck in a book, studying for mid-terms.

Isabel felt more nervous without the desk between them. She slid into a chair at one of the study tables, and they sat on the opposite side facing her. From the perch on her high stool they had seemed tall, but face-to-face they loomed over her like great cats waiting to strike. She felt outnumbered, overwhelmed and intimidated.

She searched for the right tone of voice. She decided confident with a hint of annoyance was the best way to go. "What is this all about?"

As Merlin talked, she glanced from time to time at Alfred and watched the play of emotions across his face. His arms were folded across his chest, and he looked as though he did not believe a word of what Merlin was saying. When he looked at her she detected something like disdain, and it was clear that he was unimpressed with her. Every now and then she thought there was a flash of kindness, but it would come and go as quickly as a bolt of lightening. My,my, she thought in spite of herself, he is handsome.

"Isabel," Merlin began, "have you ever had a sense that you don't belong here?"

"Belong here?" she replied, "In the library? No." She was not going to make this easy. He sounded like a recruiter, although she couldn't imagine what he would be recruiting her for.

"No, not here. I mean in your life. Have you ever felt that you don't belong in your life?"

Isabel twitched. Her mother had never been shy about telling her that she was expected to be stillborn. She had become pregnant accidentally during a one night fling when she felt angry and rebellious against her parents that involved too much drinking and not enough self-control. She had been relieved when she was told that the baby was not going to live. When Isabel was born alive, she added the innocent child to her grudge against her parents for forcing her into an untenable situation. Too proud to give the baby up for adoption, she blamed Isabel for ruining her life. I could have been successful, she would say, I could have had a career. I was smart. I had potential. Instead of a wonderful, exciting life I got you.

These men were total strangers to her. How could they know such an intimate thing? She felt queasy that someone she had never met should see into the darkest shadows of her heart and pull her most guarded feelings out into the bright light of day. "What an odd question. Why do you ask?"

"I'm going to tell you a story," Merlin said, "and I'd appreciate it if you'd let me tell the whole thing without interruption."

Isabel forced a sigh and an unconvincing, bored look at her watch. "Ok," she said, "I'll give you a bit."

Merlin gave a tolerant smile. She had the feeling that he could see right through her every deception and posture. "I'll do my best," he said, taking a deep breath and bracing himself against her skepticism. "Alfred here and I come from another, long ago time. Eleven hundred years ago to be more precise."

"You're time travelers?" she said with a skeptical laugh. Now she knew it was a hoax, maybe fraternity rush or something. But then, these guys looked a little old for that.

Merlin held up his hand for her to be quiet. "You said you'd let me talk."

"Right. Sorry," she replied, leaning back and crossing her arms over her chest. She exchanged a glance of shared suspicion with Alfred. Was it her imagination, or did she sense the tiniest bit of camaraderie with him? Perhaps they had skepticism as a common personality trait.

"Eleven hundred years ago as you mark time, a woman of noble birth was delivered of a daughter. This child was much anticipated because seers had foreseen her destiny intertwined with that of Prince Alfred," he gestured at his companion, who still sat with a steely glare and arms across his chest. "The king had so much faith in this vision that he betrothed Alfred to this girl before she was even born.

"Someone else did not want to see their union come about. Who?" Merlin asked rhetorically, then immediately answered his own question. "One filled with hatred and jealousy, determined to deny everyone else the happiness denied to him. One committed to furthering his own evil plans, who had, and has, the power to do such a thing. One filled with hatred for us all."

"Why does he hate us? What does he have the power to do?" asked Isabel, interested in spite of herself. True or not it was turning out to be a great story.

"Take the soul of that girl-child from the body of the newborn infant and cast her through time into the body of one who was never intended to be born." Merlin paused to allow the magnitude of this statement to sink in.

Isabel almost lost her composure. 'Never intended to be born.' If he was making this up, how could he know that? How could he be hitting so close? Was there any possibility that this was the truth? No way, she thought. This is not possible. In spite of her misgivings, Isabel uncrossed her arms and leaned forward on the table.

"That girl is you, Isabel. I have been searching through time and space for you for twenty-eight years, and now, here you are. We have come to get you and take you back with us."

'Take you back with us.' That phrase pushed all of her panic buttons. Isabel felt relatively safe sitting here in the library with them in her territory. But leaving with them, letting them take her anywhere, brought up images of news stories about women raped and murdered and left in fields, or woods, or by the side of the road. Isabel looked at Merlin, then at Alfred, then back to Merlin. She relaxed a little. The looks on their faces almost made her laugh.

Merlin was hopeful, but unsure of her response. Alfred looked as though he expected to be slapped, but he would take it because they deserved it for telling such a ludicrous story. They certainly didn't look dangerous. "Which fraternity are you with? This is a good prank, one of the best I've seen. Very intelligent and well thought out. Who's behind this?"

Merlin sat back and looked at Alfred who shrugged.

"You didn't actually expect her to believe it, did you?" Alfred asked. "I mean if she is everything you say she is, she is far too intelligent to accept this." He turned his attention on her. "I didn't believe it either."

Isabel appreciated the compliment, backhanded though it seemed, but she did not appreciate being talked about as though she weren't there. "Look guys, it's been real, but I've got to get back to work."

Alfred looked at Merlin with confusion. "If she thinks it's been real, then why doesn't she believe us?" Merlin shrugged, but before he could say anything, Isabel huffed and got up and walked away, carefully keeping her back to them. She went directly into the workroom where she could watch hidden until they were gone.

Chapter 6

Even though she saw them leave, Isabel did not come out from the workroom for some time. She busied herself organizing books to be re-shelved on one of the book carts, glancing out occasionally to make certain they had not returned. As she worked she thought over her encounter with "Merlin" and "Alfred." It was hard to be too annoyed with them when they had seemed so truly sincere. And to have their attention so intently focused on her was hard to resist no matter how ridiculous their story was.

She had finally decided it was safe to venture out and pulled the cart out of the workroom when the feeling hit her. It started with a tingle down her spine and a lurch in her stomach. Goosebumps popped up on her arms making the little hairs stand straight up. Breathe, she thought, remember to breathe. Her chest felt heavy, and the suddenly cold air hurt as she sucked it in. She saw Julie absent-mindedly pull her sweater around her and knew that the chill was more than her imagination.

Isabel turned slowly to see who or what had come in. She saw a man all in black standing in the doorway, looking around until his gaze finally settled on her. As he walked toward her the scene felt strange and yet familiar at the same time. Strange because he was a foreigner whose dark clothes reflected his menacing demeanor. Familiar because…why was this familiar? Was it because she had already been approached by two oddly out-of-place men today? No. This was different than that. There had been no malice in them. In fact, they had gone out of their way not to scare her.

This was more like déjà vu. Like watching your worst nightmare play out before your eyes. If this guy was part of the prank, Isabel thought, it wasn't funny anymore. His oily smirk implied familiarity, as though they had met before, but he had the advantage because she couldn't remember. She strained her brain hard to try and remember if she had ever seen him before and what connection he could possibly have to her. She couldn't imagine what it might be; her life had been totally unremarkable. Not a single shady character anywhere in her past.

"Isabel," he said smoothly, "we meet again." He spoke as he appeared, with a cultured snobbishness, as though he spent pretentious hours listening to classical music and sipping brandy. His black hair was short and slick, not a single strand out of place. His skin was flawless and icy pale as though it was a synthetic fabric stretched over an unyielding skeleton of iron and steel. Unlike the subdued passion that colored Alfred's stormy gray eyes, his were a cold, emotionless silver-blue.

"I beg your pardon," Isabel replied, trying to sound nonchalant. "Do I know you?"

"Yes indeed you do. But don't be too hard on yourself for not remembering. You were a baby after all."

"I'm sorry, I don't understand."

"I know your mother. Your real mother. She has missed you greatly." He moved closer. "I know so much about you," he said. "I know that you have never felt loved. I know that you have never felt that you belonged. I know that you are oh-so lonely."

Terror sliced through her with a sharp, precise blade. Though he was trying to sound empathetic, his eyes flashed with evil intent. Isabel hugged herself against the chill of his presence. He had power over her, the power one gains with knowledge that is not reciprocated. As he tried to intimidate her with his physical presence, she took a step back and bumped into the cart. Trapped. Trapped like an animal being backed into a cage. "Who are you?" she tried to sound annoyed, but her voice was shaking.

"I am a friend. A friend from long ago who can make everything right for you."

"I'm sorry but I don't know what you are talking about. I would like for you to leave please."

He obviously did not feel compelled to do as she asked. His confidence was as frightening as everything else about him. "You don't want me to leave, do you? Aren't you curious about what I have to tell you? About what I have to offer you?"

Still that awful smile. Still those menacing eyes. "No," she said, digging deep for courage and drawing herself up.

"If you come with me, I can take you back to those who truly love you. I can take you away from this," he swept his arm around indicating the library, "I can restore your original beauty. I can make you happier than you ever dreamed possible." His voice was smooth but she sensed condescension.

For the second time that day, Isabel was stunned by how well a stranger seemed to know her. She struggled to keep her face composed, so that he could not see the effect that he was having on her. All of her instincts were telling her to be extremely careful, that there was hidden meaning in his words. That he was pleased with himself for saying something true that actually disguised the truth. She wasn't going to fall for it. "Please leave, or I will have my friend call security." She glanced over her shoulder at the oblivious Julie, sitting behind the desk, her nose still stuck in her book.

He never looked away from her but the smile was gone. "Think of what I have to offer you, Isabel. Think of never being alone again. Think of going to a place where you most certainly belong, where you will be welcomed and loved by all who meet you. Think of it, and I will be back." He turned and walked away with measured, unhurried steps and passed through the door without looking back.

Isabel collapsed in a nearby chair. The tension left her body in one great release that left her feeling weak and unsteady. Though the stranger was gone, the uneasy feeling was not. Isabel struggled to understand why. Where did these people come from? What did they want? Their story was so preposterous that it couldn't possibly be true, so what were they hiding? How did they know so much about her life, about her deepest, most guarded thoughts? And why did they feel so familiar?

She was stirred from her thoughts by the arrival of her friend, Gwen. Gwen was everything Isabel wasn't: tall, slender, and confident. She wasn't exactly a beauty, but she exuded sexuality, and every interaction she had with men came off as an offer. Isabel had never been sure why Gwen had chosen her as a friend, except that maybe other women felt threatened by her, and so she had difficulty making friends. Isabel had no illusions as to her own attractiveness, so she felt neither threatened by Gwen nor competitive with her.

"Hey, Iz," Gwen started casually. "What are you thinking about? You look as though you've seen a ghost."

"No. Just some guys giving me a hard time."

"Giving you a hard time? Why would they do that?"

Isabel could read Gwen as though she was wearing a matrix board with a running commentary on her emotions. She sensed the jealousy and couldn't resist laughing out loud. "What? Is it so unlikely that someone would be interested in me?"

Gwen had been caught, and she knew it. She looked uncomfortable and was obviously struggling for words. Isabel let her off the hook.

"Don't worry, Gwen," Isabel said, her laugh fading away. "It was a fraternity prank."

Gwen sighed in relief. "Those guys can be pretty mean."

"Yes, they can. But I didn't fall for it," she said with some pride.

"Good for you," Gwen replied and was done with the topic. "Coming out with me tonight?"

"Geez, Gwen, you know that I hate bars. Why do you keep asking me to go with you?"

"Why do you keep saying yes?"

"Because I am afraid you will go home with some ax-murderer," Isabel replied with a smirk.

"Are you saying that I am indiscriminant?" Gwen feigned hurt.

"Yes. Yes, I am. You will go off with anything in pants. Anything male that is."

"He does have to be good-looking."

"Oh, sure. Sorry. I forgot."

"At least I have fun, you ol' stick in the mud," Gwen said good-naturedly. "Come on, Iz. What else are you going to do?"

Isabel chuckled. They had this same banter back and forth every time Gwen asked her to go out, which was at least twice a week. The same thing happened every time. They would go to a bar, usually the Purple Pelican because it was close by and had a dance floor. They would sit at a table and order drinks. Before long, some guy would come over and ask Gwen to dance. That would be the end of Gwen's company for the night. Isabel would watch for a while and then motion to Gwen that she was going home.

No one ever asked Isabel to dance. Hardly anyone ever spoke to her. She actually would have been happier to go home alone to her little apartment and be spared the forced social interaction. She only went because Gwen was her only real friend and a force of nature that would not be denied. "Fine," she answered as she always did in a defeated tone of voice, "but I have to go to my mom's first. It's grocery day."

Gwen shook her head. "Boy, you sure are good to your mom. And she treats you like dirt. Why do you do it?"

Isabel shrugged. "She took care of me for years and years. It's my turn."

"Yeah, says her," Gwen huffed. She always made Isabel feel like her mother mistreated her. It was one of the most appealing things about her friendship with Gwen. "Fine, fine," she said. "Meet me at the Pelican around seven."

"Will do," Isabel replied.

"Cool," Gwen said breezily. "It's quitting time. I'm off. Later." She blew out the door.

Isabel looked at the clock over the desk. Five o'clock. She looked at the cart of books and sighed. No time for them today. No doubt they would be waiting for her in the morning. The night shift was all students, and they seldom did more than checking out books. They were all too busy studying. Isabel didn't mind. As odd as it seemed she liked shelving books, liked being in the quiet stacks all alone. It wasn't unusual for the other librarians to have to page her because she would get interested in one book or another and lose track of time. This was something to look forward to tomorrow.

She went behind the desk to grab her purse. "Julie," she said, "time to go."

Julie stood up, stretching. "Wow," she said, "I was really into it. Did I miss anything?"

Isabel smiled. Did she miss anything? One wizard, one incredibly good-looking guy with an attitude, and one scary dude in black, who all wanted to take Isabel a thousand years into the past to be a princess or something and meet her real mother. She chuckled to herself. Ridiculous. "Nope. Nothing. It was a quiet afternoon. See you on Friday."

Chapter 7

Alfred did not appreciate the way the girl had dismissed them. He was reminded of the way Ethelbald treated him, and it made him mad. He did not like being dismissed. This girl was nobody, but she had turned her back on the son of a king. "That didn't improve our situation at all," he said to Merlin in a huff. "Now what?"

Merlin put his head in his hands, rubbing his temples as though he had a headache. "All right," he said, rubbing his eyes. "We need a plan."

"I've got a plan," said Alfred in the sarcastic voice he usually reserved for his brother. "Let's go home. We've seen her, she's seen us, and she has no interest in us. I've got better things to do than chase after some peasant who doesn't know how to behave around a prince."

"Come on," said Merlin, leading him outside. "Let's talk."

Merlin led him to a spot out of the way where they could talk without being overheard. The bright sun and gentle breeze made Alfred feel better in spite of himself. I can sit here a while and listen to Merlin talk, he thought. It is a beautiful day.

"Alfred," Merlin said, "considering what we have gone through to get here, you are not showing much effort toward accomplishing our goal."

"What is our goal, Merlin?" Alfred said crossing his arms, "Why are we doing this? You talk about free will. What if she doesn't want to go back with us? What right have we got to force her? History is already happening with her in this time and place.

She has no impact on what is happening a thousand years before her time."

"She most certainly does have an impact on what is happening a thousand years ago," Merlin replied vehemently. "She does not belong here either. She belongs with us, with you. Didn't you see how her demeanor changed when I mentioned a baby that was never supposed to be born? She knows," he said with a little too much emotion, hanging his head. "She knows and that is what is scaring her. She doesn't want to believe us because it goes against everything practical and rational she has learned to believe."

Alfred eyed Merlin suspiciously. "There's more here, old man. More that you are not telling me. What is it? Does it have something to do with you and Kathryn?"

At first, Merlin looked like a startled deer. But after thinking for a moment, he smiled a gentle, sad smile. "I loved Kathryn from the moment I first saw her. She was so beautiful, not only in her appearance, but also in her sweet gentle spirit. She was married, married to a man who would break her spirit and her body as though she were no more than a wild horse to be tamed." Merlin looked up into the sky. "God, how I hated him."

Alfred wondered at the storm blowing through Merlin's soul and wondered how it would be to feel like that about someone else. Strong feelings were unfamiliar to him, except of course for the rage he felt toward his brother and the passion that he felt for his work.

Merlin took a deep breath. "A lifetime I have loved her, and I have nothing to show for it. Nothing but one last chance to make things right." He looked at Alfred and said earnestly, "Your chance at that love, at the happiness that has eluded Kathryn and me, is sitting behind that desk in this library. This has to happen, Alfred. It has to for you. It has to for her. It has to for Britain." He sat with his hands on his knees trying to summon the words that would make Alfred understand.

Suddenly, in the middle of the warm, autumn day, a wind blew through. Not the gentle breeze that had been lifting their spirits. It was a wind that made the hair rise on their necks, and made ice form in their blood. Merlin jumped up as though he had been struck by lightning and sniffed the air like a hunter. He leaned over and grabbed Alfred by the shoulder, a look of sheer terror in his eyes. "He's here! Come on!"

"What? Who?" Alfred exclaimed on an expired breath. He had never seen Merlin move so fast.

Merlin was in a panic. He ran behind a building and pulled Alfred into the shadows with him. They had a clear view of the front entrance of the library.

"What is going on?" Alfred asked, confused.

"Malcolm has found us. Or rather, he has found her."

"Malcolm? Malcolm is here? How?"

Before Merlin could answer they saw Malcolm stride up the stairs and into the building. Alfred's eyes got wide. This whole situation became stranger and stranger every minute. It almost felt like a weird dream, except that everything was real enough to touch.

"The same way that you and I did it," Merlin answered after the door closed behind Malcolm. "He hates me, and he hates you, and he hates her. Now we are threatening to undo his evil masterpiece. He will go to no small lengths to keep us from succeeding. I fear for her safety. And we have led him right to her."

"But he has nothing to worry about. She obviously has no interest in me, and I have no interest in her." Alfred recalled that he had unusual feelings of empathy when he saw her, but immediately dismissed the thought. They were of no significance.

Merlin shook his head. "He will not care about that. He cannot risk the chance that you will come to care for each other."

"How are we going to come to care for each other? She won't even sit in the library with us. She is afraid of us."

Merlin looked surprised. "So you sensed it too, her fear. That's different for you."

"Don't put more into it than it deserves. Let's go home."

"We can't now more than ever."

Alfred was tiring of this. "Why not?"

"Because he will kill her."

Alfred was taken back. "What? Why?"

"He didn't have to kill her as a baby, because babies have very little will of their own. Their spirits are extremely easy to separate from their bodies because they are so new. The older a person gets, however, the stronger the bonds of identity are between the soul and the body. She is an adult with full control of her free will. He cannot take her spirit unless she gives it to him freely, and I doubt she will do that. His only choice will be to remove her from this life altogether by killing her body and sending her soul back to God." He paused, examining Alfred's expression closely. "I know you have no feelings for her, that she is a complete stranger to you, but do you actually want to see her die because of this?"

Alfred made a face. It was a face that admitted defeat at the same time it conveyed impatience. "No, I guess not."

"I thought not. There is a heart in there somewhere, I know there is," Merlin said poking Alfred's chest. "Now the question is what to do?" Merlin rubbed his head, as though it would make thinking easier. He glanced at the entrance to the building waiting for Malcolm to come out. "Most definitely we need to stay close to Isabel to head off attempts on her life. At the same time, we need to try and stop Malcolm. But how? How can we be in two places at one time?"

Alfred shrugged, knowing that he was not expected to answer. While Merlin was making his plan, they watched the front of the building, and in a short time Malcolm did come out, looking smug and very pleased with himself.

Finally Merlin looked at Alfred as though he had resolved the problem but wasn't too happy with the solution. "We have no choice," he said. "We have to split up. I'll go track Malcolm down. You stay here and work on Isabel." He made a face. "Please try to be charming."

Alfred gave him a "you've got to be kidding" look.

"Very well, forget charming. Please try not to offend her." Merlin said getting up.

Alfred shrugged again. "Fine," he replied grudgingly. But before he could get out the whole word, Merlin was gone.

Now what was he supposed to do? He stayed where he was in the shadows until he saw Isabel come out. He tried to follow her at a distance, to keep her in view without giving himself away. She walked toward a huge building with many floors but walls only halfway up on each floor. Above the walls he could see the tops of countless numbers of "cars."

She walked through a door and after a few seconds he stepped in behind her. He was in a large stairwell and could hear her steps above him. He followed as best he could, listening very carefully so that he could tell where she was when she opened another door and left the stairwell. He followed her out of the door and saw that he was on a floor with dozens of cars parked side-by-side all around him. He caught a glimpse of her a hundred or so feet away, getting into one of the "cars." As he watched helplessly, she drove away.

What now? Nothing to do. Nowhere to go. Then it hit him. He knew where the library was. Books. Books were always a good idea.

Chapter 8

Isabel didn't knock on the door of her mother's apartment. She had a key to let herself in. Even though she knew her mother was home, she also knew that she would never bother to get up off the sofa and come open the door. Her mother, Edith, knew that Isabel always came by on Wednesday afternoon with her groceries, but she never offered to help or said thank you. She was a queen, this was her kingdom, and Isabel was her lowly handmaiden. End of discussion.

"Hi, Mom," Isabel called pushing the door open with her foot, her arms full of groceries.

"'Bout time. I figured you forgot." Edith spoke without looking up from the trashy talk show she was watching. She was in her pajamas, a cigarette in one hand, a can of beer in the other. Her furniture was of good quality, but years enclosed in the smoke-ridden apartment had yellowed all of the upholstery and drapes. She rarely got dressed anymore, the combination of arthritis and emphysema making it too taxing on her to go out. Once upon a time, Edith had been an attractive woman. She had worked for years in the fashion industry and had always been stylishly dressed in the latest fashions. She had dated some, but never anyone who was interested in being father to her child. Edith blamed Isabel for that, never thinking that maybe she simply had bad taste in men. As her face and body aged, and she no longer felt attractive, she stopped going out. Slowly she had descended into her current lifestyle.

In the kitchen, Isabel shook her head without replying. Edith knew she hadn't forgotten. She had come every Wednesday for the last two years without fail. She no longer needed for Edith to make her a list because she wanted the same things every week. Anything new Isabel suggested was met with a disgusted, "Are you going to pay for it?" She would have, of course. She often paid for her mother's groceries without reimbursement. It was easier not to argue.

Isabel put the groceries away and cleaned up the dishes her mother had left from lunch. Then she strolled into the living room and sat down. On the TV some very well-dressed, perfectly manicured woman in big glasses was asking her guest why she slept with her daughter's husband in trade for her daughter sleeping with hers (not her father). These women had on too short skirts and stiletto heels. They had long stringy hair that they kept tossing over their shoulders like they were models posing for a high fashion magazine. They had long, bright red fingernails that reminded Isabel of the talons of birds of prey. Their heavy eye makeup made them look like raccoons. Everything about them was overdone and intense. Edith was enthralled.

"How are you today?" Isabel ventured.

"How do I look?" Edith replied without looking at her. "I'm lousy. I hate this lousy life." She flicked her ashes and took another swill of beer.

Isabel had heard it so often, it almost didn't hurt any more. Almost. She leaned her head back in the chair and wished her life away. Sorry, Mom, she thought to herself, I wish I had died too. It would have saved us both a lot of heartache. "Is there anything I can do for you?"

"Did you bring my cigarettes?"

"Yes, ma'am."

"Where are they?"

"Sorry." Isabel got up from her chair and went into the kitchen where she had left them on the counter.

"Get me another beer since you're in there," Edith grunted.

Isabel handed her mother the carton of cigarettes and the beer. The older woman took them with no thanks. She had never once looked at Isabel since she had walked in the door. It was obvious

Edith had no regard or affection for her daughter at all. In a way, Isabel envied the trashy women on the TV. At least they had something in common. At least they talked to each other. At least they had a relationship.

Isabel didn't bother to sit again. "Mom, I'm going to head out."

"Where are you in such a hurry to get to?"

"I'm going to meet Gwen out tonight."

Finally Edith looked up. "You shouldn't hang around with that little tramp. She'll give you a bad reputation."

Isabel shook her head. "Don't worry. When I'm with her, no one even notices me."

"I guess not. Plain little thing like you disappears next to Ms. Neon 'Have-sex-with-me-big-daddy'."

Isabel had to laugh. "You got it. See you later."

"Don't forget my wash."

Isabel picked up the laundry basket where her mother had left it by the door. She was more likely to trip over it than forget it. She looked back and saw that she had already been dismissed. She stepped out and closed the door behind her without another word.

Chapter 9

The small parking lot of the Purple Pelican was crowded as usual, and Isabel had to run her car up on the curb to park. She could see Gwen's car near the door and knew that she had been waiting for a while. Isabel looked at her watch. It was 7 o'clock on the dot, but Gwen had not had the extra errands that Isabel had. She would have gone home, spent an hour getting dressed, made a leisurely drive over and then sat nursing a drink, eyeing the crowd as people arrived. She would have put on a lot of heavy make-up and be wearing something short and seductive. Isabel smiled at the memory of her mother's description.

The Purple Pelican was a popular night spot for single twenty- and thirty-somethings because in addition to the indoor dance floor, it had a fenced in area filled with sand surrounded by palm trees, hibiscus and other tropical plants and hung with lights. Sometimes the area was set up for volleyball and sometimes it was cleared for dancing. Big heaters hung from the roof to warm the area in the winter. The inside of the bar was dark and intimate and smelled strongly of tar and treated wood, supporting the illusion of an old ship. The bar itself was polished cherry with brass railings and far more elegant than one would have expected in such a casual establishment. All in all it was a welcoming place, as long as you were there to have fun and not looking for any life-altering experiences.

Isabel sat a few minutes in her car. Her visits with her mother always left her disheartened, and she did not feel like company, particularly in a place where people would be so rowdy and spirited. She wished that she could disappear so that no one could see her anymore. She didn't want to talk, to try to make conversation, or to pretend like she fit in. She wanted to be left alone, to close herself up in her apartment, pull down the blinds, and to flee to her fantasies.

For now she had an obligation to fulfill. She would listen to Gwen, be shocked where she was supposed to be shocked, laugh where she was supposed to laugh, be envious where she was supposed to be envious, and admire where she was supposed to admire. Then she could go home.

Gwen was waiting at a table not far from the bar. She knew that Isabel preferred a booth because it was more comfortable, but she always picked a table because she said it made them more visible. Near the bar was important because that was the high traffic area. Being so exposed made Isabel more uncomfortable when she was sitting alone and Gwen was dancing, but she put up with it because, after all, it was entirely Gwen's show.

"It's about time," Gwen remonstrated as Isabel sat down.

"It's just now seven o'clock. Who told you to get here so early?" Isabel countered.

Gwen looked at her watch. "Sorry. How was Mom?"

"The usual," Isabel said with a shrug.

"Nice," Gwen replied sarcastically. "The bitch."

"Gwen, she is my mother."

"Yes, and she is a bitch. She totally uses you, and you let her. You didn't ask to be born. You don't owe her anything."

"Can we not have this argument again, please?" Isabel consciously changed her demeanor to be more cheerful. "Any prospects?"

Gwen relaxed. "Not yet, but it's early." She beat her straw on the side of her glass and chewed ice.

Their conversation was sparse at best, and consisted mostly of Gwen's evaluations of men as they walked through the door. Finally, her radar spotted a likely victim. She worked hard to make eye contact with him, issuing her silent invitation. Any man who received her signal knew that he was going to have sex that night. Gwen did that on purpose. She liked it. She liked the way it made her feel to have men fawning over her. She liked being promiscuous. She wasn't looking for commitment. She wanted to have fun. Isabel worried about social diseases. Gwen didn't seem to care at all.

When the object of Gwen's attention came to the table, he seemed familiar to Isabel, and she caught herself staring trying to decide where she had seen him before. He felt her looking at him and spoke to her, "Do we know each other?"

Isabel blinked. "That's what I was trying to figure out," she said with a smile. "You seem so familiar."

He squinted. "You look familiar to me too. Did you go to North High?"

"Nope."

"How 'bout Simpson First Baptist?"

"Nope." She shrugged. "Who knows? Could be anywhere."

"Yeah," he replied then turned his attention to Gwen. "Would you like to dance?"

"Sure," Gwen answered casually as though it had never crossed her mind. Nobody was fooled, but it was the way she was supposed to act. Smiling, she got up and took his hand. "See you in a few," she said to Isabel.

Isabel smiled a weak smile. She would only see Gwen from a distance for the rest of the night. She ordered another ginger ale and nursed it for an appropriate amount of time, then she waved to Gwen across the room and left.

Isabel's apartment was only a few blocks from the Purple Pelican. During the day, she would have walked, but it was a little too far to walk home alone at night. She got lucky to find a parking space on the street right in front of her building.

Home. At last she was home. Isabel loved her apartment. It was in an old building and had so much more character than the apartment clones popping up all over the place. The ceilings were high, bookshelves were built-in, the walls were plaster, and the bathtub had legs. Its ambiance made her second-hand furniture seem fashionable instead of cheap. It wasn't that she was trying to impress anyone because there was no one to impress. Only her landlord, the maintenance man, and the exterminator ever saw it. But it lifted her spirits that she could surround herself with things that she loved and not have them look out of place.

The built-in bookshelves were stacked to over-flowing with books and movies. Her favorites were nearly worn out from frequent usage, not surprising for someone who spent so much time alone.

The bay windows had white floor-to-ceiling draperies, even though the windows only went halfway down the wall. These had been left by the previous tenant, but they were lovely and heavy and in good shape, so Isabel left them. She kept them closed at the top and pulled them back with ties to let in the light. At night she loosed the ties and felt that she had complete privacy.

In the bay, she had an overstuffed chair with tapestry fabric and a carved wood frame that had no doubt made it very expensive when it was new. Her sofa and coffee table were comfortable and well used, so that anyone who happened to visit would have felt right at home. Her kitchen was dated but cheerful. Someone who lived there before had made a little green house in the window over the sink. Isabel grew herbs there, basil, dill and mint, and an African violet that was outgrowing its pot. Her bathroom, tiled with real tile, and not prefab, had a few cracks here and there, but it was clean, and everything worked, and she had plenty of hot water.

She headed for her bedroom, dropping her clothes as she walked. It was a big room that held her bed, dresser, desk, and an old loveseat. The closet had two sides, and, opening the one to the right, she put away her slacks and blazer.

On the left side was her escape. Escape from her mother. Escape from loneliness. Escape from herself.

On the weekends, Isabel liked to go shopping in second hand stores. She had found that many people took very good care of their things, and when they were ready for new, they donated them to second hand stores, which in turn used their profits to support shelters and programs for the needy. This was how she had found most of her furniture. Occasionally she found clothes in good enough shape for work or to give her a few more dressy things for going out with Gwen. Once, however, she found something completely frivolous that she could not live without.

It had been someone's wedding gown, but it was not the usual organza and lace. It was made of heavy satin in a color referred to by the bridal industry as candlelight or champagne, but most people would simply have called it ivory. The bodice was sleeveless and fitted with a deeply scooped neck, and it was covered with swirls of embroidered appliqué. Pearl-like beads had been woven into the embroidery. The same appliqué covered the bottom of a skirt that was full but had a relatively short train. It fitted her perfectly and felt wonderfully cool when she put it on.

The purchase of this dress had brought her fantasies to life. She had always been a dreamer, wishing she had been born into another life. As a child she had spent a lot of time imagining that she was someone else, somewhere else. This dress had rekindled that game for her as an adult. It gave substance and reality to her escape. With the drapes closed and the door locked, she was transported, and with the imagination of a child, she became someone else. She knew the difference between reality and illusion, but these fantasies eased her pain and refreshed her spirit so that she could get out of bed in the morning and go on.

Oddly enough, Isabel never pretended that it was a wedding gown, or she was a bride. Since she had become old enough to realize how truly lacking her family life had been, the dream of a loving home was too dear to her. She hardly dared hope that someday someone would love her and want her. Still there was a dream, a shred of hope that someday, somehow she might find someone. Someone who would want her. Someone who would love her. Someone to come home to, or who would come home to her. Isabel could not bring herself to pretend that. Its absence was too painful, and the hope of it too fragile.

Tonight she lit the candles as usual and turned off all the lights. She felt a little ridiculous, a grown woman dressing up like a little girl, and so she did not want to see herself in too bright of a light. Isabel put on the gown and seated herself in the chair in the bay. Tonight she was a queen.

The time is the 16th century. The young queen is the first woman to be the ruler in her country, a country with a long and impressive history which could be traced all the way back to prehistory. She is a great beauty, which often causes men to underestimate her wisdom and skill. Such a man stands before her now, a pompous, arrogant fool. He has been sent by his father, the king of a neighboring country, to seek a treaty with her country and create a permanent peace along their common border. Struck by her beauty but certain that any woman will fall to her knees before him, he insinuates that he can 'light the fires of her womanly passions.' One such as she would make a fine wife for a prince such as him, he says, and he could rule in her place and make decisions overwhelming for a mere woman.

She finds this offensive, but maintains her control. "Your offer of a treaty is worthy of consideration, and so I will consider it. As for the other, I seem to be doing quite well, otherwise why would you be standing before me, instead of me before you? Thank you for your offer, sir. I will call for you when I have given it more thought."

The prince is highly offended at being dismissed, and turns on his heel and draws himself up, walking out as though he has dismissed her instead. She smirks at his back and considers the matter closed.

But it is not closed. One of the prince's men comes before her and kneels in respect. "Lady," he says, "might I have a word with you in private?"

She motions for him to rise. "That would be most unusual, sir," she replies. He is very handsome, she thinks. His eyes are sincere, his countenance respectful. (Remarkable, thought Isabel, that he has taken on the appearance of the younger man from this afternoon. What was his name? Alton? Albert? Al something. Oh yes, Batman's butler. Alfred.)

"*I realize that, Your Highness, but what I have to say, have been instructed by my king to say, is for your ears and your ears alone.*"

"*Very well,*" she says, "*A brief audience. Come into my chambers.*" *She gets up from her throne and sweeps gracefully through the side door into her private rooms. He follows her there and shuts the door behind them.* "*All right, Sir...?*"

"*Alfred, Highness.*"

"*All right, Sir Alfred, you have my attention. What is it that you wish to say?*"

"*My king feared that his son would behave so, and he asked that I be prepared to speak for him if the prince offended you. I fear that he has.*"

"*Yes, in fact. I found him boorish, arrogant, and insulting.*"

"*His mother, the queen, demanded that he be assigned to this task, even though the king feared that he was unworthy of it. He has behaved exactly as expected. I apologize for the prince, for his father the king, and for my country. We have the utmost admiration for you, Your Highness. It was never our intention to offend.*"

Her mood softened in the face of his sincerity. His eyes (What color had his eyes been? Blue? Gray? Not brown. She couldn't remember exactly) *were fixed on her in such a way that she knew he found her attractive, but did not want to overstep his bounds.* "*You have my forgiveness. What exactly is it you wish to say?*"

"*This treaty is of great importance to us. As you know, we are being accosted on one side by the Germans and on another by the Spanish. If we commit to peace along our common border, we can pull out the men who now patrol it and move them to an area where they are more desperately needed.*"

"*Is there more?*"

"*Yes, lady,*" he says earnestly, "*your country has many fine products which we would like to import. Your soil produces the finest wheat and exceptionally sweet fruit. Your spinners make very fine wool. In return for this, we will trade you our famous glass, porcelain and jewelry. My king has sent you this gift as an example of our craftsmanship and token of his esteem."*

He pulls out a necklace of incredible beauty. At its center is a huge, square cut emerald of uncommon luster. To either side in graduated sizes are rubies and sapphires. They are set in fine gold filigree. "May I?" he asks, indicating he would like to put it around her neck. She nods her consent. As he moves closer to her, she suddenly becomes aware of his height and masculinity, and she feels unusually petite and feminine. He reaches around from in front of her to fasten the clasp behind her neck, causing their bodies to brush against each other. The air is suddenly charged with electricity.

He looks down into her eyes. Suddenly she is not a queen and he is not a nobleman speaking for a boorish prince. He is a man, she is a woman, and the attraction is overwhelming. She has never felt like this before. She is afraid, afraid he will realize the effect he is having on her. Afraid that he won't.

He can't help himself. He bends down touching his lips gently to hers. Passion overtakes them. His kisses become more demanding, and she responds, wrapping her arms around his neck and pulling him down to meet her. His arms go around her waist, and he lifts her off her feet, dodging her beautiful, long gown as he carries her to her bed and lays her down. They don't want to stop kissing, knowing somewhere in the back of their minds that if they do, reality will come crashing in-between them.

Reality comes anyway, in the form of an intrusive knock. "Majesty? Majesty, are you all right?" It is the voice of her chief minister.

Alfred looks at her with longing, and she smiles a weak smile. "Yes, sir minister, we are fine. You may enter."

The minister senses that something has happened, but he is too discreet to say anything. The queen has regained her composure. "Sir Alfred has brought papers from his king that are worthy of our consideration. Please review them and then meet me for supper to discuss them."

"Yes, Majesty,"the minister replies, holding the door for her guest. "Good sir, shall we get those papers?"

"Indeed," Alfred replies. He walks over to the queen and bows. "Thank you for hearing me, lady. I believe we can both benefit from this treaty." He kisses her hand, his eyes flashing with barely contained passion.

"I believe so too," the queen replies smoothly. "You serve your king well, Alfred."

Alfred bows again and follows the minister out.

That night, with the beautiful gown placed neatly over a chair and after all her handmaidens have left, the queen is alone in her bed, and she thinks of him. Touching her fingers to her lips, she remembers the warmth and softness of his kiss. Suddenly, in the darkness, he is there. He puts his finger to her lips. "I cannot stay away, mi'lady. I must touch you, must feel your body against me. Please let me lie with you until you fall asleep. I promise I will leave before anyone finds us."

She answers him with a passionate kiss. She is no fool, she knows that this cannot be, but she cannot resist the comfort of his warm body next to hers.

At this point, Isabel was lying on the sofa in her underwear. Blowing out the candles and pulling the afghan over her, she pretended to cuddle against the warm body of Sir Alfred and fell into a deep sleep.

Chapter 10

Merlin followed Malcolm and saw him pass across the bridge into their home universe. He did not have to follow him closely to know where he was going. His journey led him back to Stonehenge and back to the forest by Kathryn's house.

Merlin knew where Malcolm had set up his house, knew the dark forces that he summoned there, but he had never gone there. He never wanted to be touched by the evil that lived there. Now, however, it was a necessity.

Deep in the woods, the thick trees blocked out all that was left of the light of the dying day. In the darkness Merlin came very suddenly upon the unlit house. The windows were completely dark, and it appeared that no one was there at all. Perhaps I was wrong, Merlin questioned himself. If he is not here, then where would he have gone? Could it be that he stayed in our universe? Could it be that he is planning something bigger than I thought?

He looked in the window and saw no one. He tried the door and found it unlatched so he went in. Once inside the dying embers of the fire provided a dim light that he had not seen from outside. It was unnaturally clean. The light reflected off the highly polished jars stacked neatly on shelves next to a large table. All Malcolm's furnishings had very sharp, clean lines. There was none of the clutter that covered Merlin's own house on the other side of these woods; none of the comfortable pillows or piles of enticing books; no maps or pictures or tapestries.

Merlin went through to the back door and came into a tidy garden, designed as a perfect rectangle with a perfect circle in the middle. In each corner grew herbs and vegetables for cooking and making potions. He knew that Malcolm practiced types of magic that he had no interest in, all centered on gaining control of others. He had a potion for making people blind and one to make them fall deaf. He had recipes for concoctions that would cause a woman to get pregnant or cause her to miscarry. He could blend elixirs that would soothe the stomach or make a person wretch. Merlin had seen Malcolm do all of these things.

The center circle of the garden was surrounded by hollow tree stumps from which Malcolm had peeled away strips of bark to give each a demonic face. When lit from the inside as they were now, the faces came to life with the flickering, dancing flames. It was an eerie sight and made Merlin uneasy. He was in Malcolm's territory and didn't know what to expect. A voice in the shadows behind him struck terror through his body into his very core.

"So, Merlin, at last you have come for a visit. To what do I owe this honor?" Malcolm oozed.

"You know why I am here, Malcolm. I want you to leave them alone. I want you to let me put this right. Go find some other mischief to work."

"But this is my great work, Merlin. My masterpiece. Beautifully planned and beautifully executed. I am not about to let you undo my greatest legacy to human history." There was no urgency in his voice. He had the upper hand, and he knew it. "Why is this so important to you anyway? Isn't there something more here than your beneficent concern for humanity?"

"What do you mean by that?"

"That I know your secret, my old friend." He spat the words like a bitter herb.

Merlin looked uncomfortable, but he wasn't going to be baited. "What secret is that? Perhaps you'll share it with me."

Malcolm's voice slithered like a snake. "I've been watching her, too, Merlin. She's a little too smart, a little too learned, isn't she?"

"What are you trying to say?"

"Kathryn is beautiful and wise and kind," he gave a deep sigh. "She is everything any man could want. But she is not a scholar. Her focus is grounded firmly in the world that she can touch and see." He smirked. "And Hugh," he said with a derisive laugh, "Hugh was only capable of producing the hulking brainless wonders that are his sons."

"You underestimate Hugh's sons," Merlin replied calmly. "They are doing quite well as masters of their estates."

"Don't change the subject."

"And the subject is…?"

"Isabel's parentage."

"Just say it."

"You are that child's father, Merlin. How stupid do you think I am?"

Emotions played across Merlin's face like the shadows of clouds across a landscape. Fear, anger, sorrow, betrayal, defeat. Finally he simply shrugged his shoulders. "Yes, I am her father."

It actually felt good to say it out loud. Even he and Kathryn had never dared say the words, knowing that once words were spoken they took on a life of their own. Any one could hear them, any one could repeat them. But now, though he was relieved to have finally admitted it, it made him more vulnerable. "So now what?"

Malcolm laughed. "Now what? Do you think that this changes anything? I have known all along. All this noble talk about saving Alfred's legacy, saving souls for God, saving British history, even saving Alfred from a terrible marriage. Your beneficent quest. Ha!" He had a decidedly unpleasant look on his face. "Why do you think I hate that girl so passionately? Why you? Why Alfred? Not because I want to have power over everything I see. No. You have what I wanted. I sold my soul to be more than human so that I could have Kathryn, but for all my powers, I could not make her love me," he hissed. "She loved you. You got to have her. You made a child with her. It was you she was willing to compromise her precious piety for. I hate you, I hate that child, and I hate Alfred for having the love that I will never have." His face was red, the veins in his temples throbbing. "I hate you, do you understand? Hate beyond hate, beyond any other hate that has existed ever in the world. I will take your precious little family, and I will bring you down in the most painful way possible. I will eradicate them from history as though they never existed at all. And you? Your punishment, your eternal hell, is living without them forever, knowing that it was your actions that caused their suffering."

He paused and regained control. When he spoke again it was with cold calculation. "You and I are not so different after all, Merlin. We both act in the name of a greater cause, but hide our true, very personal motivation. You are as devious and deceptive as I am."

"I don't destroy lives," Merlin replied indignantly, drawing himself to his full height.

"So you say. What did you do to me? Doesn't my life count? You ruined my life. Not for a day, not for a year, not for a lifetime. You ruined my existence for all eternity. There is no price you can pay to make up for that. You will pay and pay and pay, from now until time itself has been reduced to a fading echo"

Merlin's hands balled into fists. He didn't know whether to lunge for Malcolm's throat or pound his body until his heart burst within him. He is playing with me, he thought, he is trying to make me lose control. He is succeeding.

He took a deep breath, unclenched his fist, and faced Malcolm with a hard, resolved expression. "We can debate that point all day, and it won't change a thing. Done is done. Isabel is born, she is missed, and she must be returned to her rightful place. In all of this she is innocent. Take your anger out on me and leave her alone."

Malcolm laughed a mirthless laugh. "That would be too easy on you. It will be far more torture for you to watch me deal with her than anything I could do to you." He looked up at the stars as if looking for inspiration. "I will dispose of her, and I will do it in my own way. I am simply biding my time, waiting for both the opportunity and the method. I am an artist, my friend. I must do this with style." He looked back directly at Merlin, his eyes filled with dark determination. "I must be on my way. You understand I have so much to do. You can see yourself out, can't you?" He swept himself into a mist and disappeared.

Chasing Malcolm is no good, Merlin continued to plan, passing into the house. He's too slippery to keep up with. If I stay close to Alfred and Isabel, close but at a discreet distance, I'll still be able to watch for signs of Malcolm and head him off before he causes any...

Merlin felt a terrific pain as something hit him on the back of the head. Everything went dark.

Chapter 11

Isabel was surprised to see Alfred the next day in a conference room on the third floor of the library. He was asleep with his head on a book on the table. She stood looking at him a moment before she woke him up. He had such a handsome face, even smashed in the binding of a book. It was a face with character, not too common, but with a strong interesting nose. His lips were full, particularly in sleep when he had no attitude to thin them out and make him looked irritated. She smiled to herself that he had not drooled on the book. She remembered last night's fantasy with those lips on hers and wondered how they would feel in reality. His hair looked soft, and she stifled the urge to touch it. It was such a nice shade of brown. His eyes were large, and she tried again to remember what color they were, but couldn't.

Isabel had no illusions, no self-deceptions that last night's fantasy had been anything but a fantasy. Still she took the large barrette out of her hair and shook it down before waking him up.

"Hey," she said softly so as not to startle him. "Hey, wake up." She shook his shoulder.

He sat up blinking and rubbing his eyes. "Oh," he said, "it's you."

Blue-gray. Alfred's eyes had been that stormy shade of blue-gray. They were not stormy now, and she made note of the depth of their blue. "Yes," she replied, trying to sound annoyed without succeeding. "What are you doing here? Did you sleep here last night?"

"Yes, I did," Alfred responded, still shaking off sleep.

"Why?" she asked impatiently.

"Because I had nowhere else to go," he said matter-of-factly.

"You look pretty well kept for a homeless person," she replied skeptically.

"I am not homeless," Alfred said.

"Then why didn't you go home?" Isabel asked with even more impatience.

"Because my home is too far away."

"Oh, yeah, right," Isabel said, softening. "You're here from the past." She wondered what his story was. Was he still following through on the prank? Was he trying to do something to hurt her? Was he crazy? Maybe an escaped mental patient? She was intrigued if nothing else, and a little flattered to be the object of so elaborate a plan whatever the circumstances. Even if he was a murderer, he was going to a lot of trouble for her. She wasn't used to being the center of attention.

They stood for a moment sizing each other up. She thought that he was not so intimidating without his friend. "When was the last time you ate?" she asked.

Alfred looked thoughtful. "By your calendar—1100 years ago."

Isabel gave him her best 'get real' look. "Very funny."

Alfred looked directly at her and said with apparent sincerity, "I was not being funny. I do not have a sense of humor. Ask anyone who knows me. And I am hungry."

"I don't suppose you have any money," she said anticipating his answer.

"No," he admitted without shame.

"Didn't think so. Come on, I'll buy you some breakfast." She couldn't believe she was doing this. Was there anyone in the world who wouldn't tell her how stupid this was?

Isabel took Alfred through the cafeteria line and watched him load up. It looked as though he truly hadn't eaten in 1100 years. Bacon, eggs, muffins, fruit—everything he saw. It was a good thing she had gone to the ATM on her way to work that morning.

"So," he said with a mouth full of muffin, "Lady Isabel, who are you?"

"Excuse me?" she was caught off-guard by his directness. Calling her "Lady" made her feel as though he could see right through her into her fantasies. She blushed.

"I've come a long way to meet you," Alfred said firmly. "I think I am right to ask about you." His manner was so confident that she felt certain he was not used to being denied. This was an unusual quality in a homeless person.

"Where is your friend?" she countered.

He sighed. "Honestly, I am not sure. Yesterday we were sitting outside your building, a cold wind blew through. He jumped up grabbed my shoulders, said 'Oh my God, he's found us!' and pulled me into the shadows to hide. He told me that Malcolm, a person of unscrupulous behavior who also happens to be a wizard, had come to stop us from bringing you back. He said 'I'll be back. Watch her.' And then he left."

"That wasn't very nice," Isabel said, going along with the joke.

"No, it wasn't," Alfred said without any hint that he meant it as a joke.

She didn't know how to take him. "Who is he exactly?"

"He told you. He is Merlin, a very great wizard and my good friend. He thinks it is very important that we take you back with us. I am following him on faith, because, frankly, I don't see the need."

She was a little irritated at his dismissal of her importance, which was odd, because she didn't believe his story anyway. Still it was creative, and she was intrigued to see how far it would go. "Back with you where?"

"Back to our time," he said impatiently. "Haven't you been listening?"

"Right," she said sarcastically, "time traveling. Sorry, I forgot."

"So I ask you again, Lady Isabel, what is special about you? What do you have to offer me?"

Had he not been so unaffected, she would have been outraged at his presumption. Mere moments before she had paid for breakfast for someone who had slept in the library because he had nowhere else to go, and he wanted to know what she had to offer him? "Breakfast, for one thing," she said smartly.

Alfred looked down at his overflowing tray and chuckled. "Yes, breakfast. Very good." He had a nice smile.

This eased the tension that had developed between them. "How is it, by the way?"

"Very interesting. I recognize these foods, but they taste very different than I am used to. The food of my time has either very strong flavor, or no flavor at all. There isn't much in-between. These foods all have some flavor, although nothing is strong. It is, however, very satisfying."

"Good. Enjoy."

"I am," he said with absolute confidence. He put his elbows on the table and leaned on his arms. Shaking a piece of bacon at her, he said, "I still want to know more about you."

"What would you like to know?" She knew all the warnings about talking to strangers. She watched the news. But it was nice to have someone ask.

"What do you do at that library?"

"I am a librarian. I find books. I check out books. I shelve books. You know, librarian things."

"How long have you been there?"

"Let's see. It was four years in June."

"Do you like this occupation?"

She smiled warmly. "Yes, I love it. Books are my life."

He nodded with understanding. "Mine, too."

"You're a librarian?"

"I should say not!" he said, overreacting a bit. "I am the brother of the king."

"Sorry. I forgot."

He nodded his forgiveness. "But I do spend a lot of time with the monks illuminating and translating books. I have recently begun a history of my people. I am currently translating the reports of Julius Caesar on Britannia from Latin into our native tongue."

"Monks?"

"Yes. The monks are the only ones who know how to read and write with any competence. Except of course for people like myself who dedicate themselves to learning. But there are not many laymen who make time for such things. And of course, the monks are well versed in Latin because it is the language of all of our sacred texts. I am trying to convert many of these texts to our language to make them more accessible to the general population."

"I guess you guys have to write everything out in longhand, huh?"

"Longhand? Explain."

"You have to write them out by hand."

"As opposed to what?"

"As opposed to having them printed."

"Printed? Is this the method of creating the books I see in your library? The small regular letters and so many words on each page?"

"Yes," she replied. "We have machines that can make many copies of any text."

"They are not beautiful," he commented honestly.

"Perhaps not. But they are practical."

He thought about that for a moment. "Yes, in answer to your question. Yes, they write them out with their hands. It is their life's work." He looked around the huge cafeteria at all of the students sitting with books spread out on the tables. "I do like that you have lots of books. Even if they are ugly."

She smiled. "Yes, lots and lots of books. Even so, books are being replaced to some degree by technology. I don't think books will ever be completely eliminated, though. Many people still enjoy sitting down comfortably with a good book to read. And books don't require a power source."

"What is tek-nahl-o-gee?"

She looked around and saw some students working on their laptops. She pointed at them, "Computers are machines that store information. Lots and lots of information. You can carry the equivalent of hundreds of books worth of information in a computer. And if you can hook up to the Internet, the resources are almost unlimited."

"The Internet?" Alfred asked, puzzled.

Isabel sighed. "Are you planning to stay in our time?"

"No longer than I have to."

"Then don't worry about the Internet."

He accepted this without hesitation. He paused, and then asked, "Do you write books?"

"No. I've tried a few times to start, but I don't think I have the talent."

He shook his head. "I don't see that it takes any special talent. I have something to say, and I write it down."

"But you've already said that very few people in your time know how to read."

"That is correct."

"So you're not exactly trying to entertain an audience, are you?"

"Why would I want to entertain them? Books are not for entertainment. They are for teaching."

"That's boring."

"Boring? What is boring?"

"Not fun. Not interesting."

Alfred shook his head. "On the contrary, it is very interesting. If we do not write down our history, it will be lost. If we do not study the Holy Books, we will not know the proper way to live."

"What good will it do anyway if people don't know how to read?" Isabel asked practically.

"I'm working on that." He shook another piece of bacon at her, "You keep turning the conversation. You are learning more about me than I am about you."

"But you are more interesting than I am," she replied coyly.

"By your own opinion. I'll be the judge of that for myself. Go ahead. Interest me."

She laughed. "There is nothing to tell. I am a librarian. I love books. I go to work, and then I go home. Nothing at all remarkable."

Alfred squinted at her. "You've captured my interest. That is pretty remarkable," he teased.

Isabel laughed again. She felt happy. "Finish your food. I've got to get back to work."

Chapter 12

All during the day Isabel could not keep her mind from wandering to the man she knew was upstairs. She kept trying to ignore her feelings, because she knew they were nothing but trouble. Romance had no place in her life, and romantic feelings toward someone would only lead to lots of pain. No one could be interested in her. She was only as interesting as she was useful, and so she had spent a lifetime making herself useful. When someone looked at her intently and asked her to tell him about herself, however, it was hard not to get taken in.

Alfred wasn't exactly charming. In fact, he was a little too direct. But Isabel liked him. She liked talking to him, and she liked looking at him. Somehow, she felt happier when she was with him. How weird was that? Some psycho she'd only known a day, and she was swooning over him like a lovesick teenager. She was too old for this, but then she had nothing better to do. He could add a little excitement into her life for as long as he was around. And as long as she was careful not to get into a dangerous situation.

Isabel avoided Gwen as much as possible during the day. If Gwen found out about Alfred, she would want to go up and check him out for herself. Once he saw Gwen, Isabel had no doubt he'd forget her. Fortunately, tonight was Gwen's Jazzercise night so Isabel didn't have to make an excuse to avoid going out.

After work, she went upstairs to see if Alfred was still there. She found him sitting in the conference room looking perplexed. He was staring at an open book with a stack of others piled next to him on the table. "I found these books but I cannot read them. The words, even most of the letters, are unfamiliar to me. Can you tell me what they are about, what is in them?"

Isabel picked up the one on the top of the pile. The Complete Works of Robert Frost. "This is one of my favorites," she said wistfully. "It is a collection of poetry by a well-known American poet."

"Read me one of his poems," Alfred said. She had a feeling he was used to people doing exactly what he asked.

"Sure," Isabel agreed. "Let me pick a good one." She looked first at the index, knowing exactly what she was looking for. "Here it is. My favorite poem of all time:

> Whose woods these are I think I know.
> His house is in the village, though;
> He will not see me stopping here
> To watch his woods fill up with snow.
>
> My little horse must think it queer
> To stop without a farmhouse near
> Between the woods and frozen lake
> The darkest evening of the year.
>
> He gives his harness bells a shake
> To ask if there is some mistake.
> The only other sound's the sweep
> Of easy wind and downy flake.
>
> The woods are lovely dark and deep.
> But I have promises to keep.
> And miles to go before I sleep,
> And miles to go before I sleep."

Isabel shut the book. They sat for a few minutes in silence. She could see that he was moved, and she felt a stirring of affection for him.

Alfred finally broke the silence. "This man was a king, I think, or at least a prince."

"Why do you say that?" That was certainly a new interpretation.

"Because he describes how it is to feel the burden of responsibility. Many times I have been out for one reason or another—perhaps hunting, perhaps traveling, perhaps anticipating a battle—and I have wished that I could linger. But obligations drive me on—'I have promises to keep'." He looked at her with weariness, "'And miles to go before I sleep'." He gave her a sad smile.

She touched him lightly on the shoulder to offer him comfort. "Let's see what else you have here," she said brightly. "Ahh, Shakespeare's Tragedies. There are several plays in here that I think you will relate to. But it's a beautiful day. Let's go to the park, and I'll read it to you."

As she led him out of the library, Isabel found the impulse to take his hand impossible to resist. It was a nice walk to the residence of the university president, the grounds of which doubled as a park for the students and staff. It seemed far removed from the hustle and bustle of the campus and its traffic. She noticed him relaxing visibly as they walked deeper and deeper into the woods and open fields. They sat by a tree at the edge of an open area. From their sheltered spot they had a generous view of the pond. They sat in silence for a few minutes taking in the activity before them. There were joggers running with easy gaits along the trail beside the water. To one side under another tree, a group of students sat discussing the open texts in front of them.

In an open area a young man was playing Frisbee with his golden retriever. The eager dog jumped up to catch the Frisbee without realizing where he was. He flopped into the water on his back. He jumped up, surprised but with the Frisbee still in his mouth. Isabel laughed, and saw that Alfred was laughing, too.

"This is a good place," Alfred said closing his eyes to focus on the breeze caressing his face. "I like it here. Read now, please." He lay back and closed his eyes.

She was amused at his command. "This is a play..." she began.

"What is a 'play'?" he interrupted.

"A story that is performed to entertain," she answered patiently.

"Oh yes, the drama. Continue."

"It is a play set in Scotland..." she began again.

He interrupted again. "What is Scotland?"

Isabel sighed. "It is a country to the north of England." She remembered that England was not called England in the time which he claimed to be from. "Let's see. It is the northernmost part of the island that your country is on."

He opened his eyes, perplexed. "The land of the Picts? They are barbarians. They kill without mercy. They rape. They plunder. They are animals. What entertainment could come from such as them?"

She put a hand on his arm to calm him. "Whatever they are in your time, at the time of this play, Scotland has become as civilized as your country. Think of the characters as Scottish rather than Picts."

"Agreed. Continue." He reclined again and closed his eyes.

She sighed and began, "Three witches speak first:

When shall we three meet again
            In thunder, lightening or in rain?
When the hurlyburly's done,
    When the battle's lost and won.
 That will be ere the set of sun.
Where the place?
Upon the heath.
There to meet with Macbeth.
 I come, Graymalkin!
Paddock calls.
 Anon!
    Fair is foul, and foul is fair.
    Hover through the fog and filthy air..."

He interrupted again. "Witches can be very bad. They can cause a lot of trouble. This Macbeth is already cursed, I think."

Isabel puffed her impatience. "If you keep interrupting me, we will never get through this."

"True enough. Go on."

He did not speak again for a long time, but with his eyes closed let her words wash over him like the gentle waves of the sea. She enjoyed reading, and he seemed to enjoy listening. They continued until Isabel noticed darkness falling. "We have to leave," she said with regret. "They close the park at dark."

Alfred got up and stretched, then offered his hand to pull her up. Capturing her gaze with his own so that she could see his sincerity, he said, "You read well. Your voice is soothing, yet you give the characters passion. Can we do this again tomorrow?"

"I'd like that," Isabel replied, trying not to appear too eager. He looked at her in a way that no one had before, and it made her knees feel weak. "You are a good audience. There is another play that I think you will like called 'Hamlet, Prince of Denmark'."

"A Dane. I hope he dies at the end."

"As a matter of fact, he does." She smiled. "Picts, witches, Danes…is there any one that you do like?"

He thought a minute. "I like you."

"Thanks," she replied, blushing, "you old smoothie. I bet you say that to all the girls."

She was kidding, but he was not. She saw from his expression that his answer was completely sincere. "Actually, I do not usually seek the company of women."

"I see," Isabel said, embarrassed. No wonder he was so violently opposed to marriage. Funny, he was so masculine that she would never have guessed. "You prefer the company of men."

He looked at her quizzically. Suddenly the light of understanding appeared in his eyes. He puffed up his body indignantly. "I most certainly do not. It is simply that the presence of most women provides a distraction that I find it easier to avoid."

She breathed a sigh of relief. "Sorry, I didn't mean to offend you. I misunderstood."

Alfred's reply was a chilly, "See that it doesn't happen again."

Isabel was disappointed and angry with herself. Here she had a wonderful afternoon with a guy whom seemed to like her, and, as always, she had managed to say the wrong thing. She knew better than to fall all over herself apologizing. Experience had taught her that made things worse. "Shall we go?" She led the way and he followed silently behind her.

By the time they got to the library Isabel was desperate. Whatever Alfred's story, whatever his motivation, his arrival was the most exciting thing that had happened to her in her entire life. She couldn't let it end like this. She wanted more time with him, more stories, more afternoons in the park, more fantasy. "I am sorry I offended you," she said trying not to whine. "Let me buy you dinner to make it up to you."

"Since I am hungry, and I am in no hurry to go back to books I cannot read, I agree. Lead on."

The tension had eased a bit, but he was still silent as they walked to the nearby pizza parlor. Isabel was amused when Alfred walked in ahead of her, head held high, obviously used to the deference of others. They slid into a dark booth, and she ordered a supreme pizza. If she was going to be his "tour guide" through the "future," she wanted to give him the full effect.

Isabel ordered herself a glass of wine but got him a dark English stout thinking it might be more to his taste. She was right.

"Very good," Alfred said, licking the foam from his lips.

"Enjoy it. The pizza here is the best, but it takes a while."

"I like this place," he said and seemed to have recovered completely from her faux pas.

They sat in silence for a few minutes then she started the conversation. "Tell me about where you come from," she said, settling in for a long story.

"What do you want to know?"

"What time is it, to begin with?"

"About a thousand years ago…"

"Around 900 AD?"

"I guess. I'm not sure about your calendar."

She looked suspicious. "You're kidding, right?"

"No, I believe I already told you that I do not have a sense of humor."

"Right. 900 AD." She sat shaking her head. What is going on here? she thought. What am I doing? He is either a great liar or a certifiable nut case. But she said, "Go on."

"What do you want to know?" he repeated.

"Who are you there? You've said several times that you are a prince. What do you do there? Do you sit on a throne all day?"

He looked at her with annoyance. "Do I look to you like I sit all day?"

"What do I know? Princes are not exactly commonplace around here in case you hadn't noticed."

"My brother, the king, he sits on his fat ass all day. I get things done."

"You don't like your brother?"

"No, I don't."

"Why?"

"Most recently because he is trying to force me to marry. He likes to try and move me like a puppet to show that, even though I am his brother and a prince in my own right, he is the one who inherited the kingdom. He hates me, and I hate him, but he can make me do anything he wants. I am powerless against him."

Married. She felt a surge of jealousy knowing that she had no right. "Why?"

He shrugged, "Because he is the king."

She nodded and waited for him to go on. It was unbelievable, but it was a great story.

"He has arranged my marriage to Elswith, daughter of the king of Mercia, the country directly to our north. It is essential that Mercia not falls to the Danes, or else they will be breathing down our necks and much harder to fight off. I see the wisdom of the union, and yet I cannot bear it. Elswith is crude and uneducated.

She flaunts herself shamelessly and gives in to her every impulse. I cannot stand to think of her as my wife."

She felt relieved but still a little jealous. "Is she ugly?"

"No, many consider her quite comely, but she has no substance. She finds everything funny and twitters like a little bird with incessant giggling."

She smiled, "And we know that you have no sense of humor."

He gave a little chuckle. "That's right. But it has less to do with that than it does with how annoying she is." He put on a falsetto, female voice. "Why should I learn to read? I am going to be queen. Everyone will do everything for me. Pouring over books will give me wrinkles. Father says reading is not for women." He gave a deep, heavy sigh. "Nothing displeases me more than the thought of being tied to her. But Baldy demands it."

"Baldy?"

"My brother, Ethelbald. He is the king, and I will do as he demands." "

"So if you are going to marry her anyway, why are you here?"

"I am here because Merlin told me I should be. And I am here because Kathryn asked me to bring you home."

"Who is Kathryn?"

"Your mother. Or rather the woman who should have been your mother. Evidently she has never gotten over your death, that is, your disappearance. Merlin has been searching for you all these years in large part for her."

Isabel felt tears threaten. The word "mother" always set off an intense emotional response in her. The fact that Alfred was talking about a mother who actually wanted her was almost too much to bear. "My mother?" This was no longer a lark. He might be crazy or he might be lying, but this was hitting way too close to home.

"She is, or was, the wife of Hugh, Lord of Eastlea. She is a great lady: beautiful, kind, understanding, intelligent. And she has been a great friend to me all my life, since my own mother died. I would do anything to insure her happiness, but before now she has never asked for anything. This is important to her. You are important to her. So here I am."

"She wants me?" Isabel's voice cracked.

"Yes, she does."

Isabel's emotions threatened to overwhelm her. She dropped her head so that Alfred couldn't see the tears welling up in her eyes.

"Where is your birth mother?" he asked. "The one who raised you? Is she dead?"

"No," she said quietly, swiping at her tears and sniffing. "When Merlin said the baby was born that was supposed to die?" She looked at him for confirmation that he remembered, "That sounds like me. I was supposed to be born dead. Edith was very unhappy that I lived."

"Edith?"

"My mother. She had big plans for her life that did not include a child. Her pregnancy was an accident, and when they told her the baby was dead, she breathed a sigh of relief. Then when I wasn't dead, she was upset."

He was incredulous. "She wanted you to die?"

"She didn't have time for a baby, and death made it all so neat and easy. Then there I was, and she is not the type to give up something that is hers. She took me home and fulfilled her responsibilities to me. She made sure I was clean and fed and clothed. She worked a lot, long hours, and as soon as I was old enough, I spent most of my time alone."

"Hmmm," he said thoughtfully, "Kathryn is nothing like that."

"Tell me more about her."

"She is very beautiful," he said, "and she carries herself like a queen." He stopped and searched Isabel's face, finally coming to gaze into her green eyes. "You don't look much like her, but there is something of you that reminds me of her."

"What does she do?"

"What does she do?" he repeated as though he couldn't imagine the question. "She does what all women of high birth do."

"Which is what?" she gestured for him to elaborate.

"She takes care of the household. Whatever that entails."

"Is she bright?"

"Bright?"

"Is she smart? Is she educated?"

"She learned to read, which is a little unusual for a woman. She does not love to learn as my mother did, but she is wise in the ways of life."

"What of Lord Hugh?"

"He died long ago. I remember him as a boor and a buffoon. My brothers held him in high esteem. They are very much alike."

"So this man would have been my father?"

Alfred looked perplexed. "Yes, I guess he must have been."

"A buffoonish father is better than no father at all."

"I don't know about that."

At that moment, the pizza arrived, and Alfred's attention was immediately riveted on the vision before him.

"What is this?" he exclaimed. The waitress looked at him like he was crazy, but Isabel waved her off.

"It's pizza," she laughed. "You have never seen pizza?" She picked up a piece and took a bite. "Watch out. It's hot."

He watched her and then copied her. He closed his eyes and ran his tongue around the inside of his mouth to taste every morsel. "This is very good."

"I'm glad you like it," she said smiling, her overwhelming emotions temporarily forgotten.

"So many vegetables and meats in one place. Amazing."

They ate mostly in silence except for the grunts and groans of pleasure coming from Alfred. Isabel was amused and touched. To see someone take so much pleasure in such an everyday, mundane thing was rare indeed.

When he appeared to be done, Isabel motioned for the check.

"Thank you for that feast," Alfred said, slamming his hands down on the table. "That was truly delicious."

"I'm glad you enjoyed it." She was sorry the meal was over. She enjoyed his company, crazy or not, and she didn't want the day to end. But she couldn't trust him yet. Everything he said was so nuts, who could know when he would change into the raving ax-murderer hiding under the surface?

As they walked back to the library across the darkened but still active campus, she resisted the strong urge to reach for his hand. She could feel that there was something special between them, and yet she wasn't quite comfortable enough to act on it.

"I guess this is where I leave you," Isabel said shyly, holding out her hand. "Goodnight, Alfred."

Alfred looked at her intently, taking her hand. "Goodnight, Isabel. This was a good day. I thank you for it."

Chapter 13

The next day, Friday, Alfred was waiting for Isabel at the table in front of the circulation desk, books stacked around him. She came up behind him and put her hands on his shoulders to surprise him. "Hi there."

He turned around and smiled. "Good morning."

"I see you found some reading material."

He nodded, looking at the stack of books in front of him. They were all books written either in Old English or Latin. "Yes, I did. I've been reading all night."

"Not literally all night?"

"Perhaps not. I did wake up with my face down in a book, so I must have slept some." He smiled again. "It was quite enjoyable." He stretched his neck around, stiff from sitting up all night two nights in a row.

Isabel hurt just looking at him. Again she had the overwhelming urge to touch him and rub the kinks out of his shoulders but dismissed it quickly as inappropriate. "I know the perfect thing for you. You need a nice hot shower. Come with me. I've got an idea." She stuck her head in the doorway of the workroom. Gwen had opened the library this morning and was sitting at the desk with a cup of coffee. "Morning, Gwen. I've got to run a quick errand. I'll be right back."

Gwen gave Isabel a sly, knowing look, as though she had learned some secret about her. "Where are you going, Iz? Does it have something to do with that great-looking guy you were talking to?"

Isabel had a moment of panic. If Gwen went after him, she would be out. She knew she had better play it cool. "Yeah, he needs to know where the gym is, so I told him I'd show him. He's new, you know."

Gwen guessed what she was up to and gave her a lustful smile. "Have you...you know?"

Isabel felt as though she had been caught, even though she hadn't done anything. "No!" she said with a little too much emotion. "Of course not. He's just a guy I met who needs some help learning his way around."

Gwen didn't buy it for a minute. "Oh, ok. Go on and take your 'friend' to the gym, I'll cover for you." She noticed that Isabel visibly relaxed and even sighed as she turned away. "Hey, Iz..."

"Yes?"

"Try not to drool."

Isabel blushed and rushed out.

She was still blushing when she walked up to Alfred, and he noticed. "What's wrong?"

This made her even more embarrassed. "Nothing. Come on."

She walked a little in front of him as they left the library so that she could get her color under control before she had to talk to him again. When she got to the place where she would turn left to go to the gymnasium, she stopped so suddenly that he bumped into her. She turned to look at him pensively.

"What?" Alfred said with a little irritation.

"Clothes," said Isabel. "You need clothes. It's not going to do you much good to take a shower and put the same clothes back on. I need to wash them. But you can't run around the gym naked."

She looked around to see what resources she had and saw the student center to her right. Inside the student center was the university store. They had clothes there. Not a big selection but at this point almost anything would do. "Got it," she said, "Come on."

Alfred followed Isabel up the sidewalk and into the large marble building. The store had just opened for the day and there were no customers there yet, so no one noticed or wondered about their odd behavior. She led him to the section filled with clothing of all types, all bearing some mark of the university. There was a much larger selection than she expected.

Isabel looked Alfred over. He looked pretty active. He would probably want to spend some time in the gym or on the track stretching his legs and working out the kinks of sleeping in the library for two nights. She chose a rack of athletic wear and began browsing through it. She picked a very comfortable looking pair of gym shorts and a sleeveless T-shirt. They were pre-washed, very soft and loose, so she didn't have to spend too much time embarrassing herself staring at him to determine his size. "These should do," she said, "You can hang out at the gym a while. There's a lot to do and it'll give you a change of scenery."

"These look comfortable," he said. "What is there to do there?"

"They have basketball courts, racquetball courts, a weight room, a track, a swimming pool, a climbing wall. Tons of stuff. I'll get you in on a visitor's pass and you can do anything that you want. That'll give me time to run to a dorm and get your clothes washed."

Alfred looked at the clothing she had put in his hands. "I need something else."

"What?" she asked distractedly looking around.

"Umm—something to go under?"

She looked at him and blushed, trying not to look down at the part he needed to cover. "That's a little tougher," she said. "They don't sell underwear here. What can we do?" Then she saw a rack of bathing suits, designed primarily for the swim team. Because of this, the men's suits were mostly Speedos. It was perfect. It would solve his problem and he could swim, too. She tried to guess at his size without having to stare at his crotch. "This should do," she said handing him one she thought would fit.

He held it up. "It's very small. Are you sure this will fit me?"

"It should," she replied looking away. "They make them tight so that you can swim faster."

"I will try," he said.

Isabel paid the cashier and led Alfred to the gym. All in all, this morning had been much more awkward than she had expected. She wanted to get him settled so that she could get back to work and regroup. She checked in at the front desk and got him a visitor's pass. Then she showed him around and let him go into the locker room to change his clothes. When she finished the tour, she asked, "Do you think you'll be all right?"

"Yes, I believe so. There is a lot to do."

"Enjoy," Isabel said smiling. "I'll be back at lunchtime." She pointed at the clock. "Around noon. If you need me you know where to find me."

"Yes I do."

She stopped at a nearby dormitory and put his clothes in the wash, using detergent that some student had left behind. Then she hurried back to work. Halfway through the morning she took the cart to shelve books and slipped out to put his clothes in the dryer. Gwen kept leering at her with a knowing smile, enjoying Isabel's discomfort. Isabel looked at the clock repeatedly, irritated to find that only a few minutes had passed since the last time she had looked. Will noon never come? she thought with frustration.

Chapter 14

Alfred did in fact find plenty to do to pass the time. The activities that used balls he watched with interest but did not try. He saw people running around a short, circular road outside, running the same route around and around, over and over again. I can do that, he thought.

He noticed right away that he looked different from the others. They all had on shoes that looked as though they were made for running, cut low at the ankle but sturdy. He had his boots, in which he not only ran, but also walked, rode, hunted and fought.

Alfred had run four times around the track when he decided that it was not interesting enough to continue. He saw some people playing tennis, and recognized the purpose of the game right away, even thought the equipment and playing court was different than he had known. This was something he could not do alone. He decided to go back inside and see what else he could find.

As he was walking in, Alfred stopped a moment to appreciate the building itself. It was huge, even though it was built into a hillside and part of it was underground. It was very utilitarian looking, no fancy columns or scrollwork. It had clean straight lines and was painted a stark, no-nonsense shade of white. He liked it.

Wandering into a smaller room, he watched a few young men lifting poles with what appeared to be very heavy weights on either end. He looked at the muscles bulging in their arms and legs. I wish I had these men in battle, he thought. A legion of these men and the Danes would turn and run at the sight of them.

Next he found a huge room with a highly polished wood floor. At either end a basket, open at the bottom, mounted on a large board, hung from the ceiling. Several young women were running back and forth on the floor, bouncing a large orange ball and throwing it at the baskets. He noticed large rows of benches, built with each row up a little higher and back a little farther than the one in front of it. It reminded him of an amphitheater, though not so beautiful. He sat down to watch them play.

The young women slipped into the background of his consciousness as Alfred's thoughts drifted to another young woman. Isabel. She confused him. On the one hand she seemed nothing like a lady. She did not wear beautiful clothes. She did not have servants. She worked to take care of herself. Peasant women did that, not someone born to nobility.

Of course, she had not been born to nobility, had she? This woman, this Edith, she had not done a very good job of polishing her daughter. She did not prepare her to attract a husband. In spite of this, Alfred thought, she is very quick-witted and well-mannered. She appears to have read and studied a great deal, and she has devoted her life to working with books.

But there is something else, Alfred thought. I like her company. I like to be with her. I am looking forward to seeing her again.

At that moment, the orange ball flew out of the game and up into the stands where he was sitting. He threw it back to the girl who was beckoning for it, then moved on to see what else he could find.

Chapter 15

Isabel found Alfred in the pool swimming laps with strong, even strokes. When he saw her, he swam over to the side and leaned on the edge. "Hello," he said with a smile.

"Hi," she replied, also smiling. "You're a good swimmer."

"Of course. It is good for making the body strong. We make games of swimming, competitions to see who is best."

She smiled, "And do you always win?"

He took the question seriously. "I do not." He paused then looked at the pool. "This is very strange. Have you ever been swimming in a river?"

"No, I haven't."

"It's very different. The current changes everything. If it is with you, you go faster. If it is against you, you work harder. Either way you risk being swept away. It is much more challenging than this." He paused and looked at her as though measuring her up. "You come and swim."

"Me? No, I can't," Isabel said, panicking.

"Oh," said Alfred matter-of-factly, "you don't know how."

"No, no," she replied quickly, her heart rushing like a trapped rabbit. "I can swim. I mean I can't swim right now."

"You don't like it?"

"No, actually, I love it," she fumbled. How could she get out of this?

"Then you don't have any swimming clothes?" he asked, perplexed.

"Actually, I keep my bathing suit in a locker in the women's locker room," she stammered. What was she doing? All she had to do was say she didn't have a bathing suit and that would have been that. What was she doing?

"Then what is the problem?" he looked at her questioning.

"I don't want you to see me in a bathing suit," she confessed, looking down.

"Why not?"

"Because I don't look so hot."

"Hot?"

"Good. I don't look good in a bathing suit."

"I don't understand. What is the problem with how you look? You are not deformed. You are not scarred or covered with sores." He paused, "Are you?"

She laughed. "No, I am not covered with scars or sores. I am fat."

"I do not understand this. You are who you are. Do you want to swim or not?"

"I give up," she said. "I'll go get my suit on."

Her suit was very conservative, a black tank, but still Isabel felt self-conscious. That feeling dissipated quickly when she saw his only reaction was a smile.

"Good," he said. "Come in."

No one had ever looked at Isabel the way Alfred was looking at her now. He was watching her closely, his eyes running over every curve of her body and following her every move. It made her uncomfortable, on one hand; but on the other, she had never felt sensuous. She began swimming laps across the pool with a strong, sure crawl. After a couple of times back and forth, she came to where he was standing and stopped to rest. It only took her a few minutes to catch her breath.

"Race?" Alfred offered with a slight smile.

She was up to the challenge. "You're on. Ready, set, go." They set off at an almost even pace, kicking and pumping their arms in synchronous motion. Alfred had the advantage of height and strength, though, and before long had pulled ahead. To her credit, he did not beat her by much.

They were both breathless from the exertion. Alfred gave her another dazzling smile. "You are very good."

"Thanks. So are you."

"Let's dive to the bottom," Alfred said enthusiastically. "I like that you can see all the way." The exhilaration of activity had changed his entire demeanor. He seemed young and carefree. She had the oddest feeling that this was the real person that he was supposed to be, and that somehow it was because of her.

"No thanks. Heights give me the heebie-jeebies."

"Heebie-jeebies?"

"You know, the creeps."

"The creeps?"

"Heights make me uneasy."

"But this is not high. It is low."

"Same difference. Go ahead."

He dove deep as she watched him through the distortion of the water. He broke the surface and gave another big smile. "Amazing!"

She smiled back. His enthusiasm was infectious, even if she didn't care to share the experience. She looked up at the clock. "Oh no, look at the time. I've got to get back."

She pulled herself out of the pool, but he grabbed her leg before she could get away. "Stay with me," he said.

She sat down and looked at him. Play hooky? She never had. But for him? Gee, what a tough choice. "Ok. Let me call and tell them I won't be back today."

Gwen enjoyed the call way too much. "So I'm not the only one willing to compromise myself to be with a guy, huh? I'm indiscriminant, am I? I've never taken off work to be with a guy I've known two days."

"Leave it alone, Gwen. I haven't issued him an invitation the way you always do."

If Gwen was offended, she gave no indication of it. "Fine, but tomorrow night you're both coming out with me. I want a closer look."

"Goodbye, Gwen."

The last thing Isabel heard was Gwen's laughter as she hung up the phone. Her irritation melted away, however, when she saw Alfred sitting on the side of the pool, waiting for her. The Speedo left little to the imagination, which was okay because his body was better even than she could ever have imagined. Lean and muscular, it was obvious that, indeed, he spent little time "sitting around." The wave of self-consciousness washed over her again. She spent plenty of time sitting around, and she looked it. She wished the towel were big enough to cover her completely.

"Done," she said, trying to sound nonchalant. "What would you like to do?"

"I'd like to see more," Alfred replied. "Show me more of this place. And read. I want you to read to me again."

"Sure," Isabel nodded. "Let's get dressed, and I'll take you downtown for a bit. Then we can come back here to the park. We can even pick up sandwiches and have a picnic."

Chapter 16

Isabel decided the train would be the best way to go. City traffic was best experienced as an observer, not a participant. Given Alfred's apparently limited time, they could skip that little adventure. Alfred was impressed with the sleek silver tubes that could move so many so quickly. "This is a very useful thing." He looked through the windows at the blur of colors as they passed. He smiled at her, "I do like going fast. But I'm disappointed that I cannot see more. Does the train ever slow down so that you can see what is outside the window?"

Isabel shrugged. "Most people who ride this train don't want to see what's outside. It is not the most beautiful part of the city." As they pulled into the station, she looked down on the nearby industrial park and the grocery distribution center closest to the tracks. Out the other side were old buildings and signs, mostly covered with graffiti. She was sure that these places were not usually included on the tours of the city.

Alfred nodded, but continued to look out with interest. Soon they passed into a dark tunnel, and he looked at her for explanation.

"We're going under the city," Isabel explained. "This way we don't have to deal with all the cars, traffic lights and pedestrians."

Alfred nodded again, taking it all in. He did not seem frightened or overwhelmed, only interested.

They came to their station, and he followed her out. She led him to a very long escalator and showed him how to use it. He followed her direction without any problem. He certainly is a quick study, she thought. I'm not sure I could function in a world so alien to me.

They blinked against the sudden assault of light and stood for a moment as Isabel decided where to go and what to do. They walked toward the downtown department stores and hotels. At the front of one large hotel was a shop that sold resort and beach wear. The mannequins in the window were very skimpily dressed. One was wearing an open bathing suit cover over a thong bikini. The other was wearing a tank with a plunging neckline, high cut legs and gaping sides held in place with laces from hip to breast. Alfred stopped, cocked his head and examined the mannequins closely. Isabel was amused. Men.

"These clothes are for swimming?" he asked without looking at her.

"More or less," she replied.

"More less than more, I would say. Why bother wearing anything at all?" He looked at her with curiosity. "Your swimming clothes were not like this. Do you also wear such things?"

She laughed and answered with an emphatic, "No, I do not. But most women who wear these are not much interested in swimming."

"I don't understand."

"They lie in lounge chairs in the sun and tan themselves."

"Tan?"

"Let the sun make their skin darker."

"Why?"

"Because they think it makes them more beautiful, I guess."

"Do you do this?"

Isabel looked at the mannequins and shook her head. "Nope. First of all I look terrible in a bikini. Second of all, I think lying out in the sun is boring."

"So you would rather swim?"

"I would rather swim. Or walk on the beach, if I am at the beach."

"These women are trying to attract husbands, I think."

She shrugged. "Some, I suppose. They are definitely showing themselves off to attract men. What they want to do with them after they get them I'll leave to your imagination." She looked at him, embarrassed, hoping he could fill in the blank by himself. Instead he looked at her with a question in his eyes. "Some women are looking for marriage, but some many just want to have a good time. Some are already married and want their husbands and others to notice them." She shrugged again. "I'm only guessing here. That's how it looks to me."

"So they are wanton?"

She thought of Gwen and smiled. "I suppose you could say that. Some of them anyway."

"Humph," he snorted with a haughty air, and shook his head. He motioned for her to move on.

They walked along slowly so that he could take in all that was going on around him: the cars, the traffic lights, the rushing people, the store windows, the street performers, the begging homeless. "I see that some things have not changed so much," he commented.

"What do you mean?"

He pointed to a young man sitting to one side on the steps of a large marble building, playing a guitar. "We also have wandering performers who will give you a song or two for a meal or a few coins." Then he nodded his head toward an alcove in a building across the street, where a dirty man in ragged clothes sat begging for money. "We have beggars, too." He looked directly at her. "See, not so different." He stopped suddenly and his expression changed. He looked as though there was nothing else going on around them. His eyes were focused, unblinking, on her.

Isabel was mesmerized by the look on Alfred's face. What was he thinking? A warm feeling started in her middle and spread through her entire body. Somehow she knew, though she was reluctant to trust her instincts, that he was glad to be with her. She shook her head and smiled as the realization hit her. She was glad to be with him, too. It felt right, and it made everything else right. She was infatuated with him, no doubt. He was so beautiful that she almost didn't care what she looked like; she was going to throw herself at him anyway. Especially when he looked at her like that. But there was more. It was contentment. Like the gears of a life which had been grinding and cranking painfully out of sync had suddenly dropped into place.

She chuckled to herself. Of course, it figured. Her soulmate was a wacko. He believed he was a ninth century English prince, for God's sake.

"What?" Alfred asked, noting her amusement.

"Nothing," Isabel said, wisely keeping her thoughts to herself. "I enjoy your company."

"Yes," he replied, "I find yours agreeable as well."

She slipped her hand into his. He entwined his fingers with hers, and they turned to walk on.

After a time, they saw a horse-drawn carriage of the kind popular with tourists. The horse looked tired. Alfred did not hesitate. He walked up to the carriage and addressed the driver. "Your horse needs tending," he said in a commanding tone.

"Get a life, man," the driver replied, unimpressed.

Alfred walked up to the horse and began to free it from its harness. "I said your horse needs tending." He removed its reins, bit and blinders. "Isabel," he commanded, pointing at a nearby fruit stand, "go to that fruit merchant and bring me an apple. Water, too."

Isabel did as she was told, too stunned at his actions to bristle at his commanding tone. When she returned, Alfred addressed the driver again. "Give me your hat."

"Who are you?" the driver replied. "Get your own hat."

Alfred drew himself up to his full height. His expression was that of one who would not be denied. "I said give me your hat."

The driver looked around at the crowd that was gathering. He handed his hat down without further comment. Alfred poured half the water into the man's hat and put it up for the horse to drink. He fed it the apple and then the rest of the water. He patted the horse's withers, and it nuzzled him. Then he led it back and harnessed it to the carriage. He handed the driver his hat. "You should take better care of this animal. You will get more work from it if you treat it with kindness." With no further comment, he walked away.

Isabel followed him. "You are an animal lover," she said having discovered something new about him.

"An animal is only an animal. But if you treat them well, they serve you better."

"It is much the same with humans, isn't it?" Isabel observed.

Alfred stopped suddenly and looked at her in surprise. "What did you say?"

"Humans also perform better when they are treated with kindness and compassion. Many employers don't seem to realize that. They take everything someone has to give until that person is all used up. Then the boss fires the exhausted employee and hires someone new."

They walked on in silence, Alfred far away in his thoughts. Suddenly he stopped and said to Isabel, "You drop words of wisdom so easily. Do you always do this?"

Isabel thought he must be kidding, but as usual the expression on his face was quite serious. "You're teasing me, aren't you?" she asked, amused.

"Teasing? No, I am not teasing. For a woman to be so wise is a great thing. So again I ask, do you speak such wisdom often?"

Isabel laughed. "Oh yes," she said, making a gesture with her hand as though her mouth was a fountain. "Wisdom spurts out of me all the time."

She took his hand again, and they resumed their walking. She was still laughing to herself at the thought of being a fountain of great wisdom. "Honestly, Alfred, you are a real hoot."

Alfred looked perplexed. "A hoot? What is a hoot?"

"You're funny. You make me laugh."

He thought about this for a moment. "I make you laugh? I never make any one laugh. In my memory you are the first person who ever thought I was funny."

Isabel laughed again. "There's a first time for everything."

Alfred nodded solemnly. After a moment he said, "I have seen enough. I'd like to go back now."

"Sure," Isabel replied and led him back to the train station.

It was a quiet ride back to the campus, Isabel and Alfred both lost in their own thoughts. What if Merlin was right? What if they were destined to be together? How could it be true? But the way it felt to be together. How could it not be true?

Chapter 17

When they got to the library, Isabel looked at Alfred's stack of books that remained on the study table from the morning. For once she was glad that Gwen had slacked off, and the books had not been re-shelved. She pulled out Beowulf. "Can you read this?" she asked.

"Yes," he replied nodding.

"Would you read to me today?"

He was pleased. "Yes."

He tucked the book under his arm and followed Isabel out into the late afternoon sunshine. They took their time walking to the park and returned to the same spot as the day before.

He opened the book and looked at her. "Are you familiar with this story?"

"A little," she replied. "I'm not entirely sure I'll be able to understand any of what you read, but I would like to hear it anyway

"This is the story of a brave warrior, Beowulf," he began, "who hears of a great monster, Grendel, who is terrorizing the kingdom of King Hrothgar. He decides to come to the aid of this king, seek out and destroy the monster."

"Wasn't Hrothgar's kingdom in Denmark?"

"It was, yes."

"I thought you hated all Danes. How do you know this story?"

"My people came from that land in the time before. Those who are there now are the descendants of the barbarians who stayed behind."

"Ok, got it. Go ahead."

He looked at the book and smiled.

"What?" she asked, also smiling.

He looked at her. "It is amazing to see this story in writing. It is one we often tell." He paused and sighed. "Anyway…

> 'Hwaet, we gardenas in geardagum,
> theodcyninga thrym gefrunon,
> hu tha aethelingas ellen fremedon!
>> Oft Scyld Scefing sceathena threatum,
>> monegum maegthum moedostla of teah…'"

He read on. His voice was deep and soothing. She closed her eyes and let the sound wash over her. She recognized very few of the words, but was able to pick one out here and there, surprised to find that aloud some seemed familiar through they had looked so strange in print. She stopped him when he got to the lines:

> 'sytham hildedeor hond alegde,
> earm ond eaxle—thaer waes eal geador
> Grendles grape—under geapne hr (of).

"Alfred," she sat up, "is that were he rips off Grendel's arm?"

"Yes, it is. So you do know this story," he smiled.

"A bit," she replied. "Just the basics, really. It's very bloody, isn't it?"

"I suppose," he shrugged, seemingly indifferent to the gore.

"Is it like that in your time?" she asked, allowing herself to bask in the fantasy of time travel.

"Sometimes. When it needs to be." He shrugged again. "Any kind of battle is bloody. By its very nature, it can be no other way."

"Have you been in a lot of battles?"

"Yes," he nodded. "Our borders are constantly threatened. We have no choice but to fight."

"Do you use a sword?"

"Yes."

"Do you ride a horse?"

"Sometimes. A horse gives you the advantage of height, but also leaves you vulnerable to bowmen with arrows. I often dismount when I am on the edge of the battlefield and go in on foot."

"I guess you have seen a lot of men die."

"Die and worse, not die. Many weapons shred the insides of the body when they strike true. Then the man's life spills out all over the ground. But if they hit him in a certain way, he does not die immediately. He simply lies on the ground, gasping for air, being trampled by the feet of those fighting around him."

Isabel grimaced. "Can't you at least drag them off the battlefield?"

"Obviously you have never seen such a fight. There is no time. If you bend over to aid the wounded, the sword of the enemy will come down on you. There is nothing to do until the battle is over. Then, we do our best to burn the dead before wild animals can desecrate their bodies."

"God," the mental image made her sick to her stomach. "You want me to go to this place?"

"I'm not asking you to go into battle," he replied.

"Still, it is so brutal. Why don't you stay here?" With me, she added silently. Stay here with me.

He shook his head. "I can't. I have things to do there, important things. Besides, while I like some things about this time, mostly it is too noisy and crowded."

"All right then, Alfred, tell me what makes it so great," she challenged.

He noticed the slight hint of a smile on her lips and twinkle of mischief in her eyes. With a light touch he traced the shape of her eyes, the bridge of her nose, and the curve of her lips.

Isabel was embarrassed by the way he was looking at her, and she wanted to look away, but she couldn't make herself do it. He was running his fingers over her face as though he was a sightless person trying to create an image for himself. She closed her eyes to focus on his touch and became intensely aware of the rise and fall of her chest. She was afraid to open her eyes, afraid that the look on his face would be gone. She jerked slightly in surprise when she felt his breath on her face right before his lips touched hers.

Their connection was soft and light, but they lingered in it. Isabel felt as though all of her life she had been standing in front of an open door facing the cold, but so accustomed to it that she never realized it could be any different. Face so close to face with him, warm air filled the space between them, and that door was finally closed, shutting out the bitter loneliness and cold. When they pulled apart, the cold came rushing back in, but she would never again be oblivious to it.

Alfred did not hesitate to close the gap between them once again. He shifted his position to pull her toward him, and then lowered her gently onto the ground. He braced himself, afraid of crushing her, but she wanted to be crushed, to feel his weight on her, so that she could believe that it was happening. She put her arms around his neck and pulled him down. They kissed again, and again, and again, slowly, deeply, relishing every moment, every second, every breath. Isabel's mind had ceased to have any coherent thoughts. It had turned into a broken record playing the same phrase over and over: Oh, God. Oh, God. Oh, God.

Suddenly, a dark shadow passed over them, and Alfred's body went rigid in her arms. She saw her fear mirrored in his eyes. "Alfred?" she said, trembling in the chilled air.

"Yes." He rolled off of her and onto his feet in one fluid motion. He reached for her hand and pulled her up to stand with him. They looked to see where the trouble was. Alfred was the first to see the man step out of the woods behind them.

Isabel recognized the man from the library. She stepped closer to Alfred and whispered, "I've seen this guy. He came to the library that first day right after you left. He is seriously creepy."

Alfred did not take his eyes off the approaching man. "I know him. That is Malcolm. The person I told you is trying to prevent us from taking you."

Isabel hugged herself against the chill. She did not need to be convinced that he was telling the truth. For the first time since this whole thing had started, she believed it was true.

Alfred had drawn himself to his full height, shoulders back, body tensed and ready to fight. His eyes were dark and stormy and his jaw was set. He looked like a warrior prince, resolved to do battle.

"Malcolm," he said tightly.

"Alfred," Malcolm replied, smiling as though he had accidentally run into an old friend. His eyes, however, were cold and dangerous. "What a wonderful surprise! Imagine finding you here."

"What do you want?"

"You know, don't you?" Malcolm said. "I've come for her."

"I don't think so. Not this time. We are not children this time. You will have to go through me to get her."

"Oh, I'm so scared," Malcolm replied sarcastically. "Do you think that you are any match for me?"

"I think that you would not engage me in a fair fight. You always hide behind your magic when in truth you are a coward."

Malcolm put his hand over his heart in a gesture of hurt feelings. "You wound me." His false joviality faded. "This time there can be no doubt. Her elimination must be unequivocal. She must be destroyed completely."

Isabel couldn't breathe. She tried to fill her lungs with air, but nothing would work. It was as though her whole body had frozen and could no longer move. She tried to feel her heart beating, but she was sure it had stopped. Alfred moved directly in front of her placing himself firmly between her and her assassin. She swayed against his strong back, closed her eyes and willed her heart to beat.

Alfred was determined. "You will not take her. Only God can take her soul."

"Yes, but if I kill her body, God will have no choice but to take her, and she will not be with you. That is all that I need."

"Why would you want to send someone to God?"

"Her sacrifice is worthwhile for the benefit we will gain. One soul for thousands."

"What are you talking about?"

Malcolm laughed. "You are such an arrogant son-of-a-bitch, Alfred. Your reign will be disastrous without her. People will turn away from God in droves. We have far more to gain by the sacrifice of her one soul than can be gained in a thousand years of mischief and misery." He paused. Obviously a new thought had entered his twisted mind. "Would you like to join her? Have you realized yet what she means to you? I would actually be doing you a favor by sending you off ahead of her." He was talking to himself, expecting no response, calculating the effects of his new plan. 'Yes, yes. I believe this is even better." He looked at them and smiled an evil, oily smile. "Goodbye, Alfred. I will not miss you at all." He did not blink, did not wave his hands, did not say a spell, but suddenly Alfred gasped and doubled over.

"Alfred!" Isabel cried out in alarm. He dropped to the ground, legs drawn up in pain, his eyes unable to focus. She knelt next to him, talking to him but getting no response. "What have you done!" she shouted at Malcolm.

He smiled and looked at her darkly. "I have eliminated one of my problems. I'll be back for you." Then he was gone.

She watched him disappear, and then put him out of her mind. One crisis at a time. She said a prayer of thanks when a maintenance man rode by. At her frantic "Please help us!" he stopped and helped her load Alfred's agony-wracked body into the back of the truck.

The ride to the Emergency Room seemed to take forever, even though they only had to go a block past the entrance to the park. Isabel ran in shouting for help. Several people in scrubs rushed outside with a gurney before she got the words out of her mouth.

When they found Alfred unable to respond to their questions, they turned to Isabel for answers.

"What is his name?" asked a breathless young woman with a clipboard.

"Alfred," Isabel replied.

"Alfred what?"

Panic weakened Isabel's knees, threatening to give out supporting her body. She knew almost nothing about him. What lie could she come up with to cover this? She couldn't think of anything. She simply had to tell the truth. "I don't know his last name."

"Do you know him at all?"

"Yes, we were together in the park. But he is a new friend. I don't know a lot about him."

"He has no wallet. Do you know if he has insurance?"

"I don't think so. He is visiting from Britain."

"We have an obligation to stabilize him, but once he is stable we'll have to send him downtown to Henry for treatment." Henry Hospital was the city-funded community hospital that served the indigent and poor.

"I understand. Please, do something about the pain." She looked at Alfred's tall body curled up on the bed and prayed that somehow he could have relief.

The nurse put her hand on Isabel's arm and spoke kindly. "They've given him some pain-killers already. He should get some relief immediately, and then they can talk to him to find out what is wrong." Even as she spoke, Alfred's body relaxed a bit. He was still in pain, but his eyes were focused. He reached out for Isabel, and she took his hand. He squeezed it weakly but seemed to find comfort in her touch. She could see that he was not only in pain, he was scared of what was happening and scared of what they were going to do to him. She reached down and brushed his hair off his forehead, smiling to reassure him.

He answered their questions as well as he could. They pulled in an ultrasound machine and were able to use it to identify his problem. They gave him a larger dose of Demerol, and his body relaxed completely. He closed his eyes and drifted off. Isabel stayed by his side, holding his hand, waiting for the results of his tests.

Finally, the doctor came in. "He has an ulcer, a bad one. It's bleeding profusely. If he doesn't have surgery to correct it, he will bleed to death."

"Please, do what you can."

The doctor looked embarrassed. "We can't treat him here because he doesn't have insurance. We'll have to send him down to Henry. I'm sorry, he really shouldn't be moved, but we don't have any choice. I've called to alert them that he's coming. Don't worry. Henry's reputation is totally unfounded. Their staff is first-rate. They'll take good care of him."

Isabel nodded. Now that Alfred was not writhing in pain, she felt a lot calmer. "I understand, Doctor. Thank you for all you've done."

"You're welcome. I'll go and call for the ambulance." He smiled again and then left them alone.

Chapter 18

Isabel sat in the quiet hospital room gazing at the sleeping Alfred. His face was relaxed in deep sleep. She continued to stroke his forehead pushing his hair aside. He had not released her other hand. He is so beautiful, she thought as she had so many times since she met him. He is so beautiful, and I am such a troll. Maybe one of his witches or wizards cast a spell on him to make him want me. How could anyone like him want me?

"I cast no spell on him to make him love you," said Merlin, entering very suddenly and apparently reading her mind. "He has come to his affection for you because of who you are. Except for your appearance you are the same person you would have been. In any body, you are most definitely Kathryn's daughter," he finished.

"Where have you been?" Isabel asked with a combination of relief and irritation. "Can't you see we are in trouble here?"

"Yes, I see," he replied. "I went to stop Malcolm before he harmed you, but he struck me down when I turned my back."

Isabel looked down at Alfred. "Maybe you should stay closer to us. You missed something important."

"Indeed. Sorry."

"No. Not sorry. Help."

"Right." He walked over to the bed and held Alfred's other hand. He closed his eyes. His face contorted with concentration. After a few moments he looked over at Isabel. "It's done," he said. "He is healed."

"Good," she said, relieved. She looked down at him. "Can you wake him up?"

"No, not in as little time as we have. The medicines have too great a hold on his system. We have to get him out of here right away before they come to take him away."

"No kidding. You wouldn't happen to have a plan, would you?"

He opened the door a crack and peeked out. "I can divert their attention so that we can roll him out in one of those rolling chairs. Where is your car?"

"About five blocks away near the library."

"Hmmm," he said thoughtfully, "Too far. I can create a distraction big enough to get us out, but not enough to cover our tracks so far pushing him in a wheelchair." His expression became determined. "Here's the plan. We'll get him in the wheelchair, and I'll create a distraction so that we can get him outside. We'll find a place to hide while you run and get the car. Then we can load him in and get away."

"Fine," she replied, glad to have something to do. "Let's do it."

Isabel peeked through the door, dashed out and grabbed a wheelchair. It took some effort for them to move Alfred's dead weight, even for Merlin who was also a big man. She tossed his clothes on his lap and threw a blanket over him, then waited while Merlin stepped out to work his magic. She heard a bang and clattering and a sudden confusion of voices and footsteps. Merlin rushed in grabbing the handles of the wheelchair and running out of the room, through the lobby and out the door.

As they walked-ran down the sidewalk Merlin looked around for a safe hiding spot. He found it in the niche of a service door. "Go," he whisper-shouted. Isabel took off at a dead run. She was no sprinter, but she made it in record time, took the stairs two at a time instead of waiting on the elevator and ran up the ramp to her car. She was still breathing hard when she pulled up to the curb to get Alfred and Merlin. She helped Merlin shove Alfred none too gently into the back seat.

"Where to?" she asked, hoping for a confident answer.

She didn't get one. "I don't know," he replied, honestly, "No place is truly safe."

"Great," she commented, sarcasm dripping from her voice. Considering he was supposed to be a powerful wizard, Merlin seemed remarkably indecisive. "We'll go to my place. At least there he can sleep while you and I plan what to do next."

The rest of the ride was quiet. Merlin was lost in his own thoughts, and Isabel's mind had completely shut down. It was good that she was going home, because she was driving totally on autopilot.

They got the still drugged Alfred out of the car with some difficulty but found that they could rouse him enough to walk up the stairs supported under both arms. Isabel led the way into her bedroom, and they eased him into bed. She tucked him in like a sleeping child, wondering at the circumstances that had led to him lying in her bed.

She found Merlin standing in the bay, looking out her window into the darkness. "See anything?" she asked, moving into the kitchen to make tea.

"No. Nothing," he replied absently. He seemed to be preparing himself, collecting and organizing his thoughts. He followed her and sat down at the kitchen table. He did not speak again until she sat down with a steaming pot and two cups. "You have come to care for Alfred a great deal."

She hung her head and nodded as though resigned to the truth. "Yes, I have." She looked toward the bedroom. "When I'm with him, I feel right somehow. Strong. Happy. Content." Her voice and expression looked anything but content.

"But you still resist," he said. "Why?"

Her eyes flashed with anger. "Why? Come on, Merlin. Give me a break!" She got up and began to pace frantically from one side of the kitchen to the other. "Do you realize what you are asking? You are a wizard? He is a prince from a thousand years ago? You want me to go 'back' with you? Do you hear how that sounds? I would have to be totally looney toons to believe it." Her voice rose in pitch with each emphatic remark.

"So you think we are lying." Merlin said calmly.

"No," she nodded, hanging her head in defeat, "I don't think you are lying. But how could you be telling the truth?"

Merlin looked at Isabel with compassion. "I will tell you. I will make you understand."

"Please," she pleaded, settling in her chair for a long story.

Merlin looked into his cup as though for inspiration. He began, "Isabel, do you believe in God?"

She didn't see what that had to do with anything, but it was an easy enough question to answer. "Yes, I do. I'm not much for organized religion though, so don't try and quiz me."

He shook his head and smiled gently. "No, I won't." His smile disappeared and he became serious again. "Think of God as an artist. He creates matter from his own imagination and then manipulates it in some way to create a work of art. Your Big Bang is a perfect example of this." He paused to see that he had her attention, and then he continued.

"Your people wonder 'Is there life on other planets?' Of course there is. Many different forms of life exist throughout your universe. But your universe with all of its suns and moons, planets and peoples is only one of many universes that God has created.

"Think of it," he said emphatically. "God has eternity past and eternity future in which to work. He has created quite a portfolio. Each of his universes is a separate work with its own physical laws and beings. I am from one of those other universes.

"In my universe we have a very limited physical presence. Our bodies are loosely connected particles without specific shape or form. We would seem to you to float from place to place. We have an awareness of the others around us, and when we communicate, we hear the other person in our minds. We don't have eyes because there is nothing to see. We don't have ears because there is nothing to hear. Do you understand?"

"Sort of," she replied hesitantly.

"When we passed through to get here, Alfred told me that it felt to him as though he had become a cloud. He felt that way because you become, in essence, a floating mind.

"God created bridges for us to travel to other universes. We pass easily from place to place, not only into your world but into many others. We each have our favorites, and mine is Earth. My presence here and the popular stories of my time with Arthur are only two of the times I have interacted with humans. I haven't always been famous," he said with a smile. He got a weak smile from her in return.

"Our evolution has also included learning to control and manipulate matter with the only tool we have at our disposal: our thoughts. That skill, in addition to the difference in the composition of our bodies, gives us what appear to be magic powers." He shook his head and laughed. "Magic powers. Our magic is nothing more than our ability to move around the physical elements of your universe at the atomic level. Surely that makes sense to you?"

She nodded. Her body was going numb, her mind separating from it. This was a crazy story, and she was bothered that it was starting to make sense. "So how do Alfred and I fit in? You are speaking of universes, and we are just two people."

"It's true that in the vast scheme of God's creation, you and Alfred seem to be a small concern. But here, now, on this Earth, you are of great importance. Your lives will impact the lives of countless generations after you, from Alfred's time to your time and beyond. I care deeply about humans, and that is why I choose to spend so much time among them. More than that, I care deeply about you and Alfred and your mother, Kathryn. For me all the great vastness of Creation, all the beings and planets and galaxies and universes, boil down to this moment and your decision on this one thing."

Isabel sat back in her chair to put some space between her and his intensity. Each new thing she learned about this situation was more overwhelming than the last. What he said made a certain sense. Part of her wanted to ask so many questions, but another part thought she couldn't stand to know any more. She still hadn't responded to him when there was a knock at her door. She looked through the peephole and saw…Santa Claus? The situation kept getting weirder and weirder.

"Who is it?" Merlin asked suspiciously.

"Santa Claus?" Isabel replied weakly.

Merlin did not seem surprised. He opened the door without hesitation. The man who stepped in was not wearing a red suit, but in every other way, from the kind face to the little round belly to the white beard, the man was Santa Claus. He did not, however, look very jolly.

Merlin was not happy to see him, though they spoke in the tone of old friends. "Kris, I cannot leave now."

"Merlin," he responded firmly, "you have no choice. You either come now, or you will find your way blocked when you try to come home."

"But I have to pass through to return these people to their right time!" Merlin said emphatically.

"In that case, you had better come and explain yourself." Kris softened a bit. "The assembly is waiting for you. They are demanding, but they are not unreasonable. If you explain, they may even help you. Malcolm is not popular with any of us either, you know."

"What about these children? Who will protect them? Will you?" Merlin pleaded.

"I'm sorry Merlin, I can't. But Malcolm too has been summoned. Evidently this whole business has become messier than it should have been. They will be fine for a little while. Come quickly, and you can return that much faster."

Merlin sighed in resignation. He turned to Isabel who was swaying a little, and took her by the shoulders. "Stay put. I will return as quickly as I can. If Malcolm does show up, head for the bridge as fast as you can. Alfred knows where it is."

"If Alfred wakes up."

Merlin smiled. "He will and soon. Tell him I'll be back as soon as I can." He turned to follow his friend out the door.

"Hey," Isabel stopped them as they were leaving, "are you Santa Claus?"

The old man smiled a most beautiful smile. "I am indeed. Merlin is not the only one with a deep affection for humans."

And then they were gone.

Isabel stood staring at the closed door. Now what? she thought. I could run. I could leave my car and all my things and simply disappear. Alfred is asleep, and he wouldn't know until he woke up. That would give me a pretty good lead.

She walked into the bedroom where Alfred slept soundly, and her heart softened. She couldn't leave. She couldn't leave him to face all of this alone. She remembered his kisses in the park, the weight of his body, and the tickle of his breath on her cheek. I will probably never find that again, she thought. How can I give up even one moment of this feeling?

She slid into the bed and put her arm around him. He shifted to settle in against her. In his sleep, he put his arm over hers, pulling it more tightly around him. She found she couldn't keep her eyes open. As she drifted off to sleep she recognized a vague, far-off thought that she should probably stay awake and keep watch, but she couldn't resist the lure of sleep.

Chapter 19

Merlin had spent so much time living with humans that his original form no longer felt natural. He loved the solidness and sensations of having a body. True, having no physical needs had its advantages. Living in this universe was the equivalent of an intellectual buzz, a constant high of frenzied mental energy. Sometimes when Merlin had some difficult problem to solve, he would come back and exist quietly separate from the others, turning his entire being to thinking things through. For the most part, however, he preferred to spend his time on Earth.

The usual cacophony of voices had quieted because of the import of the occasion. The only sound was the rumble of voices far distant whose members had no loyalty to this group. The inhabitants of this universe had divided themselves loosely into two factions: those who used the bridges to interact with other species in a positive, friendly, helpful way; and those who sought power and domination over weaker and less developed cultures. The control and domination bloc had recalled Malcolm at the same time that Merlin had been summoned.

Their universe had very few laws. There was little need in a place where there could be no violence. The only things to steal were ideas, and killing was possible but purposeless. There was one law, however, that all had agreed on: no humans were to be brought into their universe and then allowed to leave.

There were many reasons for this. Many civilizations were not as advanced or as well intentioned as theirs. Should someone gain knowledge of the bridges without the wisdom to use them properly, disaster could strike throughout Creation. Many peoples, such as humans, were not yet ready to meet with and work with those from other universes or even other planets within their own universe. Someone who learned how to use the bridges could travel to other places and times and bring back technology or knowledge inappropriate for the original culture. Taking this same situation in a different direction, a person from another place who had knowledge of the existence of different universes could use that knowledge to make him- or herself powerful within his or her own culture. A power that may or may not be used properly. Not to mention the possibility of one race forcing a weaker one into slavery.

Merlin knew all of this. He knew the reasons for the law and fully agreed and supported it, except in this case. He knew that if he had tried to convince the others of the need for justice, they would have enforced the directives of their own existence. Now that events had been set in motion, he hoped they would let him finish.

The group that called Merlin was not a governing body but a democratic assembly. It was led by a panel of their wisest and most experienced members. Their role was to help define issues and give advice on how to handle them. Merlin knew, however, that ultimately his fate would rest in the hands of all.

Odin was widely recognized as the assembly's leader, because of his natural wisdom and broad spectrum of experiences. It was he who spoke for all of them. "Merlin," he said, "you have broken our only law."

"Yes, Odin, I know." Merlin was polite but not humble. He was certain that he was right.

"Why did you do this?" asked Odin.

"I have good reason." Merlin replied.

"That reason is?"

"Another of our kind worked a terrible injustice on these humans. I am trying to put it right."

"Malcolm?"

"Yes."

Another who went by the name Balder spoke. "Malcolm can be called to answer for his actions, Merlin, but you should not have brought humans here. Humans are among the creatures who are most likely to respond badly to exposure to our universe. You may have caused great damage."

Merlin had the strength of his convictions and did not back down. "It was necessary to move Alfred through time to put the situation right."

"You could have done this without him," she accused.

"No. You know how the humans are after their industrial revolution. Most of them no longer believe in spirits or magic. It was necessary for her to have a compelling reason to suspend her disbelief. I felt that as kindred spirits their affection for each other would develop quickly, and I was correct in that belief. They are reaching the point at which they cannot bear separation."

"Many of us have interacted with humans," commented Odin. "In spite of all they have to offer, they are a violent and unpredictable people. We cannot right all of their wrongs. They have free will as we do. They make their choices and must then live with them."

Merlin was getting frustrated. "You have done things on Earth that have changed human history."

Odin sensed his frustration, but was unrelenting. "My interactions were incorporated into human history, and I never brought any of them here. I gave them no awareness of the vastness of Creation or the diversity of beings that inhabit their own universe and the multitude of others. We behave this way with all people. They must be allowed to find these things for themselves in their own time."

"You know that in principle I agree with you totally," Merlin argued. "But this situation warrants an exception."

"And the fact that she is your daughter has no bearing on the situation?" commented another, Gaia.

Merlin sighed. "Of course it does. How could it not? Others of you have had children on Earth and in other places. Surely you understand the attachment."

Odin spoke again. "We do understand, but that does not justify your actions. None of us did what you have done. I feel that we must close the bridges to you, Merlin, if you intend to repeat this reckless incident. You must either stay, or go and never return."

Merlin would not back down. "Her soul," he pleaded, "he took her soul. The very essence of you, of me, of any of us. What Malcolm has done, he did with the full intention of giving evil free reign over those who had no use of their own free will. Let us at least allow human history to unfold as its people will it. Allow me to put these two back in their right places. Then I promise I will do no more."

There was a hum of conversation. He could sense that the others were considering his argument.

"How do you know they will not reveal us?" Odin asked.

"Reveal us? Alfred already half doesn't believe it. He knows that to say what he has seen would put his very sanity in question. Not to mention the threat to everything he holds dear if the truth of his sacred texts is called into question."

"And the girl?"

"She is my daughter. She will understand. If she gives me her word, we can trust that she will not betray us."

The assembly considered Merlin's words. It seemed that most were sympathetic to Merlin's cause. Malcolm and the others had caused trouble for many of them. Many hoped that this plan could be thwarted and a victory be struck for those whose intentions were good. Merlin could sense that the tide of opinion was turning in his favor.

"You will be allowed to return them," Odin said sternly, "and we will hope that your faith in their discretion is justified. But let that be the end of it. Do not compromise us any further."

"Thank you." Merlin was relieved. He moved quickly to the bridge. He wanted to get back to Alfred and Isabel before Malcolm had a chance to do more damage.

Chapter 20

Alfred was dragged into consciousness by his tight, growling stomach, but he refused its demands like a petulant child. He was not leaving his comfortable cocoon no matter how his hunger nagged. Recognizing the rise and fall of breathing against his back, he shifted to face the sleeping Isabel. Pictures flashed into his mind of their interlude in the park, of their fervent kisses and the passionate press of their eager bodies. He should have been appalled by his wanton craving for her, but his self-control had finally met its match. He could resist his body's hunger for food, but this craving was not to be denied. Before he could act on his impulses, however, his tantalizing memories were driven out by horrific flashes of rage and blinding agony. He sat up abruptly, no longer concerned about disturbing her. "Isabel," he said hoarsely.

Isabel's mind had been half awake all night, so consciousness came on her quickly. She sat up and searched his face for signs of the excruciating pain of the night before. "What's wrong?"

"Where am I?"

She relaxed and rubbed her eyes. "This is my apartment. We brought you here from the hospital."

"We? We who?"

"Merlin. Merlin came to the hospital and healed you, and then he and I brought you here. We didn't know what else to do," she shrugged.

"Merlin was here? Where is he?"

"Honestly, I don't know. Some guy came and told him he had been summoned somewhere. He told us to stay here, and he would be back as soon as he could."

"What happened?" Alfred asked, still trying to get a firm grasp on consciousness.

"What do you remember?"

"I remember the park. Being with you. Malcolm coming. Pain." He squeezed his eyes shut and tried to penetrate the fog in his brain for his last conscious visions. "After that only strange lights. Strange faces." He tried to rub away the throbbing pain in his head. "And then nothing. Waking up here."

Isabel nodded. "That actually kind of sums it up. Malcolm ripped a hole in your stomach, and it was bleeding. That was what caused the pain. A maintenance guy came by and helped me get you to the hospital."

"Hospital?" he interrupted.

"Yes. It's a place where you go when you are dangerously ill. The strange faces you remember were the doctors and nurses. They were going to take you downtown to another hospital to operate on you."

"Operate?"

"Cut you open to fix what's wrong inside."

Alfred shuddered, remembering battlefields and bodies littered like carcasses with their insides spilling out.

"But Merlin came and healed you. We didn't know where to go so we brought you here."

Alfred threw the bedclothes aside. The rush of cool air raised the hairs on his back, and he felt for the opening in his shirt.

"That's a hospital gown," Isabel explained.

"Where are my clothes?"

"Over there on the loveseat."

Alfred stood up and stretched. The gown pulled open and exposed his bare back. Isabel looked away thinking he wouldn't see her, but he saw the blush of her cheeks in the reflection in the mirror. "Why do I feel numb?" he asked.

She sighed. "You were bad off so they gave you a lot of morphine to kill the pain. That's how come you've slept so long. It'll wear off soon enough." She pointed to the bathroom, "You can go in there to change."

Alfred came out to find Isabel standing over the stove making something that looked delicious. He was so hungry that roasted sticks and leaves would have looked good. He breathed deeply of the steam as she set the full plate in front of him.

"What do we do now?" he asked with a mouth full of food.

"We wait, I guess," Isabel shrugged. "That's what Merlin told us to do."

"What else did Merlin say? Where was he hiding while all of this was happening to us?" Alfred did not try to mask his annoyance.

"When he went to stop Malcolm, he was waiting for him. He ambushed him and knocked him out."

"I'm surprised he left him alive."

"He explained to me where he comes from and why he can do what he does. It made so much sense, I had to believe him. Of course, after Malcolm's little show, I can hardly deny it."

"So you are ready to come with us?" Alfred asked hopefully. He was ready to go home.

"I don't know," she hung her head, once again showing her doubt. "I believe you, and yet how can it be true?" She looked up at him. "I want to be with you. I love being with you. But how can I trust this?"

Alfred didn't know what to say. If he weren't living it, he wouldn't believe it either. He turned his attention fully on his food.

Sensing his discomfort, Isabel changed the subject. "Tell me more about where you come from."

He sighed in relief. "What do you want to know?"

"I know that it's bloody," she said clearing the table, "and I know that it's quiet, and that's about all."

"So," he repeated, "What else do you want to know?"

She smiled. "You're a prince, right? So you must be the son of a king and queen, right? Tell me about your family."

Isabel led the way into the living room, and sat on the sofa, pulling her legs under her.

"I am the son of King Ethelwulf and Queen Osbera of Wessex, the most powerful and important country on the island of Britannia. When my father died, my brother Ethelbald became king. I hate him."

She chuckled, "So you've said. Why do you hate him?"

"I told you, he's going to make me marry that wench Elswith."

"There's no other reason?"

"There are plenty of reasons to hate him," Alfred said earnestly.

"And they are?"

"For one thing, he married our stepmother. I hate her."

She laughed. "There you go again. Why do you hate her?"

Alfred did not find this funny. "She is a wench, too, but a cunning, clever wench. She hates me."

Isabel laughed out loud. "We have established that you all hate each other."

He still did not see the humor. "There is too much to tell, but I will tell you enough so that you will understand."

Isabel settled herself against the cushions to prepare for a long tale.

"When I was twelve years old," Alfred began, "my father decided we should journey to Rome. My mother had been long dead, but she had a heart-felt wish that I be blessed by His Holiness, the Pope. My father had ignored this wish as he had all of her needs for the last years of her life. As he got older, he became more concerned with the fate of his immortal soul and regretted he had denied her this pious wish.

"He left my brother Ethelbald as king in his stead, and we set out on our pilgrimage." His eyes misted over as though he was looking into the past, watching a replay of this trip. "We saw so many amazing things. We stopped in the court of the Frankish king, Charles, and he met us with great hospitality. While we were there, we attracted the attention of the king's daughter, Judith, who was barely older than myself but clever far beyond her years. We left with the promise of stopping there again on our trip home."

His face relaxed into a spiritual trance, as though he was gazing on Heaven itself. "I had been told that Rome had declined greatly since the height of the empire, but to my provincial eyes it was overwhelming in its magnificence. The marble buildings and great statues were crafted with such skill and precision that they seemed to be life frozen in place and turned to stone. To stand in the Coliseum is to feel the lingering power of lives won and lost in by the great gladiators and the ferocious beasts who met them there. The walls of the Baths wept from the steam of the hot, soothing waters. The palace of the Pope was beyond description. The pristine white walls and untarnished gold trim seemed to be the gateway to Heaven itself. I was already tall and manly in my own country, but in this holy place I felt like a child barely balanced on unsteady legs.

"The Pope met us himself. I had not anticipated that they would know us, never mind treating us with such great esteem. I could see that in spite of the distance Britannia was considered a territory of consequence. I thought to myself, if our good will is so important, why should we be subjugated to the rule of others? Why shouldn't we determine our own destiny? Why shouldn't we become an important power on our own? I found my life's quest that day.

"The Pope was so impressed with my learning and piety, that he anointed me his Spiritual Son. I have tried since that time to live up to his expectations for me. That is why I am so serious about my work."

When he paused, Isabel commented, "Wow, all that when you were twelve?"

"I have always been of more serious mind than my brothers," Alfred replied.

"We stopped at the Frankish court on our return as we had promised. Judith and her father were lying in wait for us like predators on the hunt. They wanted their share in the rising power of Britannia. Judith seduced my father, working him like an experienced whore. She played perfectly to the old man's vanity, beguiling him with the offer of her young body. My stupid father fell easily for her charms, and before we left that court she was his wife.

"Judith." He spit her name like he was expelling a bitter fruit. "She left my father sleeping in their marriage bed and came to me in the night. 'He is old,' she said, 'and I am young. He cannot satisfy me,' she oozed, dropping her gown and stroking her body to inflame my desire. 'You are young and strong,' she ran her hands over my entire body from my shoulders to my legs and everything in between. I grabbed her wrists and pulled her hands away. 'No,' I said, 'you are my father's wife. I will not lay with you.' She taunted me, 'Don't you find me beautiful?'"

Alfred looked directly into Isabel's eyes, "She is beautiful, I will tell you that. Even now, so many years after, she is beautiful. But her physical beauty belies the dark soul of a handmaiden of the Devil himself. She is the siren embodiment of that deceitful serpent that caused the fall of Man."

Alfred pressed his temples. "I sent her away that night, and many more after that. She could not believe that I would not fall under her spell. The more she pressed, the more determined I became. Finally she looked elsewhere to satisfy her physical hunger, but she never stopped hating me for resisting her. Hating that I might tell my father of her impurity. Hating that I was more righteous than she. She hates me still.

"From that time, she set about undermining my father's affection and trust of me. She wanted to ensure that I would not reveal her indiscretions to him." Alfred shook his head. "She needn't have worried. My father did not hold me in high regard, in spite of the Pope's kind words. He considered me weak and spoiled. He would have chosen her attentions over my affection under any circumstances. I knew this better than she did, and so I kept my mouth shut. Once she realized this, her only use for me was to humiliate me to amuse herself."

Alfred stopped and drew a deep breath. He was not used to talking so much, and he was growing tired of it. He wanted Isabel to know what had happened, however, and so he pressed on, trying to shorten the tale with fewer details. "Word reached my brother that we were returning with a wife for my father, and that he had declared her equal ruler with him." Alfred shook his head, "The vixen. That would never have happened when my father was young and strong.

"Ethelbald had a taste of power, and he did not want to give it up, particularly to a woman. We were met with troops charged with keeping my father off British soil. 'We will not serve a foreign queen,' his general conveyed his message. 'You have proven yourself old and foolish. You will not rule this land.'

"As word spread, there came to be two camps of warriors in the field by the shore: those loyal to my brother and those loyal to my father. My father looked out and saw that this battle would divide our country, weaken us, set brother against brother, and leave us vulnerable to attack from without. He sent emissaries to Ethelbald and asked for a truce. They divided our country in half with a kingdom for each of them. They determined to fight together against invaders. When my father died, his half would go to my brother. Then the land would be united again under one ruler.

"My brother, not wanting to deplete his resources with a long civil war, agreed. And so it was until my father died." He shook his head again. "Judith wanted to hold on to her power, and so she worked her spell on my stupid brother before my father's body was cold. Within the month, she was queen again, except now she is married to my brother who hates me as much as she does. They entertain themselves by working mischief on me." Disgust distorted his handsome face.

Isabel sighed and shook her head. "That is quite a story."

Alfred shrugged. "It is as it is."

They sat quietly for a moment. Isabel opened her mouth to speak, but he held up his hand to cut her off. "I am tired of talking. No more talking now."

Alfred sat back and relaxed, eyes fixed on Isabel. He marveled that again she had enticed him to tell a long story. Again she sat through the whole thing hanging on his every word. Every time he looked at her he liked her more. Every time he looked at her, he wanted her more.

His intense gaze was making Isabel fidget. She broke the tense silence. "So Judith is very beautiful."

"Yes," Alfred replied slowly, his eyes never wavering, "Many think so." He shifted across the sofa closer to her and took her hand, entwining their fingers. "But you are so much more. You are bright and quick-witted, kind and understanding. You do not appear at first to be a great beauty, yet the more I know you the more beautiful you become."

Isabel got up and smiled down at him. "Now I know you are joking." She walked into the kitchen and began to prepare tea.

Alfred followed her. "Why would you doubt me?"

Her back to him, she answered, "Because there is nothing beautiful about me. I can look in the mirror. I am a troll."

Alfred stepped closer to her so that he was standing directly behind her. "But you are beautiful, Isabel. You are beautiful in so many ways." He turned her around to face him, but she hung her head, not meeting his gaze. "If you are to be my wife you must be more confident."

Tears spilled out of Isabel's eyes and trailed down her cheeks. Alfred lifted her chin and gently wiped her tears. He looked at her for a long moment, his eyes running over her face as though he was trying to memorize it. He bent down slowly and touched his lips to hers.

He took a breath and kissed her again, more firmly. She wrapped her arms around his neck, molding to his body like warm clay. He circled her waist, pulling her more tightly to him. Their kisses were long and passionate, sharing every breath. Finally there was no more air to share, and reluctantly they pulled apart.

Isabel dropped her head against Alfred's chest and filled her lungs. "I will never be a princess, Alfred. I will never carry myself like a queen. Had I been born in your time I would have been trained to that life. But I wasn't. I am a little nobody librarian. I am fat. I am ugly. I am totally unremarkable."

"Fat?" Alfred asked, "Why do you keep saying that?" He moved his hands over the curves of her back, her waist, her hips. "I cannot tell you, Isabel," he said in a low voice, "I cannot tell you how I have never found a woman irresistible, but I cannot resist you." He leaned down and kissed her again. "I want to be with you as badly as I have ever wanted anything in my life." He led her back to the sofa and pulled her down with him, leaning her back as he had in the park. All thoughts of his precious piety and chastity had been stripped away leaving only the instinctive urges of his body.

At that very inappropriate moment, the phone rang.

Chapter 21

Isabel was not going to answer the phone. Go away, she thought, go away and leave us alone. But when the machine picked it up, she heard her mother's cranky, demanding voice and could not deny it. Much to Alfred's annoyance, she reached behind her and picked up the receiver. "I'm here, Mom. Sorry. I was in the bathroom," she lied.

"Where have you been?" her mother demanded.

"I've been busy." Alfred was distracting her, kissing her eyes, her ears and her neck.

"Busy with what?" her mother asked with derision.

"Just stuff, Mom. What's up?" She needed to get off the phone.

"Where are my clothes? You took them on Wednesday and never brought them back. Don't you think I need my clothes?" There was no warmth or appreciation in her voice.

Isabel sat up suddenly, pushing Alfred off. She looked to where her mother's laundry basket full of dirty clothes still sat. Oh no, she thought, there's been so much going on, I forgot. She didn't want to try and explain, to set the beauty of the last few days before her mother to be ridiculed and belittled. "Sorry, Mom. I've been tied up. I'll get them over there sometime today."

"That would be helpful," her mother replied sarcastically and hung up.

Isabel remembered Merlin's request that they stay put, but she didn't see how they were any safer in her apartment than they would be anywhere else. She had to take care of her mother's clothes. She turned to Alfred, who was looking none too happy. "We're going to the laundromat."

"What? What's a lawn-dro-mat?" He still wasn't happy, but he was interested.

"A place where people wash their clothes." She pointed to the laundry basket by the door. "I've got to wash my mother's clothes and get them back to her. I was supposed to have done it two days ago."

"You have no choice?"

"I have no choice."

"Very well then. We will go to the lawn-dro-mat."

Alfred gallantly carried the basket the two blocks they had to walk. Isabel felt frightened and exposed on the street. Eager to be back under cover, she set a quick pace. She was glad to find that they were the only people spending Saturday morning washing clothes.

"I know these machines," Alfred commented. "Merlin and I stole our clothes from one like them when we arrived."

Isabel laughed. "That's not very princely."

"No, but we didn't have much choice," Alfred said matter-of-factly.

"I guess not." Isabel started the routine of washing clothes. Alfred watched her with interest.

"I have said before," he commented, "there are many things about this time that are very useful. I think women would like this very much."

"Women and men," she corrected.

"Men wash clothes?" Alfred asked with surprise.

"Sure," she nodded. "Lots of men live alone. Lots of women work and men share the chores. Lots of men do wash."

"Humph."

Isabel put in the last piece and let the door drop into place. "Now we wait."

"How long?"

"We'll be here a couple of hours. Let's see what's on the TV." She found the remote on the side table in the waiting area and started flipping channels. Alfred was interested in all of it: the cartoons, the movies, and the music.

He watched her carefully, and it took him all of a minute and a half to learn how to use the remote. He asked to see it and then proceeded to turn the channels quickly, stopping briefly when something caught his eye, then moving on. This proves it, Isabel thought, amused. Remote control is a gender specific, genetically controlled trait. She watched him for nearly half an hour before she felt she had to jump in. "Alfred," she said, "can we pick something, please?"

He looked at her mystified. "How do you choose? There are too many choices, too much to see."

"You get used to it after a while. Soon you'll get to where you think there's nothing on." She noticed that he looked a little dazed. "Maybe we should turn it off for a little while."

"Maybe so. How?"

Isabel pushed the off button and took a deep breath. At just that moment, the washing machines buzzed, and she got up to put the clothes in the dryers. He watched everything she did closely, until she stood up and looked at him with a smile. "Now we wait again."

He reached for her hand and pulled her into his arms. "Princesses, queens, do not wash clothes. I think we can find better things for you to do."

She wrapped her arms around his waist and looked up into his face. "Oh yeah? Like what?"

His face lit up with a mischievous smile. "Let me see." He leaned down and kissed her lightly.

A new voice interrupted, "Iz, is this what you've been doing? Now I see why you wanted to skip work." Gwen had walked in, making even jeans and a T-shirt look like an invitation.

Isabel and Alfred stepped apart. Gwen would no doubt steal Alfred's attention. He was a man, and he couldn't help himself. She had seen it time after time with Gwen, almost like magic. She walked into a room and set her attention on a man, and he was hers by the end of the night. Always. Isabel had never seen her turned down.

"What are you doing here, Gwen?"

"I went to your apartment to see what was up with you, but obviously you weren't there. I saw you here when I walked by. Are you going to introduce me to your friend?" she asked seductively.

Isabel sighed. Her bubble of happiness had burst. "Gwen, this is Alfred. Alfred, this is my friend, Gwen. She and I work together at the library."

"Hi, Alfred," Gwen oozed, "I wondered who could make our Isabel play hooky. Have you two been having fun?"

"It's been very educational," Alfred replied diplomatically.

Isabel was surprised and pleased to sense Alfred's resistance to Gwen's charms. "It's been great," Isabel said, relaxing a little.

"He's here from out of town, and you're in the laundromat? How come?" Gwen was not taking Alfred's hint. He was obviously not interested in what she had to offer. Evidently she thought him worth some extra effort. Alfred was tall and handsome, exactly the kind of man Gwen liked best.

Gwen's confidence stood out starkly against her own self-doubt. She said quickly, "My mom needs her clothes. We're doing them real quick, and then we're going to run them over to her."

"Oooooo, the laundromat and then the Wicked Witch of the West. Glad to see you're showing him all the best parts of town," Gwen said sarcastically. "Where are you taking him after that, the landfill?"

Isabel ignored Gwen's sarcasm. "No, we're planning a quiet evening at home."

Gwen had gradually worked herself around to where she was standing between them. She started playing with the buttons on Alfred's shirt. "Quiet evening at home? What kind of a tour guide are you? You need to bring him out to have a good time." She looked up at Alfred. "Alfred, do you dance?"

"Not usually, no." He was not falling into Gwen's trap.

"You know, I've never seen Isabel dance either. You can try it out together tonight. If you're not sure of yourself, I'd be happy to dance with you first so that you can get a feel for it."

Isabel knew that Gwen wanted him to get a feel for more than how to dance. "I don't think so, Gwen. Thanks anyway."

Gwen became adamant. "I won't take no for an answer," she laughed, walking out the door. "See you there at the usual time." In a whirlwind, she was gone.

"She is your friend?" Alfred asked skeptically.

"Yes, such as it is. I don't have many friends. Gwen gives me someone to hang with."

"Hang with?"

"Be with. Do things with. So I don't have to sit alone in my apartment all the time."

"Humph," he said again. "Sometimes it is better to be alone."

"Sometimes," she agreed, "but when you are always alone sometimes it is better to have company, even Gwen." She sighed, "Let's try the TV again. This time I control the remote."

When the clothes were finished, they went straight from the laundromat to Isabel's mother's apartment. She was sitting in the same spot as on Wednesday, drinking beer and smoking a cigarette just as Isabel had left her. The only evidence that she had moved was the different pajamas she was wearing. "Hi, Mom," Isabel said with forced cheerfulness.

Edith looked up at Alfred as he walked in behind Isabel. "Who are you?" she said scornfully.

"Mom, this is my friend, Alfred," Isabel introduced him hesitantly. She could never predict how her mother was going to act or what she was going to say. The more time she spent alone, the crasser and more impolite she became.

"Alfred." Edith spoke his name as if it was something she had to spit out. "Why is Alfred here? Why did you bring a stranger to my apartment to see me in my pajamas? Couldn't you have warned me he was coming?"

"I'm sorry, Mom. He's visiting from out of town so I didn't want to leave him sitting alone. I didn't think it would be a problem. We won't be here that long." Isabel went into her mother's bedroom to put away the clean clothes.

Isabel's whole demeanor changed. Her shoulders sagged, and she hung her head at her mother's sharp rebuke.

"Why are you with my daughter?" Edith said, looking him up and down. "You don't seem like the type that would be interested in her."

"I actually find her company quite enjoyable," Alfred said with tolerance.

"So she's giving you what you want, eh? Figures. Can't imagine any other way she'd get a date." Alfred was looking at her with an expression of disgust. "What is your problem?" she asked looking for a fight.

"I am thinking that I cannot believe that someone as kind and thoughtful and intelligent as Isabel came from you."

"You would speak to me like that in my own home! Have you ever raised a child by yourself, mister? Did you ever give up all your hopes and dreams to raise a child you didn't ask for? I think not. You will not speak to me like that. Who the hell are you, anyway? What do you know?" Edith took another swill of beer and draw on her cigarette, using it to light a fresh one before putting it out in the overflowing ashtray. A day's worth of alcohol fueled her anger to an unreasonable state. "Isabel!" she screeched, "Isabel!"

"Yes, ma'am," Isabel replied in a low voice as she came in from the bedroom.

"Get this son-of-a-bitch out of my house! He cannot speak to me this way in my own home! Take him out of here and never bring him back. If you take up with him, you can consider yourself done with me! I will not tolerate such disrespect, do you hear? Do you hear me?"

Isabel was impressed to see that the angrier Edith got, the calmer Alfred became. She pushed him out of the door ahead of her and called back, "Goodbye, Mother." She could hear her mother's loud rumblings through the door. 'That little whore. Got a man the only way someone like her could. She couldn't learn from my mistake, didn't listen to what I have told her all her life. Men are scum, and they only want one thing. One thing…' Her voice trailed off as Isabel and Alfred stepped out of her building into the glow of the afternoon sun.

"She is an evil woman," Alfred commented calmly.

"Not evil," Isabel replied, "just disappointed."

"How could she be disappointed in you? You are her superior by far."

"Thank you for saying so," Isabel shrugged. She was not about to engage him in a debate comparing her with her mother.

"She may have been the mother of your body, but she bears no relation to your spirit. In that respect you are very like Kathryn."

Isabel had no reply. This whole conversation was bringing her too close to tears.

"There is far more to you than meets the eye, Lady Isabel." His eyes had taken on a mischievous sparkle.

"What do you mean by that?"

"Simply that you have designed your appearance to hide the person within you."

"What? What are you talking about?"

"Why do you have that gown in your closet?"

"Have you been going through my things?"

"Yes," he teased. "For what purpose do you wear that dress? It is wrinkled. It has been worn."

"I don't know what you are talking about." Caught, her heart pounded painfully against the inside of her chest.

"There is a strong, passionate person hiding beneath your skin, Isabel. I feel it in your body. Sometimes I hear it in your words. I would like to see you in that gown. I think that you would look like a princess."

Isabel blushed and changed the subject. "Do you want to meet Gwen tonight?"

"I don't care to see Gwen again, but it would be interesting to see another place." He knew that he had her.

"Then we'll go, but you can't wear these jeans. Let's go get you something better."

Chapter 22

It was Saturday night, and the parking lot at the Purple Pelican was jammed to overflowing. Isabel had to park in the empty lot of the bank across the street. This accorded Alfred the full impact of the nightclub's appearance. It was colorful, it was crowded, and it was loud.

As they went in, Isabel noticed that once again Gwen had a parking space near the front door. Wonder what time she got here, Isabel thought, shaking her head. Gwen was a woman on a mission, and that mission was men. Not to marry, not to love, just pure unapologetic lust. She loved for men to look at her. She loved for men to want her. She loved finally, inevitably, to give men what they wanted most.

Gwen was waiting for them at her usual table by the bar. She smiled a sly smile as they walked up, as though she could see into their minds and read their thoughts.

"Hi, Iz," Gwen cooed. "I wondered if you would really come. I'm glad you did. Now I can get to know this guy." She motioned to the other chairs around the table. "Com'on and sit."

A busy waiter threw cocktail napkins on the table in front of them. "What can I get you?"

Alfred looked at Isabel for direction. "I'll take a white zinfandel," she said, "and get him a Guinness."

"Got it." The waiter rushed away.

"You order for him and everything," Gwen said mischievously. "You guys are moving fast."

Before Isabel could say a word, Alfred said shortly, "Isabel is being a good guide. If she visited me I would do the same for her." End of subject.

Isabel thought Gwen would be offended, but it was amusement not anger that she saw in Gwen's face. She was amazed at how cool Gwen could be. It was one trait that Isabel really admired.

Gwen continued the conversation with a very casual tone, but the expression on her face was anything but casual. Isabel found the intensity of Gwen's interrogation a little embarrassing, but Alfred seemed to take it in stride. Even though Alfred wasn't giving in to Gwen's charms, still Isabel was jealous. These were two strong, confident people, equal to each other in word and action.

"So Alfred," Gwen asked, "where are you from?"

"I am from Britain," he replied. "From a place called Wessex."

"That's funny," she observed, "You don't have much of an accent."

"You don't think so?" he replied evasively.

"Why are you here? I mean, you met Isabel after you came here, didn't you?"

"Yes, I did."

"So why did you come originally?"

Alfred thought carefully about his answer. "I was curious," he said finally.

Gwen sat back in her chair and looked like she didn't buy it, but she said nothing. After an uncomfortable moment or two, she asked seductively, "Has your curiosity been satisfied?"

"Yes," he said looking at Isabel. "It has been more than satisfied."

It was an honest answer given simply without embarrassment or innuendo. The emotion subtle, but still Gwen looked like she would be sick from its sweetness. "How 'bout a dance, Alfred?" she said, pushing away from the table.

"No. I don't want to dance with you."

Again Gwen should have had her feelings hurt, but she seemed to throw it right off. "Let's find someone else then." She looked around the bar and caught the eye of a man, who had been watching her. "He looks good."

He looked familiar to Isabel. "Isn't that the guy from the other night?"

"Hmmmm," Gwen purred, "so he is. He was certainly good enough for a repeat performance. Will you guys excuse me?" She got up and sashayed across the room.

Alfred looked after her. "There's more going on with her than she's telling."

"Why do you say that?" Isabel tried to joke though she too felt uneasy, "Do you think she is also hiding a passionate personality?"

He smiled warmly and took her hand. "No, not at all. Still," he said looking back at Gwen, "something about her is not right."

Isabel didn't know what to say, but at that moment the band started Bob Segar's "We've Got Tonight." "Let's dance," she offered.

"I don't know." He looked out at the dancers on the floor. They hardly seemed to be moving at all. After a moment he said, "Why not?"

He led her out to a dark corner of the deck. The "beach" was crowded, the floor inside was crowded, the part of the deck that was well-lit was crowded, but Alfred found one little spot in shadow to give them privacy. He looked at her with an unspoken question.

"This is easy," Isabel said, "You put your arms around my waist." He did and pulled her close. "I'll put my arms around your neck." She could feel herself blushing. "Now we sway to the music, back and forth, and we can even turn if you want."

Alfred, the quick study, took only seconds to master twenty-first century dancing. Then he was able to turn his full attention on Isabel. "Isabel," he said in a low voice.

"What?" she answered looking up at him.

"Don't make me go back alone."

"Alfred, I …" she stammered.

"Isabel," his voice was still low, but had a slightly pleading tone to it. "I cannot be without you. Please." He choked a little on it, and she had the feeling he didn't often say please. "Please come back with me."

Isabel thought her heart would burst. What if she woke up tomorrow, and he was gone? How would it be to wake up every morning for the rest of her life thinking of what might have been? How would it be to come here, or go do wash, or go to the park, and know that he would not be there, would never be there?

She decided. "Let's see," she teased, "indoor plumbing, grocery stores and cable TV versus outhouses, walking everywhere and having to kill or grow my own food. Women with equal rights versus women as a slave race. Hospitals, doctors and insurance versus…versus…versus what?"

Alfred shrugged.

"Let's look at it from a different angle," she said. "Here loneliness. There you. Here a mother who hates me. There a mother who's been waiting for me for twenty-eight years. Here books. There you. Here movies. There you. Here everything but you. There you. Hmmm," she said, "tough choice." He looked disappointed, so she decided not to milk it any more. "I think," she paused for effect, "I choose you."

"You're going?" He sounded like a child who found out he was going to Disney World.

"I'm going," she said with a beautiful smile.

Looking around to see that they were still hidden from prying eyes, he leaned down and kissed her, hugging her tightly. His embrace revealed feelings too strong for words. He looked into her face for assurance that she was committed to her decision. Her sparkling eyes left no doubt.

Then over the top of her head, he saw Merlin come in the front door. "Merlin is here," he whispered.

"What? Where?" she replied, unwilling to leave his arms.

"He just walked through the door."

She turned and looked, then sighed. "Alfred, when we get where we are going, can you find a place where people won't keep dropping in?"

He chuckled, "Indeed I will. If I have to, I will build a house from the inside with no windows and no doors. Then we can do what we will without any intrusion."

His suggestive tone made her eyes light up again and her breath catch in her chest. "Let's get going."

They walked across the bar to join Merlin who did not look happy. "Is this what you call 'staying put'?" he rebuked them.

"Sorry," Isabel replied. "My mother called and needed her clothes, and then Gwen came to the laundromat, and one thing led to another sort of out of control."

"Do you know what danger you have put yourselves in? Malcolm could be anywhere, could be anyone," Merlin said looking around. He was jumpy and uneasy. "In fact, I believe he is here. I'm almost sure of it."

"What, here?" Isabel was shocked. She and Alfred both looked around the room but saw no sign of Malcolm. "Can you guys change your appearance?"

"Yes."

"Can you recognize him?" Alfred asked.

"I don't know. Maybe," Merlin was distracted as he scrutinized every person in the room.

"Merlin," Alfred said in a low tone, "Isabel is ready to go with us."

That got Merlin's attention. He squinted as he looked into Isabel's face, as though he could see inside her mind and be sure she meant it. "You are ready?"

"I am. Nothing there can be as bad as my loneliness here."

Merlin rubbed his hands together. "Excellent. Let's go."

Isabel had a flash of panic. "Now?"

"Yes, now. Malcolm is close. We've got to get away before he has a chance to do something."

Isabel wanted to go, but she needed to tie up loose ends. "What about my mother? Who will take care of her? I need to make arrangements."

Alfred put his arm around her. "That witch is stronger than you think. I doubt she'll let herself suffer long. She'll catch someone in her spider web."

"What about my job? My apartment? My things? What will happen to them?"

Merlin spoke to her kindly. "You don't need those things. They are completely unimportant. Life here will go on hardly noticing you are gone, Isabel. You never belonged here to begin with."

With Merlin's hand on her arm to comfort her and Alfred's arm around her shoulders to give her strength, Isabel felt as though she was in a cocoon of warmth and love. She drew herself up. "Right. Let's go." She looked around but Gwen was nowhere to be seen. Probably making out in some dark corner, she thought. As they were walking out the door, she stopped suddenly.

"What?" asked Alfred almost tripping over her.

"Bathroom," she replied. "I need to go to the bathroom."

"Now?"

"I don't think this journey will have any place to stop, will it?"

Merlin shook his head. "Go then, but make it fast."

Isabel pushed the bathroom door shut, leaning against it so it could hold her up. She looked in the mirror. "Are you doing this?" she said out loud to her reflection. "Can you really be doing this? Are you really going to travel through time and be a princess on the other side?"

She leaned against the sink. "Oh God," she said out loud to no one, "no way. I don't care how real it feels, this must be a dream. That means I have to wake up, and that means he will be gone. A phantom vision of what will never be. But I will still miss him as though he was real." She covered her face with her hands.

Isabel looked at her reflection again. "Hey," she said, brightening a bit, "maybe I'm in a coma. Maybe I'll never wake up. Maybe I'll live this whole great, exciting life and never realize that I'm actually lying in a hospital bed in a sanitarium somewhere. I can live with that. Please, God, please let that be it."

At that moment, Gwen walked through the door. "Iz, what's up?"

"Nothing," Isabel lied, trying to sound casual. "How's it going ith the guy?"

Gwen ignored Isabel's feeble attempt at avoiding the subject. "Something is up. I saw you and Alfred talking and hugging as though you've made some kind of decision. I saw that old guy walk in, and you guys rush over to him. You were starting out the door without so much as a goodbye. Try and tell me again that there's nothing going on."

"Alfred thinks the bar is too loud and crowded. We were just going with his friend to a quieter place."

Suddenly Gwen's demeanor changed. Her eyes turned dark and her expression cold. "You're lying, Isabel," she said in a voice that made gooseflesh break out all over Isabel's body. "You are lying, and I know that you are lying. You have decided to go back with them. Merlin is taking you now."

"What?" Isabel's heart skipped a beat. "How do you know that? How do you know Merlin?"

"I have connections, Isabel. Connections that do not want you to leave here alive." Isabel couldn't tell if the terrifying menace had dimmed her vision or genuinely darkened the bright bathroom. Gwen pulled the door open, and the guy she had been dancing with stepped in. His eyes flashed red.

The dream was turning into a nightmare. "Who are you?" Isabel croaked.

"Don't you recognize me, little girl? I am the man who knows all your secrets. I am the one who sent you here. And I am the one who is going to put you away." As Isabel watched, he began to change. Individually the changes were minute, a little around his eyes, a little around his mouth, a gentle darkening of his hair, his shoulders slimming ever so slightly, his height diminishing a bit. Taken all together, they created the appearance of a completely different person. Malcolm.

Like at the park, he didn't move or blink, but suddenly Isabel felt as though all of the bones in her body had been disconnected. She collapsed on the floor in a heap. She was still conscious and could hear what they were saying, but she could not move or speak.

"Malcolm," Gwen said with scorn, "do you intend to carry her?"

"Me? No."

"Neither do I. Don't you think you had better make her able to walk out of here?"

"Good thinking."

Isabel felt the strength return in small measure to her legs though her kidnappers still had to drag her limp body.

Gwen said, "Now what? We can't stroll out past Merlin and Alfred."

Malcolm peeked out the door. "There's an exit right here at the end of the hall. We'll go out there."

Gwen shook her head. "That's an emergency exit. As soon as we open the door the alarm will go off."

"So? Your car is right outside, isn't it?" he snapped as though she was an idiot. "We'll move quickly, throw her into your car, and drive off before they even have the presence of mind to move."

Gwen nodded. "You're good."

Merlin and Alfred were walking over to knock on the bathroom door when they saw Gwen and Malcolm come out with Isabel propped up between them. "Malcolm!" Merlin yelled, not caring who heard. They ran as fast as they could through the crowded bar, but as they burst through the door Gwen was peeling out of the parking lot.

Hearing the alarm, the policeman who was working crowd control came running out, weapon drawn.

"They're kidnapping that girl!" Merlin yelled.

They were moving too fast for anyone to catch them, but the policeman maintained his cool and memorized the car type, color and license plate before it disappeared into the darkness. He jumped into his car to find that Merlin and Alfred were taking the back seat. "You can't ride with me! It's too dangerous!"

"That woman is my wife," Alfred exclaimed. "Go!"

With no time for argument, the police car sent gravel flying as it sped out of the driveway after Gwen, sirens blaring. He got on his radio and gave the dispatcher the information on the car he was chasing. Alfred and Merlin heard her immediately put a call out to all officers in the area. The radio crackled and buzzed with voices reporting sightings and pursuit. With that help, they were able to follow her to her destination, Wigless George Park.

Chapter 23

Gwen pulled out of sight and killed her lights. Several patrol cars rushed past, sirens still blaring. In front of them loomed the mountain-sized rock. It had been named Wigless George Mountain by angry colonists during the Revolutionary War who claimed it looked like King George without his wig on. Many efforts had been made to give it a more dignified name, but the locals and the tourists liked it and so it stuck. Spring through fall a laser light show was projected onto its smooth, bare, northern face. Malcolm had decided that was the perfect place for him to put on his own show.

The trail to the top was closed at dark, so Malcolm and Gwen were able to drag Isabel up without any interference. They heard policemen come and go but always hid in the shadows until the way was clear. Isabel, still partially paralyzed, was powerless to help herself or yell for help in anyway. Even the use of her legs was so inhibited that they barely held her upright, never mind being of any use to defend herself. Still she had enough sensation to feel every bump, scrape, cut and bruise she got as they literally dragged her up the steep, rocky slope. The uneven ground was difficult even for those who wanted to climb it. She fell as much as she stood, and they took no care to help her.

When they reached the top, Malcolm dropped her against the cable car station. A crowd was gathered on the expansive lawn at the foot of the mountain, waiting for the show to begin. Malcolm looked down on them with a satisfied smile. "They're going to get more of a show than they ever dreamed," he said, rubbing his hands together.

He walked over to Isabel and crouched in front of her. "Removing your soul was an act of pure genius, Isabel. And I'm not boasting. Others who are expert on these kinds of things have said as much. Not only did it set your country--your real country— on a path to centuries of chaos, but it ruined the lives of you, Alfred, Kathryn and Merlin. I was so pleased with the results," he said smugly. "But now I am afraid you have become a problem again, and this time a more permanent solution is required."

Terror began its frantic, feral dance as Isabel knew that she would never see the light of another day. Her limp body was beyond her control, and she was powerless to do anything to forestall her fate. This was the end of her life.

"I can see you are afraid," he smiled, "and of course you should be. But you should also be proud. You are going to be one of my most magnificent works ever. Those people below will be talking about this for the rest of their lives, passing the story on to their children and to their children's children and so forth. They will never forget you, Isabel. You will be famous. Why, you should thank me. I am taking you from being a little nobody with nothing, to being a celebrity."

He laughed at his own joke while Gwen fidgeted nervously. "Would you like to know what I am going to do?" Malcolm said as though Isabel was capable of responding. "Of course you do." He took a deep breath and then began waving his arms around as though he was conducting an orchestra. "I am an artist you see, and my medium is magic. Magic used for retribution. Magic used to punish those who dare to get in my way. I am going to turn you into a shooting star, my Isabel. I am going to set you on fire and then LAUNCH," he said this with a great flourish, "yes, LAUNCH, you into the air over the side of the mountain, over the heads of the people below. You will hang in the air a moment like a flaring firework and then plunge through the sky like a shooting star." He was giddy, overcome with his own brilliance. "It will be spectacular." He turned and faced them both, "I shall stay a few days to bask in the acclaim of my spectacular show. To be sure, no one will know that it was me, but I will be able to move around incognito and gather their exclamations of horror and surprise."

"Can we just get this over with, Picasso?" Gwen asked nervously.

He continued talking out loud to himself. "Now let's see. The fire is no problem, but how should she be launched? I can hardly throw her, and simple magic would be so boring. We need some kind of device." He began looking around.

Isabel looked up at Gwen and communicated with her eyes. They pleaded for help, pleaded to be released. Gwen had no doubt what that look meant, but she had no intention of helping. "You want me to let you go? Sorry, girlfriend, no way. Did you think that I was really able to attract all those men just myself? Nobody can do that, not even me. Nope. These guys that Malcolm works with, they offered to make me irresistible if I would keep my eye on you. Can you guess when that was?" Gwen looked to Isabel for a response, knowing that she wouldn't get one. "College. Can you believe that? I couldn't imagine why a little nothing like you needed watching, but who was I to argue? In return they made it so I can have any guy that I want. Not love, mind you, they can't do love. But I wasn't interested in love anyway. I want them to want me. I want them all to want me. Why would I tie myself to one man?

"The great thing about it is it's all so scientific. They changed my body so that I put out little undetectable electrical impulses that stimulate just the right part of a man's brain to make him want my body. Is that not cool? Don't know why it didn't work on Alfred."

Gwen paused and looked calmly into Isabel's terrified eyes. "Sorry, Iz, I'm not giving that up for anybody. Not even for you. I will say, though, that I appreciate your doing all the stuff you did without complaining. You're not a whiner, I'll say that for you, trailing around behind me for years, watching me have all the fun."

Malcolm came over and interrupted Gwen's monologue. "I'm so glad you are having a chance for some girl talk, but I'm afraid it's time to begin." He motioned to an inconspicuous shed off to the side. The lock lay on the ground, and the door was standing open. "That shed is filled with gun-powder and fireworks. If we put enough of it under one of these trash cans we can launch it like a rocket. We'll put her in the trash can and set her on fire and then shoot her across the sky. It will be magnificent."

He began contentedly working to make good his plan. "Come here and help me. We must get this done before the light show is over. The whole effect will be spoiled if there is no audience."

Isabel wished she could pass out, but her brain was not cooperating. Everything else about this dream had felt so real, surely she would also feel this painful death. She had always been afraid of burning, but she had comforted herself that if her building burned she would probably be killed by smoke inhalation before the flames got to her. Now she was faced with actually feeling the flames consume her, watching her skin and flesh melt down to the bones. If her brain was the last to go, if her eyes could still see, she would know it all as she shot through the sky. She would see the horrified faces of the crowd as she crashed through them to shatter her bones on the hard earth below.

She had a vision of the pictures she had seen of Joan of Arc, standing bravely tied to a stake on a pile of kindling, face upturned, resigned to be martyred for her cause. Isabel was not so brave. If she had the use of her mouth and voice, she would be pleading for her life. If she could drop to her knees and beg, she would without hesitation. If she could get up, she would run. She would run in any direction as fast as she could without even stopping for a breath. Her life may not have been great, but she was not eager to give it up. She watched helplessly as Malcolm and Gwen prepared the instrument of her death, and prayed over and over for salvation to appear.

Isabel did not know, could not see, that Merlin and Alfred had found their way to her and were crouched just out of sight, deciding how best to save her. Malcolm had shouted his plan to the cosmos, and so they knew exactly what he planned to do. They could see Isabel's immobile body, but could not guess what state she was in, whether already dead, or unconscious, or simply paralyzed with fear. They did notice that she did not appear to be bound and so she would at least be easier to carry away.

"What can we do?" Alfred whispered urgently. "I have already tried to fight Malcolm. He can fell me before I even raise my fist."

"Yes…I mean…no," Merlin stammered, distracted. "I will have to fight Malcolm. You will have to get Isabel and run with her."

"Can you defeat him?"

"I don't know." He looked at Alfred in the darkness, his face lit by the colorful flashes of the lightshow starting below. "But I can distract him." He looked back to the situation progressing before them. "I will occupy him, and you take Isabel and run. Go as fast as you can back to the bridge. I will come to you as quickly as I can. Let me see what is wrong with Isabel. It is hard from so great a distance." He concentrated hard, searching with his mind for her consciousness. "She is conscious," he said finally. "She is paralyzed. I can fix her problem in one simple movement."

Even from their distance, they could see Isabel flexing her arms and hands. Much to their relief she did so discretely and did not jump up or try to run.

At first, Malcolm and Gwen were too busy to see that they had been joined by Merlin and Alfred. Gwen saw them first and motioned to Malcolm.

"Merlin," Malcolm growled, "you cannot hope to win here. I have the edge, because I have nothing to lose. But you, you have much to lose don't you? Have you told them yet? Have you told them the truth?"

While Merlin drew Malcolm's attention, Alfred worked his way over to Isabel. He crouched beside her and ran his hands gently over her battered body, checking for broken bones. Would she be able to run? Would she be able to move at all? She had a huge gash across her right cheek running from outside her eye to her nose. Blood had dried in drips across her face. Her sweater had several tears, and yarn had started unraveling and was hanging down. Dried blood was caked around the edges of the holes. Her pants were torn and dirty, and though he could see no blood, he suspected that underneath them her legs were battered and bruised.

Caressing the cut on her cheek, he sought confirmation in her eyes. He lifted her gently to her feet, supporting her weight as she found her balance. When they heard Malcolm's question, they stopped. "What truth, Merlin? What is he talking about?" Alfred asked. Isabel was still too weak to speak.

Merlin drew his body to its full height and tensed his jaw, but he said nothing.

"Tell them why you are here, Merlin. Tell them why you are really here," Malcolm said with lecherous glee.

Merlin still said nothing.

"Alfred," Malcolm teased, "did you think that you were here for the good of your kingdom? Did you think you were here to make life better for future generations? Did you think you were here at the will of God? You are not. It has all been a lie. Merlin has his own selfish reasons for this little production, don't you Merlin? Tell them. Tell them all of it."

Merlin clinched his fists but still said nothing.

"No? Then I shall tell them for you." Malcolm began pacing like a professor giving a lecture. His face too was flashing with lights from the show below: red, green, orange, yellow and blue. "Kathryn is your mother, child. I've only spent minutes with you and I can see that, although I must congratulate myself on completely eliminating her beauty from your face. But that idiot Sir Hugh could never have produced someone like you. You are far too intelligent and insightful to have even the smallest part of him in your spirit. No. Your father was a man of special gifts, a man not even of this world, isn't that right, Merlin? Did you use those special gifts to lure Kathryn into your bed? How did you do it?"

Merlin's ashen face reflected the light show like polished marble, his body tensed into the hard posture of carved stone. Alfred, Isabel and even Gwen were mesmerized by Malcolm's speech.

"I tried, you know," he said to Merlin. "Kathryn is why I became one of you. In return for working evil wherever I could, I was given the power of your beings. I was going to use that power to make her love me instead of you. Sir Hugh, he was no problem, she never loved him. I might not have her hand, but I could have her heart and her body. Isn't that what you did? But she would have none of it. She did not want me. No matter how handsome or how powerful I made myself she wanted only you. And then you created this child with her. She was having your child! Can you imagine what that did to me? Can you imagine how my rage burned?"

He turned on Alfred and Isabel. "Do you see now? Merlin and I are not so different. Each of us was working outwardly for a greater cause while secretly our motives were very, very personal. Isabel, Merlin searched for you, he needed you, because you are his child. He wanted back what I had stolen from him. And I wanted you gone because you represented everything I could never have. Kathryn's love for Merlin. His ecstasy in that love. The joy of sharing a child. My hatred knows no bounds. I will do anything to destroy you all." He took a deep breath, "Except of course for Kathryn. I will have her. With you out of the way, my old friend, I will find a way."

Isabel leaned heavily on Alfred for support. As the realization settled on her that she was looking at her father, a father who loved her so much that he came across a thousand years to get her, blocking her body with his own from the man consumed with the desire to eradicate her existence, she felt strength well up from a depth she never knew she had. She relieved Alfred of the burden of her weight and stood on her own feet, ready to run, ready to fight, ready to do whatever had to be done to survive.

Merlin saw that Alfred and Isabel were not upset by Malcolm's speech. He regained his self control and faced his opponent once again. "Look at them, Malcolm. Your speech has gained you nothing. They have discovered their love for each other, the love you tried so hard to eradicate. You have failed. Why they are here, how they got here, these things do not matter to them. Let them go. Your battle is with me. They have done nothing to you."

Malcolm laughed an evil oily laugh. "Done nothing? Their very existence is an arrow through my heart. I can only get relief by removing the arrow forever. They must die, and I will make sure that you live long enough to see their agonizing demise."

Chapter 24

"Can you run?" Alfred whispered.

"If it will get me out of here, I can fly," she murmured back.

"Good. As soon as Merlin gets Malcolm in a place where he can't come after us, we'll run for it. Run as fast as you can and don't stop to look back."

"I'm with you."

As they watched, Malcolm reached up and grabbed a handful of air. He molded it as though he was fashioning a slab of clay into a perfect ball. Opening his hands, he revealed a glowing blue sphere hissing with bolts of electricity. He launched it like a stone straight at Merlin.

Alfred wasn't sure what he expected to happen when Merlin got hit with the ball of electricity, but the effect was beyond anything he had imagined. The lightning bolts chased up and down Merlin's body until finally there was an explosion out from his middle. A mass of sparkling particles shot into the sky and rained down on the crowd seated on the lawn below. Merlin did the same thing to Malcolm and the same thing happened.

Malcolm and Merlin fired the glowing missiles with such stunning speed that the individual balls became blurred into flowing streams of blue light. As the piles of silver and gold ash piled up on the ground around them, the crowd shifted its attention upward ignoring the laser show in favor of the spectacular fireworks they had not been expecting.

In spite of the explosions coming from their bodies, the battle between Merlin and Malcolm raged on without pause. Alfred and Isabel were so astonished at the spectacle that they almost forgot to take their chance at escape. Alfred, ever the soldier, came to his senses first. He grabbed Isabel's hand and, crouching down, ran across the top of the mountain to the path down the other side.

Gwen saw them and started yelling for Malcolm. "Malcolm, look!" she cried. "Look! They're getting away!"

Malcolm turned to look at her mid-throw and sent one of his balls of energy soaring at Gwen. She caught it full force in her chest and instantly fell to the ground.

Isabel tumbled down the side of the mountain totally out of control. She would push herself up, take a step or two, and then lose her footing and slide, loose rocks chasing before her. She could barely make out Alfred's silhouette ahead in the dark, but it really didn't matter. There was only one way down.

She was bumped, scratched, cut and bruised, but she was determined to get to the bottom. When she did slide into place beside Alfred, they turned together to look back. The spectacular fireworks still lit the sky. Gold and silver ash was raining down on them. Isabel feared what was happening to Merlin. How long could he take Malcolm's barrage and still come out alive?

Isabel looked into Alfred's face and saw that he also was concerned. "We have to do what he asked," Alfred said finally, "or else his sacrifice is for nothing. We've got to get back to the bridge." Isabel nodded weakly and led the way toward the park entrance.

They ran or walked as Isabel was able. Alfred's boundless energy kept her moving far beyond what she was otherwise unable to do. They came to the highway and began to run on the shoulder, feeling it was the quickest way to reach their destination. Finally her legs felt as weak as when Malcolm had rendered them useless. She could not will them to take another step, and she collapsed on the side of the road in a puddle of pain and exhaustion.

Whether it was divine intervention or just a stroke of luck, at that moment a car stopped. It was an older model compact car, paint flaking off the roof and hood, bug guts cemented permanently on the front grill. The lone occupant, a young man in old faded jeans and a Rolling Stones t-shirt, rolled down the passenger side window with an old-fashioned crank handle. "You folks need a ride?" he asked, cheerfully ignoring the obvious.

Isabel spoke up. "We do. Where are you going?"

"I'm going back to school, ma'am."

"To the university?"

"Yes, ma'am."

Isabel looked at Alfred. It was hard to know who to trust, and yet they had very little choice. "Yes, please may we have a ride? That's where we're going, too."

They climbed into the back seat, and the boy pealed out. No doubt they would get there a lot faster this way.

"Did you folks see the fireworks on the mountain tonight?"

Isabel nodded weakly, then, realizing that the driver couldn't see them in the dark, replied, "Yes, we did."

"Wasn't that something?" he continued enthusiastically. "I never saw anything like that before."

"Me either," Isabel said truthfully.

"My name is Michael," he said cheerfully.

"I'm Isabel, and this is my friend, Alfred."

"Nice to meet you. If you don't mind me saying so, you folks look a little beat up. Were you in an accident?"

Isabel thought about her answer. Alfred was obviously going to be no help. He was staring out the window determined to say nothing. But we can't be rude, she thought. This guy took a chance stopping and picking up two strangers. At least we can be polite. "Yes," she replied. "But we are meeting someone at the university, and we have no way of getting in touch with him. That's why it is so important that we get there."

"No problem," he said, satisfied. The conversation lagged, and Isabel felt herself starting to doze off. It seemed like no time before they pulled into the familiar campus. Michael dropped them in front of the library as they requested.

"I'm sorry I don't have anything to give you," Isabel said, embarrassed that she couldn't give him any sort of tip.

Michael shook his head and put his hands up. "I wouldn't take it anyway. I'm glad I could help." He sped away across the quiet campus and disappeared in the darkness.

Taking charge, Alfred led Isabel by the hand to the shadows behind the dormitory where he had first entered this world. She crumpled into a heap against the marble wall and watched him pull his original clothes from their hiding place in the nearby gully. He put them on, discarding the tattered and torn rags which had been nice, new clothes when she bought them for him hours before. Now it was past midnight, and that afternoon shopping trip seemed as though it had happened centuries ago. He sat down close to her, their legs touching.

Safe at least for the moment, physically and emotionally exhausted, Isabel began to sob, silent, body-racking sobs. Alfred put his arms around her. When her tears were spent, cocooned in his embrace, she drifted off to sleep.

Isabel woke when Alfred stirred, and her eyes opened wide when she saw Merlin. 'You're alive?" she said with wonder.

"Yes," Merlin sighed weakly, "I am alive. Barely, but I am alive."

"What happened?" asked Alfred.

"Let's save that story for later, Alfred," Merlin said quietly. "Now we must go. Malcolm is defeated but not destroyed. He could return at anytime to finish his job. We need to get out of here before something else happens."

Alfred and Isabel nodded. They were past ready for this adventure to be over. They turned in the direction that Merlin indicated and saw that the rising sun was about to shoot its morning rays between two old trees standing nearby. Merlin waited on the light and then stepped through and disappeared. Alfred grabbed Isabel's hand and pulled her through after him, taking her to meet her destiny before she had a chance to change her mind.

Merlin had not had the time to prepare Isabel as he had Alfred. She panicked as soon as the darkness enveloped her. She couldn't see, couldn't hear, couldn't reach out to touch and couldn't cry out for help.

Thousands of voices overwhelmed her mind, as though everyone in a huge crowd was talking all at once. She couldn't understand even one of them. She tried to cry out but found she had no mouth to speak. Fortunately in her panic she simply froze in place and so did not get lost before Merlin had a chance to help her. "Isabel," she heard, "Isabel, I am here. Think what you want to say and concentrate on me," said Merlin's voice, "I will hear you."

"Merlin?"

"Yes, child."

"I'm scared."

"Don't worry. See how you feel so light? You are all together, but spread out. You move as your mind wills. Focus on my voice and move toward me."

Isabel did as she was told and was surprised to find that it worked.

"Good," Merlin said. "Very good."

"Where is Alfred?" she asked.

"I am here, Isabel," Alfred replied.

"Isabel," Merlin asked, "do you feel that you can follow me?"

She reached out with her mind again and sensed his nearness. "Yes."

"Good. Let's get you out of here."

Sensing Merlin in front of her and Alfred behind, she felt them 'floating' together like a group of clouds. The cacophony had receded into the background, and no one else tried to speak to them. Their trip was a quick one, and soon she was following Merlin back into the light, feet on solid ground. Alfred came right behind her.

Isabel looked around. She recognized immediately where she was although she had only seen it in pictures. "We're at Stonehenge," she said hoarsely.

"Yes," Merlin smiled kindly. "I'm glad you recognize it. Rest a bit. We are in no hurry, now that we are home."

She sat on the cold, damp ground and leaned against one of the huge stones. I'm leaning against one of the stones of Stonehenge, she thought. Stonehenge. Through the spaces between the stones she could see the broad, green Salisbury Plain stretching out in every direction. Whether we have traveled in time or not, she thought, we have certainly traveled in place. She felt dizzy and disoriented, so she closed her eyes and focused on the dewy grass beneath her and the cold stone at her back. It certainly felt real, yet her mind still could not accept it. Perhaps, she thought as she drifted off to sleep again, perhaps when I open my eyes it will all be gone.

Chapter 25

When Isabel opened her eyes, the scene had changed a little, so she felt she must have dozed off. Two horses had appeared, and Merlin and Alfred were sitting by a small fire talking in low tones. Isabel stretched and found that every bone, every muscle, every nerve in her body ached. By sheer force of will she pushed herself up and joined them at the fire. Its warmth felt good where it touched her, and she longed for an electric heating pad, one that she could lie in like a sleeping bag.

"Awake at last," Merlin said cheerfully. His appearance, however, was anything but cheerful. He no longer looked robust and vital. His hair hung limply, its luster and fullness gone. His skin had no color except for dark circles around his sunken eyes. Isabel thought he looked almost transparent, like a sheet that has seen one too many cycles of the washing machine. Instead of his usual proud posture, he was stooped and weary.

Isabel looked at Alfred to see if he shared her concern. She was even more alarmed by what she saw in him. His posture was ramrod straight, his face expressionless. He did not meet her gaze.

"Here, have some water," Merlin said kindly, offering her a leather pouch with a mouthpiece at one end.

Isabel drank her fill and returned it to him. He poured some out on a piece of cloth and offered it to her. "You are a bit of a mess," he said.

Still Alfred did not look at her.

Isabel wiped her face. She knew from the stinging that her face was covered with cuts and scratches. The cloth came away stained with the red-brown of old blood.

Merlin took it from her, poured more water on it and rinsed it out. Isabel took it and wiped her elbow through the hole in her sweater. It hurt so badly tears filled her eyes. Though she couldn't see the cut clearly, she felt sure she needed stitches. Stitches she would never have. She hoped she wouldn't get an infection and have to have her arm amputated. Oh God, she thought, done is done. She sighed. "Now what?"

"We were discussing that," Merlin said. We were so focused on our goal that we never thought to plan what to do when we got back."

"I think, until we decide what our best course of action is, you had better stay hidden," said Alfred, finally looking directly at her. His face, his eyes, gave no hint of the feelings between them that had seemed so powerful just the day before.

"Agreed," said Merlin, nodding. "We can take her directly to Kathryn's to rest and get more appropriate clothes."

Isabel looked down at her tattered and torn twenty-first century clothes and realized for the first time that just getting here was not the end of the road. She had a long way to go before she would fit in. "Kathryn is my mother, right?" she asked awkwardly. The words sounded odd.

"Yes, Kathryn is your mother. Your real mother," said Merlin, nodding. "She'll take good care of you. She's the perfect person to teach you what you need to know."

"Sounds good to me. Let's go." Isabel stood up.

Alfred and Merlin didn't move.

"First we must plan," Alfred said flatly. "This situation is very complicated."

Isabel sat back down. "Tell me about it."

"First," said Alfred, "we must make it so that you do not appear so strange. Not just the way you are dressed. That is easy. But you must be at ease with this life and this place." He shrugged.

"Time with Kathryn can take care of that," commented Merlin.

"Yes, but how much time? The date Ethelbald set for my marriage is only three weeks away."

"Isabel?" Merlin asked seeking her thoughts.

"Learn fast. Got it. What next?" She was determined not to let her fears and doubts overwhelm her. She had to keep control.

Merlin smiled at her response, but Alfred seemed to have returned to his 'I have no sense of humor' attitude. "Next we have to decide how to change things so that Ethelbald will agree to let me marry you instead of Elswith."

Isabel wished that Alfred could have made that statement with a little more feeling. He said it as though he was trying to decide what strategy to use in battle. His whole demeanor had completely changed. She was receiving none of the feelings of warmth and affection that had made her agree to come with them. Doubt overwhelmed her confidence. Maybe this had been the wrong thing. Maybe she didn't belong here anymore than there. Maybe she was a misfit no matter where she was. She wanted to run, to hide, to disappear, but she didn't know where to go.

"I don't know how to fit her in," Merlin admitted, his head hanging, body and mind spent beyond exhaustion. Looking at her with a weak but reassuring smile he said, "Let's take her to Kathryn and then decide what to do. Perhaps something will come to us along the way."

Alfred looked at Merlin thoughtfully. "You're right. We have to do something. We'll start with that and pray for guidance with the other."

They put out the fire and mounted their horses. Alfred offered Isabel his hand, and, after a bit of awkwardness, pulled her up behind him. Isabel found she could not control her giddy, hysterical laughter, but Alfred did not find it funny. Her laughter died quickly when faced with his humorless expression. Boy, she thought, is this what life with him is going to be like?

They set off east across the Plain. Carrying an extra person slowed Alfred's horse considerably, so they set a slow pace. In the distance, Isabel could see low hills with gentle slopes. They were following an ancient road of broken stone, grass growing around the edges and in the cracks. She could see that the road climbed the hill and disappeared on the other side. Groups of trees were scattered here and there. A small creek suddenly appeared with no source that she could see and trailed alongside the path.

The farther they went, the stiffer Alfred became. He seemed to be trying to put as much distance between them as possible, a ridiculous gesture as they were riding the same horse. She had to hold on to him to stay on the horse, but did not receive any comfort from the embrace. She could have had her arms around a telephone pole and felt more warmth. She felt another wave of doubt and wondered if she had imagined the chemistry between them.

They had been riding for sometime in silence when Isabel noticed stone ruins coming up ahead of them. Isabel was struck by the thought that there were even older times and older peoples to leave ruins in what was for her an ancient time. A thousand years before her had seemed so old. In the scheme of the history of the world, Alfred's time was actually pretty recent. She had studied history, of course, and had known the facts, yet here it was, a reality she had never really perceived.

When they came to the decaying walls, Alfred tugged on the reins of his horse to stop. Merlin, riding just ahead of them, looked back and pulled his horse to a halt. "What is it?" he asked.

Alfred seemed very imperious sitting tall and stiff in the saddle. "I believe it would be a better use of our time if I left you and went to Winchester alone. I need to see what has happened since I left and judge the atmosphere there. Judith and Ethelbald have had three days to come up with new ways to make my life a misery." He paused. "Also on my own I may see some way to achieve our goal." He turned slightly so that he could see Isabel out of the corner of his eye. "We are coming to New Sarum. It would be best if you avoided being seen for now, even in so small a town. You and Merlin need to leave from here and keep your distance from the settled area so that no one will see you."

"I guess you're sorry now that you brought me."

Alfred either did not understand or did not care what she was really asking, so he gave her a very terse reply. "We are doing what we must do."

Merlin was not happy that Alfred was sloughing them off, but he had to agree. "There is wisdom in what he is saying," Merlin sighed unhappily. "Come, Isabel, you can ride with me."

Isabel's feelings were hurt, but she could not deny that the plan made sense. Saying nothing, she got off Alfred's horse and accepted Merlin's hand so that he could pull her up behind him. Now she had a good view of Alfred, and could see that his jaw was clinched with resolve, and his expression had no warmth at all. She had no doubt that he intended to marry her. He would find a way to make it happen. She wondered what the quality of that marriage would be. Would he always view it as simply doing his duty? What had happened to her being the only woman he could not resist? What had happened to the tantalizing promise of a sanctuary with no windows and no doors? Had it all been a dream?

"I will see you at Kathryn's in a day or two," Alfred said and rode off without further comment.

Chapter 26

Merlin started off in a more southward direction, though Isabel could tell that they were still headed east. They rode for a while in silence, but unlike Alfred's rigid back, Merlin seemed to be leaning against her. She thought of how tired he must be and wondered what other effect his battle of last night must have had on him.

Just as he was leaning against her, Isabel was leaning against him. She was exhausted, physically and emotionally exhausted. She had a passing vision of the movie *Forrest Gump*, of the scene where Forrest and Bubba are in Vietnam and Bubba says, "I'll lean against you and you lean against me then neither one of us has to sleep with our head in the mud." She sighed. She would never again know anyone who had seen that movie or any other.

When they came to another stream, Merlin stopped and dismounted. He drank right out of the stream. So did his horse. Animals drank this water. Who knew what else they did in it? Isabel's twenty-first century sensibilities screamed. What about pollution? What about chemicals? What about bacteria? She realized again where she was. There would never be a water treatment plant. There would never be a filtered faucet. Too thirsty to go without, she drank her fill. The water tasted a little odd but not bad. It was cold and refreshing, and she splashed some on her face to help her perk up.

"We need to get going," Merlin sighed. "I want to get to Kathryn's today so that we can get a proper meal, clean clothes and a decent night's sleep."

"Too bad you can't call her on your cell phone to tell her where we are and when we'll be there," Isabel commented.

Merlin smiled feebly. He looked even paler and wearier than before. Isabel had the feeling that he was trying to get her to Kathryn's before he collapsed.

"I'm with you," Isabel said, forcing a smile. "Lead on." She clambered up first and Merlin climbed in front of her.

For a long time they didn't speak. Then Merlin gave a deep sigh again, and reading her mind, offered words of comfort. "You worked your magic so quickly on Alfred in your time because he was in unfamiliar territory. Now he is back, and old habits die hard. He will come around again, but it will take some time."

"Do you really think so?" she asked.

"Yes," he said kindly, "you belong together, as I knew you would. He knows that still, but he is a man who drives himself relentlessly to achieve his goal. He is skilled at ignoring distractions."

"I hope so," Isabel said in a low voice. She struggled again to force down her fears and doubts. A new thought occurred to her. "So you are my father?"

"Yes," he replied somberly.

"I don't understand. How is that possible?" She couldn't wrap her mind around it.

"The essence of the person who you are was created to be here, in this time, the child of Kathryn and myself," Merlin replied.

"But I thought the essence of a person is tied to his or her physical being."

"Have you ever felt the distinction between your body and your thoughts?" Merlin asked.

"Oh, boy, have I," Isabel replied emphatically. "I am the queen of not fitting into my body." She mumbled to herself, "Now I know why."

"The body is simply a receptacle for the soul. The nature of soul is determined by two factors. First is the essence of who you are. That never changes. It is who you are when you are with

God, and it is who you are no matter how many lifetimes you live. It is you for all eternity.

"The other factor is determined by heredity. That is what makes you a unique individual in each lifetime that you lead. Your parents contribute that part. You take on some combination of your family's traits, talents and characteristics. Thus your fundamental nature remains the same but also evolves each time you are born. Have you ever noticed that some people seem to possess natural wisdom and knowledge, even beyond what they are taught in life? That is because their souls have lived many lives and gathered many different experiences. These traits are determined before you are born and are imprinted on you to shape your personality for this particular lifetime."

"So the physical plays no part at all?"

"Some, but only as people's environments are shaped by their physical presence. Haven't you ever noticed how people who suffer great tragedy seem to have extra strength others lack? How disabled people overcome their handicaps to lead magnificent lives, often lives more spectacular than those of others without such afflictions? It makes sense that God molds that soul, that personality, separately from its body to give it the extra strength that it needs, and yet it is tailored to that specific physical presence. Should that soul be taken from its intended body, as yours was, then all of its magnificence is wasted."

"So my being, the 'essence' of who I am would have been the same if I had grown up here instead of there?"

"Yes and no," Merlin said patiently. "In this particular case you grew up in an environment which stripped you of your confidence and discouraged the use of your natural abilities and talents. That is the true evil of Malcolm's plan. He did not simply take you from those who loved you. He cast you into a situation that alienated you from your true self.

"On the other hand," he continued, "he was not able to extinguish your natural nobility, your compassion, or your intelligence. These qualities may not have been honored in your environment, but you nurtured them nonetheless."

It's true, Isabel thought, compassion and intelligence were not Edith's defining qualities. She had never fully realized how little she had in common with her mother. As far as her twentieth century father, she had to wonder how compassionate and caring a father could be whom you have never seen and who has never inquired as to your well-being?

"And none of this is changed by the fact that my dad is an alien?" Isabel asked.

"Souls are souls. All souls of all creatures in all universes come from the same God. From the biological perspective, had you kept your original physical presence, my body would have made yours different. Still, because of the nature of my physical being, I feel that some of the elements of my make-up stuck to your soul when it was moved. When I look at you I see something more than others see. Something 'magical'."

"Did you love my mother very much?"

"I still do. Our transgression against her marriage vow was wrong, and we have paid dearly for it. Hopefully we can have some peace together once you are in your proper place. Hopefully, we paid enough by losing you for twenty-eight years."

"I'm glad you're my dad," she said squeezing him in a gentle embrace. "Thank you for caring enough to come all that way for me."

"You're welcome," he said patting her hand. "I am proud of the person you turned out to be, although I had nothing to do with it. You are even more than I had hoped for."

"Thank you," she said.

They continued in silence. When Isabel tried to ask another question, Merlin stopped her. "I promise you answers, Isabel, all that I have to give. But I am too tired now to talk any more. Can you save them for later?"

Isabel nodded and spent the rest of journey mulling over the things that he had told her.

They rode on for the better part of the day, stopping occasionally to rest the horse and stretch their legs. She noticed that gradually the land was getting flat again, and there were more trees. The trees got thicker and thicker until they were picking out an old overgrown path through a forest. It was cool and moist and so thick that it filtered the bright afternoon sunlight to a dusk-like twilight. The forest seemed huge, and as daylight was fading, the longer shadows made it look infinitely deep and impenetrable. It was beautiful but eerie, and Isabel was anxious to be through it.

She had no idea how long they had ridden when they came out of the forest quite suddenly. Rolling hills and green meadows spread before them. Though darkness was creeping up into the horizon as the sun set behind them, she could still see that in the distance there was a beautiful clear lake reflecting the deep blue of the darkening sky. Merlin quickened their pace along the edge of the forest. A building appeared nestled against the thick stand of trees, growing larger as they approached it. "Is that it?" she asked.

"That's it," he replied breathlessly, showing the first bit of energy and enthusiasm she had seen in him that day. He spurred the horse to go faster.

Chapter 27

Drawing closer, Isabel could see that the building was a large manor house. Its walls were made of rough, uneven stones, as though it sprung into existence from nature itself. There were very few windows, and those were small and unadorned from the outside. English ivy grew up from one corner spreading to both sides, enhancing the natural aspect of the house.

Merlin drew up the horse in the front yard, a large area of beaten earth where no grass or other plants grew. A middle-aged man appeared seemingly out of nowhere to take the horse. "Please tell Lady Kathryn that we have arrived," Merlin said wearily.

In spite of her exhaustion, Isabel was curious about her surroundings and walked about the yard exploring. To three sides the view was magnificent. Rolling hills spread in every direction down to the lake. Here and there were groups of sheep grazing peacefully. A small house was off to the left in the distance, and she could see a cozy plume of smoke rising from the chimney.

She turned to face the house. To the left was a grove of healthy apple trees; and further down were the white boxes of man-made bee hives. To the right and set back was an addition to the main house with its own separate chimney, doorway and windows. A neat garden filled the yard created between the side of the big house and the front of the smaller wing. Beyond the garden she could see a small animal pen.

Isabel sighed. It was a more beautiful place than she could have ever imagined. She closed her eyes and turned her face to catch the last warm rays of the setting sun. With her eyes closed she noticed what Alfred had told her about so many times. It was quiet. Really, really quiet. No distant sound of traffic or construction equipment, and no background hum of electricity.

Isabel opened her eyes and turned back to the house just as Kathryn stepped out. She was stunned by her beauty and remembered Malcolm's words: "At least I eliminated Kathryn's beauty from your face." She had long, wavy blond hair that softly framed her face. Her eyes were the warm blue of topaz, clear and bright like the distant lake, and emphasized by the remarkable color of her long, sky-blue gown. She was petite both in stature and figure, and Isabel felt like a hulking brute standing near her. Her angelic appearance made her initially appear to be above the common world until she drew close and smiled. Her smile was warm and real and her eyes shone with life. It was Isabel who had put the shine back in those eyes; in the eyes of a mother who had found a child she thought forever lost.

Kathryn looked at Merlin for reassurance. "Is this her?" she asked.

He simply nodded.

Kathryn reached out to squeeze his arm then turned her eyes back to Isabel. "Hello," she said in a voice barely above a whisper, "I am Kathryn. What is your name?"

"Isabel," Isabel choked out, her throat constricted with emotion.

"Isabel," Kathryn repeated. "What a lovely name. It is so nice to meet you, Isabel."

Isabel didn't know what to say. Malcolm's derisive comment kept playing over and over in her mind like a scratched record. She blurted it out before she even thought of what she was saying, "I can see what Malcolm meant when he said he had eliminated your beauty from my face." She blushed, embarrassed by her lack of eloquence.

Kathryn smiled at Merlin and then embraced Isabel tightly. Isabel was afraid to hug too hard, afraid she would hurt the smaller woman, but she found that Kathryn was not as fragile as she looked.

Kathryn drew back and looked directly into Isabel's eyes. "You are the most beautiful thing my eyes have ever seen," she said in a voice slightly above a whisper. "That is another thing that Malcolm is wrong about." She put her arm around Isabel's shoulders. "Let's go in and get you cleaned up," she said cheerfully.

They stepped through the front door into a great room which seemed to take up the entire bottom floor of the house. Directly across the room in front of them was a huge fireplace with a fire so large that Isabel could feel its heat all the way at the front door. There was very little furniture in the room: a large table surrounded by benches and two chairs with little footstools on either side of the fireplace. There was a basket of fabric on the floor next to one of the chairs. On the walls to the right and to the left hung two huge tapestries, both hunting scenes. There were two windows on the front wall and two windows on the back wall on either side of the fireplace. She noticed a door standing open near the back on the right and decided it must lead to the addition she saw outside. In the same spot on the left was a doorway without a door.

With what little she knew of this time period, she had expected the house to reek. It did not. It smelled wonderfully of apples and cinnamon, baking bread and something else savory, maybe stew or soup. Suddenly Isabel realized she was hungry.

"You must be hungry after such a long trip," Kathryn said. "You can have some bread and cheese now, before you clean up, and by the time all is done, dinner should be ready." She walked toward the open door to the addition and called, "Millie, would you bring our guests bread and cheese and some water, please?" She motioned to the table and led them over to sit down. Merlin, exhausted, used the table to prop himself up. Kathryn looked at him with concern but maintained her composure.

A young woman arrived with a loaf of bread and a slab of cheese on a board with a knife. An older woman followed with a pitcher of water and three cups. This second woman looked at Isabel intently. "This is our girl, isn't it mi'lady?" she asked.

Kathryn eyes reflected surprise, though her expression once again remained composed. "What makes you say that, Millie?"

"I can just tell. Once you've birthed a child and been the first face its eyes see, it kind of belongs to you, if you know what I mean. You see yourself reflected in their eyes for the rest of their lives. Her outside looks wrong, but her eyes are the same, if you know what I mean." She took Isabel's hand and examined it then looked again into her eyes, squinting as if that helped her see more deeply. "No, mi'lady, there's no doubt. That's our girl all right." She patted Isabel's hand and returned to the kitchen.

Kathryn shook her head. "Sometimes I think there's some witch about Millie, the things she knows."

They sat in silence for a moment or two, and then Kathryn turned to Merlin. "Where is Alfred?"

Merlin smiled. "You would not have recognized him with her, Kathryn. After only three days, he was a different person. He actually smiled a time or two." Kathryn chuckled and shook her head in exaggerated disbelief. "They loved each other quickly and deeply, as we believed they would." His smile disappeared and he sighed. "When we returned, he changed back, as suddenly as someone shutting a door. He showed her no warmth at all," he said looking at Isabel with compassion. "I wouldn't be surprised to find that she is now sorry she came with us. She is hardly getting what she expected, I imagine."

Isabel smiled weakly. "I am a little discouraged by how distant he's become, and I am afraid that the relationship we developed is gone forever. But being here with you makes it all worthwhile."

Kathryn reached across the table and covered Isabel's hand with her own. "Good," she said, "I am glad." She noticed that they had stopped eating. "Come now let's find you both some clean clothes."

The open doorway on the other side of the room led to a stairwell. Isabel and Merlin followed Kathryn up the stairs to the second floor. There were only four large rooms upstairs, and Kathryn led them each to a different one. Isabel was relieved to see a large tub of steaming water waiting for her and clean clothes lying on the bed. "We have only peasants' clothes that will fit you for now, but I will put the women working on new clothes for you right away. It will take precedence over everything else they are doing. Would you like for me to stay and help you? Or I can send one of them up to help."

Isabel turned red and felt embarrassed. "No, no please," she said with a little too much enthusiasm, "I can do it myself. Thanks though, really." She was eager not to offend, but she had always been obsessively modest, and the thought of strangers undressing and bathing her sent her heart racing in a near panic attack.

"All right then, my precious one," Kathryn wrapped Isabel in a warm, loving embrace. "If you need anything, I'm close by. Just call, and I'll come right away."

"I will. Thank you. Thank you so much for everything," Isabel replied, tears welling in her eyes.

With a final squeeze Kathryn left, shutting the door behind her.

Isabel was glad to be alone for a bit, though she didn't want to be long away from her new-found family. She sat on the bed to gather her thoughts and mull over what was happening. She examined the clothes that had been left for her. There were some loose short pants for the undergarment, and a knee-length, straight, white blouse with no collar and a simple "V" opening at the neck. A brown, ankle-length tunic went over the underclothes and a leather tie was there to belt it at the waist. There were some other items that she thought might be stockings, but she had no idea how to wear them, so she left them off.

Everything was made of different gauges of wool, the shirt and undergarments fine and soft, the over tunic rough and more textured. The slippers were also made of the coarse, brown wool.

Isabel undressed and used the washcloths provided to soothe her entire body with the blessed hot water. She didn't find any soap, but the dirty condition of the water when she was done let her know that she was certainly much cleaner than when she started. She was battered and bruised from head to toe as a result of her adventure on the stone mountain, but there was no serious injury that wouldn't heal. Washing without a mirror, she could feel the sting of the cuts she could not see on her face as she wiped it. She wondered if they were going to leave scars, and how bad those scars would be.

Her elbow required the most attention. The piercing pain blinded her as she pulled out the fibers of her sweater that had become embedded in the dried blood of the open gash. When the pain subsided enough for her vision to clear, she saw with relief that it wasn't as bad as she had thought. She smiled at her own melodramatic musings from earlier in the day. I guess I'm not going to lose my arm after all, she thought.

Refreshed, Isabel put on the clothes as best she could and folded her dirty ones into a neat pile on the floor. She couldn't imagine that they could do anything with them but burn them, but she didn't want them to think she was a slob before they could even get to know her.

The rough slippers had been lined with soft fleece and felt wonderful on her feet. Looking out the window, she could see very little in the dark except for the phantom images of the bare yard below. She could tell by that, however, that she had a front facing window and would probably be able to see the distant lake in the daylight.

She went downstairs to find that Merlin had already come down and started to eat. A full, untouched bowl of stew sat in front of Kathryn, her spoon sitting idly by, her every thought focused on the well-being of the man in front of her. She looked up and smiled when she saw Isabel come in. "Alysonne," she called, "Isabel is ready now."

Isabel had hardly settled on the bench before a steaming bowl of stew was placed in front of her. A fresh loaf of bread and generous slab of butter sat enticingly on a nearby cutting board. The stew had a stronger taste than she was used to, but she adjusted to it after only a few bites and ate the whole bowl, sopping up the remaining gravy with a chunk of bread. Alysonne appeared to remove the bowls and brought in what looked and smelled like apple cobbler. Isabel put some on her plate, but couldn't decide whether to eat it or simply savor the smell. She thought that she should try to be refined like Kathryn and not eat so enthusiastically, but it was too good to leave.

"Now come and sit," Kathryn indicated the chairs by the fire, and Isabel noticed that a third one had been brought in. "I must have your story, or as much of it as you can tell me without being too tired."

Isabel was surprised to realize that she didn't feel tired at all. The good food and loving company had energized her. Merlin, on the other hand, seemed hardly able to hold his body upright. He dragged himself to his chair, and sat mostly with his eyes closed so that Isabel could not tell if he was sleeping or not.

She told Kathryn of her first impression of Merlin and Alfred and of finding Alfred sleeping in the library. They laughed together over Alfred's awkward experiences, and Kathryn nodded wisely when he acted as she would expect him to. Occasionally Isabel would look to Merlin for his comments, but he never opened his eyes.

As she drew near the end of the story, Isabel found that she had become so relaxed that she too was having difficulty keeping her eyes open. Kathryn stood up and touched her on the shoulder. "Come now, to bed with you. I'll have the rest of your story in the morning."

Isabel shook herself awake. "I'm sorry."

"Good gracious, sorry for what? You have had quite an adventure. We will have plenty of time to spend together. For now I will be happy to have my beloved daughter sleeping under my roof at last." She hugged her again, and released her with a little push on the back in the direction of the stairs.

"Yes, right, thank you," Isabel replied sleepily. She looked back and saw Kathryn kneeling by Merlin's chair. "Do you need for me to help you with Merlin?"

"No, we'll be fine. I'll see you in the morning."

Exhausted, Isabel stumbled a bit walking up the stairs. She pulled the tunic off and lay down on the soft bed, pulling the quilted covers over her. She heard Merlin's heavy steps outside her room. Her last conscious thought was to wonder if Merlin and Kathryn would sleep together, his body being healed and his strength being restored in the warmth of her embrace. Mom and Dad together, she thought, and drifted off to sleep.

Chapter 28

From the moment his foot touched the ground at Stonehenge, Alfred had felt his burden returning as if someone was piling stones on his back. With Isabel, in her time, this life had seemed so far away. He had been totally focused on their mission to recover her. Here, now, his responsibilities crushed him like one of the pillars of Stonehenge falling on his back. For one thing, bloodthirsty invaders could come from anywhere at any time, and the Mercians were no longer able to hold their own ground without the help of Wessex. That meant many trips north at his brother's bidding.

At home, Ethelbald and Judith constantly schemed to hinder and humiliate him. Knowing that he was going back to face their contempt and manipulation, his defenses slipped into place like the drawing of a curtain.

Just as these obligations parried for his time, Alfred's passion for his books and translations loomed even larger. He had a plan in mind, a vast, life-consuming plan, and he knew that, while the monks shared his enthusiasm for the work, they did not share his vision. He had to be a constantly visible presence, issuing orders and leaving instructions to keep the work moving constantly ahead.

In addition, the marriage issue still loomed large. Isabel can do these things with me, Alfred thought, lulled into almost a trance-like state by the movement of his horse beneath him. She can help me. I must think of a way to make this work. I have the right, no, the obligation, to marry a woman who can help me achieve my goals. It is important that I follow the will of God in this situation, but what is that will? Surely not marrying Elswith. She is completely unworthy. Isabel is a much more suitable wife for me. She is intelligent, honest, and pure.

Pure? Alfred thought. He remembered her subtle, clean fragrance and the smooth softness of her skin. He remembered the weight of her head on his chest and the way her body seemed to fit perfectly against his, like two pieces of a puzzle. He had always considered such base thoughts to be sinful, but with Isabel it felt like a sin *not* to be with her.

He waved his hand to wipe the visions of her away as though he was clearing cobwebs. I cannot let myself dwell on that, he thought. I must resume my responsibilities. There is no place here for softness. We have too much to do. Isabel will understand that as soon as she learns. As soon as she learns it all.

 Alfred traveled roughly the same distance as Merlin and Isabel, but because he was alone he made the trip at a much quicker pace. Early in the afternoon he realized that he was going to get to Winchester too early to escape seeing Judith and Ethelbald that day. He changed his course and stopped at the monastery a small distance from the castle to see how work there was progressing. Pleased to see that they had made excellent progress in his absence, he got something to eat and a change of clothes. He left again at twilight so that he could ride into town, store his horse in the stables, and sneak to his room without being seen.

Alfred made a very small fire in the fireplace in his room and sat on the floor staring into the flames. He found himself wishing that Merlin would appear through his door as he had so many times before. He needed desperately to talk to his longtime friend and counselor, but Merlin was with Isabel because he himself had sent them off together.

In spite of his self-discipline, Alfred could not forget his time with Isabel. The visions of her that he had brushed away before came crowding back in the dark loneliness of his room. He couldn't forget how she looked and felt in his arms when they danced, couldn't forget the sound of her voice or the fragrance of her perfume. I am ruined, he thought. I can no longer devote myself to anything else if she is not with me.

No matter how many scenarios he visualized, however, he couldn't find a way to take Elswith out of the picture and put Isabel in without having to explain who she was and where she had come from. Even then, if Ethelbald knew that Alfred actually wanted to marry Isabel, he would do everything in his power to see that it didn't happen. Alfred finally dozed off into a restless, fitful sleep, working on the problem even in his dreams.

Instead of a solution, however, he dreamed a dream he had many times before. He was running at top speed onto the battlefield to join a ferocious battle. Even from a distance, he could see the ground was wet and red from freshly spilled blood. Men were falling with spears and arrows protruding from their bodies and steam rising as their inner heat met the cool air. Behind him swarmed a large garrison of reinforcements that would turn the tide of battle for Wessex's beleaguered soldiers. As he ran, he was seized with a great uneasiness. He stopped running, hesitated and then turned to look behind him. Always before in this dream, there had been no one. No garrison, no reinforcements. No sign of anyone at all.

But when he looked back this time he was not alone. Isabel stood in the distance. She did not wave him on and did not call him back. She was simply there. Yet somehow in his dream he knew that he felt better for it. He turned back to the battle and drew himself up. Now he had a personal reason to fight. Now he had something important to protect.

Alfred woke up on the cold floor, the fire long since burned out. He remembered everything immediately, the fire, the floor, his dream. He also remembered that no answers had come. He got up and stretched, taking a few deep breaths, then, bracing himself for the inevitable, ventured out in search of hot water and breakfast. That immediately alerted everyone to his presence, and in the blink of an eye one of Ethelbald's servants tracked him down and summoned him to the great hall.

Alfred found the scene much as it had been before. Ethelbald and his two other brothers, Ethelred and Ethelbert, were all standing over the big table at the end of the room pouring over a map. Judith was sitting in her chair, saying nothing but listening to every word. There was a sense of urgency that hadn't been there before. In fact, they were so engrossed that they didn't notice him come in. "What has happened?" he asked putting aside his personal feelings and adopting the serious mood of the others.

Ethelbald looked up. The look on his face made Alfred certain that there would be no pleasantries this time, false or otherwise. "While you have been off pouting, little brother, the Danes have made another foray, this time hitting one of our towns on the coast. These men from the north are no better than wild animals, plowing down every human soul in their path without regard for man or woman, child or elder, strong or weak. My captain tells me there is nothing left but mutilated bodies and ghosts." He sighed and shook his head. "They are getting closer."

He looked directly at Alfred, "It is imperative that this alliance be made with Mercia. Lincoln and Nottingham have both fallen, their abbeys have been looted, and their clerics have either been driven out or murdered. The king has had to move his governing seat all the way back to Worcester. You must get up there now. We must stop this."

Ethelbald paused for emphasis. "You must marry Elswith. Burhred is weak, but he is proud. He will not surrender his power to us unless it appears he is still in control. Only as his son-in-law can you take charge and still save his honor."

Alfred did not speak immediately. Although he hated Ethelbald, as a soldier he served him loyally and without hesitation. He could see that the mischief was gone from his brother's eyes. This was serious business and all personal issues had been put aside. Ethelbald as king was commanding him to do what was in the best interest of his country.

Alfred glanced down at Judith. There was plenty of mischief in her eyes. She was getting what she wanted: Alfred married off to a despicably immoral woman and condemned to a life of distasteful irritation. Looking him up and down, she smiled slyly. Her mind was obviously not on the battle plan on the table.

Judith's appearance caused Alfred to have a memory flash of sitting with Isabel and telling her about his step-mother. He remembered where that conversation had led, and bowed his head so those present would not see the expression on his face soften.

His brothers could not have cared less about Alfred's expression, but Judith did care. With his head bowed she could not see his eyes, but the usually tight lines and permanent frown of his mouth had eased into a sad smile. She sat up in her chair, her expression changing from satisfaction to outrage. It gave Alfred his own sense of satisfaction to see that he was causing her such aggravation.

Having gone so long without comment, Ethelbald looked at Alfred and said with irritation, "Well?"

Alfred's reverie came to a sudden end. "Of course, Ethelbald, you know that when it comes to protecting Wessex, I serve you without question. Elswith still disgusts me, but I will go there and do what I must." What am I going to do about Isabel? he thought. I cannot go and marry Elswith having brought Isabel here for nothing. Even as he moved to the table and looked at the map, half of his brain continued to work on the problem. Like yesterday, like last night, no solution presented itself. He looked down as Ethelbald pointed out where the most recent raid had taken place and where they suspected the next would come. He showed him how the eastern border of Mercia was being slowly moved westward. There was no denying the situation was grave.

"I need for you to leave as soon as possible," Ethelbald said firmly.

I need more time, thought Alfred. Please God, he prayed silently, give me an answer. Then, whether divinely inspired or not, an answer came to him. "I need men," he said, "I need a troop of at least thirty men to travel with me."

Ethelbald shook his head. "No. No men. Only you. There are already men in Worcester, although God knows what kind of shape they are in after so long under Burhred. You will be able to get there faster alone, and one man does not make an easy target."

Alfred knew that argument was pointless. He surrendered his point but still held his head high. "I need three days."

"Three days? Three days is too long. You must leave now."

"I have said that I serve you loyally, and you know that is true. I will not argue with you about taking a troop with me. But I have affairs to put in order. These things may not be important to you, Ethelbald, but they are important to me." Alfred hid his anxiety with the arrogant demeanor that everyone expected. He might serve his brother as king, but he had not totally surrendered his will. He needed more time, and he would have it. "Give me two days."

Ethelbald pursed his lips and rubbed his head in aggravation. "Very well, two days. You will leave the day after tomorrow in the early morning. Go now and do what you must."

With that, Alfred was dismissed. He turned and walked out without even bothering to hate Ethelbald. He had far more important things on his mind.

Chapter 29

Isabel slept soundly and remembered none of her dreams if she had them, and so when she woke up she felt disoriented and confused. She opened her eyes without moving any other part of her body and stared straight ahead trying to decide where she was and how she got there. In a matter of seconds it all came rushing back: Alfred and Merlin in the library; the days with Alfred; the battle on the mountain; Alfred's attitude change; coming to Kathryn's.

Still unmoving, Isabel listened for sounds that might clue her in to what was going on. There wasn't much to hear. Finally Isabel got up and pulled the tunic over her head. Hmmm, she thought, no toothbrush. She wondered if there were toothbrushes at all. Certainly no toothpaste. No toothpaste, no toothbrushes, no bathroom. She looked around and saw that the basin and pitcher of water from the night before had been refilled. She splashed her face and rinsed her mouth. Putting on her slippers, she ventured out to see who was about.

There was the ever-present fire in the great room fireplace, but not a soul to be seen. The door to the addition was once again standing open, and Isabel could hear muffled voices from the other side. She was comforted by the familiar smell of garlic and onions. It was stronger than she was used to, but familiar nonetheless.

Isabel wandered through the door and saw that, as she expected, she was in the kitchen. Though it was early morning, the women in the kitchen were already hard at work. She recognized Millie kneading dough on a flour-covered table. Another woman who looked like a middle-aged version of Millie was chopping meat and vegetables and putting them in a large pot nearby. The two were having the cheerful conversation that women tend to have when they are cooking together. They looked up and smiled when they saw Isabel.

"Good mornin' mi'lady," they said in unison.

"Good morning," Isabel said hesitantly with a shy smile of her own.

"Did you sleep well?" asked the younger woman.

"Yes I did, thank you," replied Isabel.

"Missy," Millie said with respectful familiarity as though she had know Isabel all her life, "this here's my daughter, Mavis. That was her daughter, Alysonne, brought you your stew last night."

"Nice to meet you, Mavis," Isabel said shyly.

"And you, mi'lady," Mavis said with a nod.

Isabel looked around. "Where is Kathryn?"

"She's out in the garden," replied Millie, indicating the door to the outside.

Isabel walked out into a beautiful, cool fall morning. In the sunglow off the mist, Kathryn looked like a creature newly arrived from heaven, her blond hair a glowing halo in the dawn.

Kathryn turned to look at her as she stepped close. "Good morning, dear one," she said. "Did you sleep well?"

"Good morning," replied Isabel. "Yes. Thank you for your hospitality."

"Hospitality? Goodness, this is your home." She put her arm around Isabel's shoulders. "There has always been an empty spot here where you should have been. And now here you are."

Isabel put her arm around Kathryn's waist and stood silent, willing herself to be strong. Finally she brushed the tears off her cheeks and asked, "Where's Merlin?"

Kathryn's brow furrowed and her sparkling eyes darkened. "He had to go back from whence he came. He's weak and wounded beyond our meager ability to heal. He had to go home." She sighed and shook her head. "I am so worried about him."

"When will he be back?"

"He doesn't know."

Isabel's tears welled up again. This was Merlin's plan. Without him, she didn't know what to do. She stood with Kathryn staring at the lake, her appreciation of its beauty compromised by her uncertain future.

After a time, Kathryn broke the silence, "Merlin told me about Alfred's hasty departure."

Oh no, Isabel thought, something else to make me cry. She was trying hard to get her emotions under control, but the lump in her throat prevented her from giving any kind of reply.

Kathryn looked her straight in the eye. "You are not to worry about that. That is Alfred's way. If he said he would be here, he will be here."

"Yes, but will he want me?"

"Want you? That's not really a factor, is it? You are here, and Alfred is nothing if not honorable. He will fulfill his promise to you and that will be that."

"But I want…we were…it was…I mean…it seemed like it was going to be more than that," Isabel stammered.

Kathryn smiled. "I know, Merlin told me. You didn't know Alfred before, so you have no judgment, but your effect on him was so much more than we could ever have hoped. Now you need time. You both need time." She drew herself up. "Come now. Let's go have some breakfast, shall we? You and I have plenty to do to occupy that time. It will fly by, you'll see." She took Isabel's hand and led her back into the kitchen.

Isabel and Kathryn sat at one end of the huge dining table in the great room and shared a light breakfast of hot tea and bread with butter and honey. Kathryn was so warm and welcoming that Isabel's shyness slipped away. In the time it took to eat breakfast, Kathryn had become the best friend she had ever had. "Was Alfred always so stern?" she asked.

"No, of course not," Kathryn replied quickly. "Once he was a boy just like any other." She paused and looked thoughtful. "No, not just like any other. Losing his mother so young was a terrible blow. He had always been a serious little thing, and after that he was a little man, more mature than any of his older brothers. He was only five years old, you know." Her voice trailed into a few moments of silence. Then remembering herself, she said, "Unfortunately he made that trip to Rome and met the Pope." She looked at Isabel with a grimace. "He was never the same after that. The Pope went and adopted him as his spiritual son and that was the beginning of his whole attitude change. It gave him his life's mission in the service of God. Don't get me wrong. Serving God is a good thing, but he takes it a bit too far. Sometimes his company is less than desirable," she finished, irritation rife in her words.

Isabel chuckled.

Kathryn smiled at her with a question in her eyes. "What?"

"You irritated—it's just funny. You don't look like the type to have such a common emotion."

"No? What type do I look like?"

"You look angelic. Serene. Like nothing would bother you."

Kathryn smiled. "Thank you for that, but it's all an act. It's the result of being well brought up, trained to be the wife of a powerful man. The truth is that my feelings are much baser than you probably think. I hide them, but they are there." She looked into the fire. "Merlin uncovered them. He's the only one who ever even tried. He sees more than most people, you know?"

Isabel nodded her head slowly. "You loved him a lot, didn't you?"

"Oh, my dear, I love him still. I had no idea how rich life could be until he touched my heart," Kathryn said with misty eyes. "And then he gave me you...twice. I love your brothers though I never felt more than duty to their father, but they do not brighten the world for me as you do." She cupped Isabel's face in her hands. "When I look at you I see all the happiness my life could ever hold."

"A month ago, I would have said I did not understand what you are saying, but since I have met Alfred that has all changed. He sees, or saw, the passion that I have hidden all my life. He called me on it and challenged me to set it free."

"Alfred said that?"

"Yes, he did."

"My, my, my. You did have some effect on him. I can't wait to see how different he is."

"However he had changed, he's changed back now." Isabel shrugged.

Kathryn smiled kindly. "You're here, aren't you? That's a step in the right direction. The alterations will take some time to be lasting. But they will, you'll see." She sighed and decided to change the subject. "Tell me about your time. How is it different from here?"

Isabel chuckled, "The question with the shorter answer is 'How isn't it different from here?' The thing I miss most so far is the bathroom."

"The bath-room?"

"Yep. The water runs right in, all you have to do is turn a knob. One knob gives you hot water, and one gives you cold. And toilets," she paused to think of her description, "in toilets you put your...your...um," she tried to think of a delicate way to say it, "your...um...you know, you relieve yourself, then you push a lever and whoosh," she made a whoosh gesture, "it's gone."

"My, my," said Kathryn.

"Any food you want, you go right to the grocery store and buy it."

"Gro-shree store?"

"Yep. You go there and they have anything you want: all kinds of meats, vegetables, fruits, milk, bread. You give them money, and they give you food."

"Like a market?"

"That's right, like a market. But much, much easier. Any food you can imagine from anywhere in the world is available without any effort on your part."

"Any food?"

"Any food you can think of and a lot that you can't."

"My, my," said Kathryn.

"And when you have someplace to go you get in your car and go."

"Car?"

"It's a carriage with no horse. It goes by itself."

"You don't have to push?"

Isabel laughed. "You're not supposed to have to push. Sometimes they break down, and you do wind up pushing." She paused and looked thoughtful. "Alfred said they were loud and smelly, and he was right. I don't really miss cars. And this food is good, too. I can do without the grocery stores. But the bathrooms—those I miss."

Kathryn nodded, "I can see why. Hot water without waiting for it to heat up, as much as you want. I would love to have that. Your world sounds wondrous."

"I suppose. But it's history to me now—sort of." She was struck by the oddity of her situation. Her past was in the future, and her future now existed before she was born. She leaned on the table and dropped her head onto her hands.

"What's the matter, Isabel?"

Isabel looked at Kathryn and felt a little surprise that she was still there. "This place is overwhelming," she replied. "I keep wondering when I am going to wake up from this dream. When am I going to look up and all of this be gone?"

Kathryn reached across the table and squeezed Isabel's arm.

Isabel knew she needed to say something, but she didn't know what to say. Finally she said, "I don't know how I can believe any of this, and yet it is all so real. In many ways it is more real than anything else that has ever happened to me. Since I met Merlin and Alfred, I have felt…I don't know…connected. I never felt connected to anyone before. Even my mom. I have had more conversation with you in the last half hour than I have had with my mom in the last five years. Now I'm starting to wonder if that life was the dream. But that can't be, can it? If it was, then I would know everything about here already."

"Let's get busy learning what you need, shall we?" said Kathryn cheerfully.

Isabel picked up on Kathryn's change of tone. She sat up and took a deep breath. "You're right. Let's do it."

"First, clothes." She called Millie. "Millie, please take Isabel's size and bring us the fabric we have to choose from." Millie curtsied in and curtsied out, returning a few minutes later with Alysonne carrying the fabric. After the measurements were taken and the fabrics were chosen, Kathryn told Millie, "Making Isabel's clothes is your top priority. Send Peter to fetch Sarah and Celwyn to come and help." Millie and Alysonne hurried out, excited by the sudden rush of activity.

They spent the rest of the day covering details. Kathryn showed Isabel where the privy was behind the house and assured her that it would be so in most places. They discussed what to do during that time of the month. ("Rags?" Isabel asked. "It is a woman's burden," Kathryn replied matter-of-factly.) They also discussed other matters of hygiene, like how to care for your teeth so they don't turn brown and fall out; how to keep your body smelling sweet; how to care for clothing that you wear over and over again. She showed her the creek that was the source of water for the house and the large reservoir where they stored it so that they didn't have to run back and forth every time they needed water.

Isabel had expected to be disgusted, but instead found that it was all very interesting, and actually very clever considering what they had to work with. Kathryn's house was well-maintained, but with only Kathryn living there and so few visitors, a very small staff was required. Millie, who at one time ran it all with a much larger staff, was nominally in charge, but she was growing old and too tired for so much responsibility. In truth things in the house were run by her daughter, Mavis. Mavis' husband, James, was in charge of the outside, which included caring for the household livestock and the horses. Mavis' and James' daughter, Alysonne, helped in the house. Their son, Peter, helped his father with the animals. There were others of course, farmers and their families living in farms scattered all over the vast holdings of Lady Kathryn and her sons. They were far distant, however, and the hustle and bustle of their activities created no stir at the big house on the hill.

The day flew by, and in no time Isabel noticed that the sun was going down. Kathryn took her up to her room, and she found a new gown and its accessories there, a truly lovely one in pale blue. Kathryn helped her dress, showing her order in which it all went on and the appropriate way to wear it. It was awkward, but after it was all together she loved it. It was a much better look for her than blue jeans and T-shirts.

After a filling dinner of stew and bread, they settled in the chairs in front of the fire. Kathryn picked up her needlework. "I will teach you this," she said kindly, "but not today."

Isabel nodded and then sat for a bit staring into the fire. Finally she said, "Is this what you do every night?"

Kathryn didn't look up from her canvas, but replied, "What do you mean?"

"You sit here every night after dinner doing nothing?"

"I'm not doing nothing," Kathryn replied evenly.

"True, but this is what you do night after night after night?"

Kathryn looked up. "Because I am here alone, yes, this is what I do most nights. But I am proud of the tapestries I make," she said indicating the two large ones hanging on the walls. "One of mine hangs in the king's great hall, the one I gave him as a wedding gift. I have to admit though, Millie and Mavis worked on that one and these others with me. Often they come in after supper and sit with me and work. What do you usually do?"

"Watch TV or maybe put in a movie or read."

"Explain those things to me."

"They are all forms of entertainment," Isabel replied. "You can do them alone or with others." She realized she wasn't being very clear. "TV and movies are like plays. Like the drama. And reading. Books are a lot easier to come by than they are here, and there are a lot more of them."

"We often have stories," said Kathryn. "Either one of us tells one or sometimes a traveling story-teller will exchange one for food and a good place to sleep. I love a good story. Do you have any to tell?"

"No," Isabel replied quickly, "I am not a story-teller." As she thought about it, however, she realized that all of the movies and television programs she had seen and the books she had read were completely unknown in this time. She had a wealth of stories to tell, if she could manage to do them justice. "Actually, I know a lot of stories, but I'm not sure how good I'll be at telling them."

"Please try. I'm sure you'll do fine," Kathryn encouraged her.

"Alright," Isabel replied. Then she tried to think of a story she knew well enough to tell with confidence. She decided to start simple and see how it went, so she picked the story of Cinderella. It was easy, it was short, and she had lived it a hundred times in her dreams. "Once upon a time," Isabel started, "there was a girl named Ella who loved her father very much. Her mother had died when she was small, so that the girl knew her mother only as an angel in heaven. Her father, on the other hand, was her parent, her teacher, her playmate and her best friend. As she grew older, her father became concerned that there should be a woman in his house who could teach his Ella to be a fine lady. Because of this he married a woman of good family, a widow, who had two daughters of her own about Ella's age."

Kathryn listened enthralled, occasionally looking up from her work when the story got exciting. Isabel found herself warming to the task, and decided that she would spend some of her unoccupied thinking time remembering story lines and plots and thinking how best to tell them aloud.

When she finished, Kathryn put her needlework down and sat back in her chair as though she was exhausted. "That was a wonderful story, Isabel. You are a gifted storyteller."

Hmm, thought Isabel. I have been here one day and already I have discovered a hidden talent. "Thanks," she said to Kathryn, "you are a great audience."

"Good," Kathryn smiled, putting down her needlework and rising from her chair, "then we shall have a story every night. I shall take that happy thought to bed with me and dream sweet dreams of your Cinderella."

Isabel followed her up the stairs to their rooms.

"Goodnight, sweet Isabel," Kathryn said. "Thank you again for a wonderful story."

"Goodnight," she hesitated and then decided to try it, "Mother." She waited to see how Kathryn would react.

A smile lit her face and sparkling tears lit her eyes. She kissed Isabel on the cheek. "My little one," she whispered, "home at last."

Isabel melted into her embrace like a small child soothed by a devoted mother. She had never known such love or comfort. She had never known what it meant to be wanted. She had never been in a place that felt so much like home.

Chapter 30

Isabel was wakened in the middle of the night by commotion in the courtyard. She opened her eyes to find that it was so dark she had to concentrate to make sure they were really open. She felt her way over to where she knew the window was, and found that she could see moving shapes, presumably humans and horses, but more than she could see she could feel tension and apprehension. When her eyes were better adjusted to the sparse light, she made her way to the door and down the stairs into the great room.

In the firelight, Isabel saw a determined-looking Alfred talking urgently with a concerned Kathryn, who was still clad in her nightdress. "What is it?" Isabel asked anxiously. "What has happened?"

"We have to go," Alfred said matter-of-factly.

"Go where?" Her voice was a little shriller than would have liked.

"To Mercia. I have to go and you have to go with me."

"Why?"

"Ethelbald is sending me to marry Elswith right away. I haven't yet been able to plan a way out of it, but I will have more options if you are with me."

"Alfred," Isabel said uncertainly, "I can't. I'm not ready. I need more time."

"Time is something in very short supply, Isabel," Alfred said sternly. "You must come, ready or not. Everything we have done to get you here will be worthless if you don't."

Kathryn moved to Isabel's side and put her arm around her shoulders. "Here I have just found her and you would take her from me?" she asked, unfazed by Alfred's tenacity. She was used to dealing with stubborn, powerful men.

"Kathryn," Alfred said without emotion, "she is here for me, and you know that. That she can be with you, her mother, is secondary." He turned his intent gaze on Isabel. "You have one day to get ready. One day. I have to go back to Winchester because I have other things to do there before I leave. I will be back this same time tomorrow. Be ready." He wheeled around, rushed out the door and was on his horse and out of sight before Kathryn and Isabel even had a chance to draw a breath.

Kathryn sighed. She looked into Isabel's face and saw the panic in her eyes. She smiled gently. "Don't worry. At least he gave us a day. The way he was talking, I thought he was going to carry you off in your nightdress."

Isabel smiled weakly.

Kathryn summoned cheerfulness she did not feel to calm her daughter's fears, said, "No more sleep for us tonight." She took a candle from the mantle and handed it to Isabel. "Go up now and get dressed. We have a lot to do."

Isabel thought she had dressed quickly, but when she got back downstairs, Kathryn was not only dressed but sending Millie and Mavis out to make her more clothes. She smiled when she saw Isabel, "They're going to make you traveling clothes, and whatever else they can before Alfred returns. At daylight, James will bring around a horse for you, and we'll see how well you ride."

"How well?" said Isabel with a smirk. "That's easy. Not well. In fact, I don't ride at all."

"That is our major task for the day then," Kathryn said. "You must be able to sit a horse for the long ride to Mercia."

"How long?"

"I'm not sure exactly," Kathryn replied honestly. "Maybe a week."

"A week. Great."

Kathryn smiled. "You'll do fine. It'll be like your...what do you call them?...oh yes, cars. Horses aren't very noisy but they can be very dirty and smelly. You should feel right at home."

Isabel chuckled in spite of her anxiety. Then she turned to Kathryn with a half-smile. "So did you find him greatly changed?"

Kathryn also chuckled. "No. He is the same arrogant whelp he has always been. But he did take the time to come and warn you. That says something. You are on his mind, and he has some respect for you. That's impressive."

The day passed even faster than the one before it. Isabel spent hours getting to know her horse and learning to ride. James taught her not only how to stay on but also the feeling of riding and the importance of developing a relationship with the horse. Kathryn gave her one of her finest mares, a horse of gentle spirit who was also the mother of champion racers. She could carry Isabel with great speed, but she would take care that her rider didn't fall off. Freawyn, as the horse was called, seemed taken with Isabel right away, as though she had been waiting for the return of a beloved, long-lost mistress. She was patient with Isabel's awkwardness, and by day's end, Isabel had become an adequate rider, though her legs felt bowed and sore. Nonetheless she felt that she had made another great friend.

In late afternoon, Isabel went into the great room to find their supplies laid out on the banquet table. There were dried meats and fruits and pouches filled with water. Her lovely new gown was folded neatly to one side, next to two substantial-looking blankets. There was a folded pile of miscellaneous rags which two days of instruction told Isabel were for everything from bathing to bandaging. There was large sharp knife which she felt sure was for more than cutting her meat, and she grimaced to think what other uses it might have.

Kathryn walked in from the kitchen. "What do you think?" she said confidently. "I think you will be prepared. Thank goodness Alfred gave us a day's notice."

"Wow," Isabel said in quiet awe. "This is a lot of stuff."

Kathryn smiled. "You have more clothes, though we didn't have time to make you another gown, so you'll have to make do with the one you've got. You will find traveling clothes up on your bed. The under garments are the same, but there are pants and a shorter tunic. I'm afraid beautiful gowns are not made for riding. We'll pack the tunic you have on; it is the clothing of a peasant, so I don't want you to be seen in it, but it will serve if these others get wet. You will find a cloak there, too, one of mine. It is much warmer than I have needed for some time, and I will be so happy for someone to have use of it. The further north you go the cooler it will be, particularly at night." Kathryn sighed. "Come now and have a bite to eat, then you can change your clothes and we will finish packing."

Overwhelmed, Isabel followed Kathryn obediently into the kitchen.

Chapter 31

By the time Alfred rode from Kathryn's at Eastlea to the monastery in Winchester, the sun had come up and then some. He had committed to leave for Worcester the next morning. He had put Isabel on alert to be ready; and he knew that Kathryn would take care of packing their supplies. His mind had dismissed all those concerns. When he arrived at the monastery, his thoughts were completely occupied with the task at hand. He had to find a way to keep the work on his books moving along. It was his passion. It was his obsession. It was his legacy.

Already the monks had worked a week without his supervision. This time it was impossible to say how long it would be before he returned. Alfred needed to be certain that there was someone in charge who shared his commitment and who would push ahead and keep the others on task.

There was no question that the monks would continue to do as Alfred had bid them. They were nothing if not obedient, but by and large they did not share his enthusiasm or his sense of urgency. They lived very quiet lives in an isolated place. They had little regard for the passage of time, and they could not see the importance of creating a library of books in their native tongue.

He could motivate them, however, with the issue of faith. The peasants were still a little too close to their old religion, the one of druids and mischievous spirits and false gods. The brothers understood that the words of Christ needed to be accessible to them to reinforce the foundation of Christianity and sever all ties with paganism. That they understood, and it was enough to keep them working, but it was not enough to create a real passion for their work.

There was something more, though, an unspoken fear which haunted Alfred that caused him to try to charge them with his passion. What if the Danes actually succeeded in their mission of conquest? Should all of Britain fall, should the Danes overtake and destroy them, there needed to be a record of their lives, a record of their greatness. Otherwise they would suffer the same fate as so many peoples before them, disappearing into the dust with no evidence that they ever existed at all.

The monks, however, were for the most part satisfied having their important texts in Latin. They all read Latin, and most of the lay people they were supposedly writing for couldn't read anyway. They were not so far-sighted as Alfred, but they did as he told them. He had, after all, been adopted by the Pope, and he was the brother of the king.

Alfred knew he needed someone to lead in his stead, to encourage them to work hard and strive for excellence. He knew the perfect man for the job: Cuthbert, a young monk named after the beloved saint. The problem was Cuthbert's age; he had come to the monastery two years before at twelve years of age and now was an unimpressive fourteen. He was wise beyond his years, one might even say divinely so, but many of the older men considered him inexperienced and untested. It was unlikely that they would follow his lead. There needed to be someone else, but who? Alfred went looking for Cuthbert to seek his help in selecting his spiritual lieutenant.

He found the boy working in the garden. "Why are you here, Cuthbert? Why are you not working in the library?"

Cuthbert smiled gently, his eyes wise. It was as though a much older soul had been put in his young body. "Even I must have some time outside, my lord. My eyes blur and my hands cramp from the constant writing and drawing." He looked up and closed his eyes against the warm sun. "Occasionally I need the sun to revive me and drive me on."

Alfred did not smile, but he was struck as always by the boy's poise. Though he certainly meant no harm to any at the monastery, still most of them feared him and approached him with bowed heads. Not Cuthbert though, not ever. "Brother Cuthbert, we have grave matters to discuss."

The gentle happiness on the young monk's face changed quickly to steeled resolution. "What? What is it?"

"Ethelbald is sending me back to Mercia in the morning. The situation there is very dangerous, and I have no idea how long I'll be gone. I am supposed to marry the king's daughter and take charge of the defense of that land. They are an important buffer between us and disaster, and they are not strong enough to stand alone."

Cuthbert nodded slowly. They had received word of the Danish attacks, and of the gruesome fate of the clerics they found. Those brothers and sisters suffered torture of the most heinous, soul-destroying kind, writhing and begging for mercy from agonizing dismemberment and evisceration, their monasteries decimated beyond recognition. "Then you must go. How can I help you?"

"It seems few understand the importance of the work we do here, but it is essential that it be continued while I am gone. If something happens, and I never return, I can die in peace if I know that the work will go on. You understand why it is so important, but I am afraid that without me here, your brothers will be less than diligent."

Cuthbert shook his head doubtfully. "Alfred, my good friend, you know that they give me no authority. I can promise that I will work and work hard, but I cannot promise that they will follow my leadership."

They moved to a nearby bench. When Alfred sat, he sat on the edge as though at any moment someone would release his spring, and he would shoot up into the air. "Who else can help us? Who will be taskmaster in my stead?"

"I do not know," Cuthbert replied sadly. "Perhaps if we ask the Lord for guidance, He will present us with the answer."

They looked up to see an older man strolling toward them. "Who is that?" Alfred asked. "I don't remember him."

"That is Brother Swithun. He is come to us recently from the North. I believe he escaped a Danish attack, but I am not certain. He has kept very much to himself since he arrived."

Brother Swithun had obviously been looking for them. "You are Prince Alfred," he said as he walked up. "Some of the brothers mentioned they had seen you arrive. I have been waiting to speak with you."

"With me?"

"Yes. They tell me you are the one who drives this library," Swithun said with energy and enthusiasm. "You are the one who has set its tasks. You are the one with the vision." He bowed. "I come to offer my service to you."

"What service is that?" Alfred asked trying to maintain a calm demeanor in spite of his excitement.

"I have spent my life in the translation and illumination of great books by great men. Everything I accomplished, every manuscript I finished, was burned by the Danes when they burned our library. It was a terrible blow, more difficult even than losing my life would have been. If my existence here is to have any meaning, I must start over, so I am presenting myself to you."

Alfred looked at Cuthbert, who nodded his understanding. "Did you know, Brother Swithun, that you are the answer to a prayer?" Alfred stood up and the three men walked together into the library.

As they walked between the tall desks, each occupied by a monk intent on his work, Alfred saw that in spite of his concerns, the quality of their work was impeccable. The beauty of their illuminations would inspire thoughts of the great God, even for those who could not read the texts.

Swithun commented on the quality of the work. "When I arrived and saw what goes on here, it was as though I had been given a vision of Heaven itself. I asked how this miracle of learning had come to be, and I was told that you were its driving force. Your passion demands the very best and your vision spurs them on."

"Mine is a mission from God himself, Brother Swithun," said Alfred. "I can take no credit for its success. I am afraid that while I am gone, the work will not be…" he searched for the right words. "The work will not be so passionately pursued. Cuthbert shares my vision, but his youth works against him. You are the one. You are the answer to our prayers. You and Cuthbert together can see that this continues in my absence." He stopped and looked Swithun directly in the eyes, "That is, if you are willing."

Swithun chuckled. "Willing?" He bowed again. "Your mission is now mine."

Alfred, Cuthbert and Swithun sought out the abbot. Alfred wanted no doubts about his wishes and no hindrances to their efforts. The old abbot was put off at first, thinking that Alfred was putting Swithun in his place. Nothing could have been further from the truth. Alfred wanted to ensure that Swithun would not be weighed down with administrative duties. Once that misunderstanding was settled, the abbot gladly gave Swithun and Cuthbert responsibility for the library, so that he could focus on the myriad other details of running the monastery.

They persuaded Alfred to eat before he left, then accompanied him to his horse. "It is a sacred trust I leave in you, brothers," Alfred said.

Cuthbert answered for both, "We will not fail you."

Alfred nodded and was off, spurring his horse at top speed for the castle at Winchester. He would go and take his leave of the king, secretly return to Eastlea for Isabel, and then begin his journey to Mercia with all of its uncertainty.

Chapter 32

Alfred arrived at Eastlea as the first light of dawn was peeking over the horizon and found that everything was ready for their journey. As he drew up and stopped, Alfred's horse, Rofan, neighed in greeting to Freawyn, recognizing his mother. Alfred patted Freawyn on her withers as he walked by, and she nuzzled him in reply.

He walked into the great room to find Isabel sitting, staring into the fire, already dressed in her traveling clothes and obviously waiting for him.

"You didn't sleep?" he asked without greeting.

"No," Isabel replied, rubbing her eyes. "No, I didn't."

"It would be better if you had," Alfred said practically. "We have a long way to go."

"Yes, it would have been, but it didn't happen," Isabel said with irritation. "Can you blame me?"

Alfred shrugged and turned as Kathryn walked in from the kitchen and greeted him. "You are here," she said. "Good. We have had an anxious night, and you should be on your way."

Isabel stood up and saw that Alfred was looking at her clothing. "These are my new travel clothes. Mavis and Millie made them for me yesterday."

"They won't do."

Kathryn looked indignant. "What do you mean they won't do?"

"I mean, I need for her to look like a man."

"You didn't say that yesterday."

"I'm saying it now." Alfred's tone left no room for argument. "I need for her to look like a man. The less attention we draw on our journey the better. People are more likely to notice a soldier traveling with a woman than one traveling with a servant."

Kathryn looked at him with exasperation. "This is what she has, and we were hard pressed to make that. What do you want me to do?"

Alfred looked around and saw James outside with the horses. "Give her something of James' to wear. You can pack these for later."

Kathryn was appalled. "James is three times Isabel's size, Alfred. His clothes won't even come close to fitting her."

"Peter is too small. James will have to do."

Kathryn called Mavis and sent her to retrieve some of her husband's work clothes. It turned out that simply changing Isabel's tunic for the simpler, more masculine one was enough. Kathryn also gave her an old cloak with a hood that had belonged to one of her sons. Isabel tucked her long hair back in the hood. Finally, Alfred was satisfied

Mavis bundled up Isabel's other clothes and packed them away in the pack on Freawyn. Alfred mounted Rofan, ready to be away. Isabel shook hands with James, Mavis and Millie and thanked them for their hard work and help. She turned to Kathryn and embraced her. "I can't believe I have to leave you so soon. You are the best mother I could have ever had."

"Now your place at my table will be empty once again," Kathryn replied cupping Isabel's face in her hands. "Farewell. Return to me safely, dear one."

Isabel found the all too familiar lump rising in her throat and nodded without reply. With James' help, she mounted Freawyn and followed Alfred out of the courtyard, looking back only once to wave goodbye.

After some initial anxiety, Isabel realized that Freawyn knew to follow Rofan and so all she had to do was hold on. Whatever pace Alfred's horse set, her horse matched. It's like cruise control for horses, she thought, smiling at her own joke. A joke that no one else would ever get. She sighed wondering if she was going to spend the whole trip looking at Alfred's back and his horse's rear.

They were approaching a familiar line of trees, and she knew they were going to take the path through the forest on which Merlin had brought her here. As they rode in Isabel noticed again how dark it became from the lush vegetation. Here and there beams of early morning sunlight filled with dancing specks of dust and insects broke through the branches. She inhaled deeply and took in the fragrance of wet dirt and decomposing leaves. "Are there animals in this forest?" she asked breaking the silence.

"Yes," Alfred replied. "The New Forest is known for its fine hunting."

"And this belongs to Kathryn?"

"Literally yes, to Kathryn and her sons, but not really. Parts of this forest are very mysterious. Merlin lives here as does Malcolm and who knows what else. Parts of it are filled with magic. Most hunters know when to go no further or risk their very souls."

Isabel looked to her right and noticed that she couldn't see far before the trees grew too thick to see through. She heard breaking limbs, rustling leaves and the chattering of birds even though she couldn't see any of the animals making the noise. It was a little creepy. She was glad she wasn't alone.

Ahead Alfred rode through one of the sunbeams, and she saw the light bounce off his shirt and noticed for the first time that he was wearing an overshirt made of metal links. "What is your shirt made of? It reflects light like a mirror."

"I'm wearing my mail," he replied matter-of-factly.

"Mail? Like chain mail?" She searched her brain for any information she had ever learned about armor. She knew that the metal links made the shirt more flexible than the armor suits of the chivalric age, but it seemed that the open chain would allow well-placed stab to pass through. For all her education about the middle ages, however, the apparatus of war was not her specialty, so she decided not to ask.

"Yes. It protects me in battle."

For the first time she noticed the long, lethal sword hanging off his horse. "Are we going into battle?"

"Not intentionally. Not before we get to Mercia." He looked around. "Still, the Danes could be anywhere. And there are other dangers."

She waited, but he did not elaborate. After a few minutes she said, "Should I have a mail shirt, too?"

Alfred humpfed. "You are not a soldier. You are not even a man. If danger comes, get down and stay out of the way, I will take care of it."

"You really have this whole macho thing going, don't you?"

"Macho thing?"

"Yeah, me Tarzan, you Jane. Me big strong man, you weak helpless woman."

"I don't understand. Who is Tarzan and who is Jane?"

"They're characters—story characters. The point is, women are not as helpless as you think."

"Are you saying you want to fight?" he asked scornfully.

Isabel ignored his condescension and considered her answer. She most definitely did not want to fight. She would feel safer with some of that chain mail, but she couldn't imagine herself wielding a sword. She willed herself to shut up and save the women's movement for a less dangerous time. "No," she replied, "I don't want to fight."

"So what is the problem?"

"No problem. Sorry I even mentioned it." They fell back into silence.

It felt as though they rode for hours. Near as she could tell through the thick canopy of trees, it appeared the sun had climbed considerably higher into the sky, so Isabel thought it must be close to midday. She was yanked back to reality when Freawyn stopped suddenly almost pitching her over her head. Alfred was dismounting Rofan. Looking beyond him she could see that a creek cut across their path.

"Let the horses rest and drink their fill," Alfred said.

Isabel dismounted, and Freawyn joined Rofan at the creek without any urging. She followed Alfred to the shallow bank and sat on a rock across from him. He took a long deep drink and encouraged her to do the same. She looked at the horses and wondered again, as she had with Merlin, how many other creatures drank from this stream, how many lived in it, and what else they did in it. She made a face and decided it probably wasn't going to be any better anywhere else. The water at Eastlea was straight from the river, and it had not made her sick. She wished she had time to boil it first, but time was in short supply.

Isabel thought this would be an opportunity for conversation, but obviously Alfred didn't agree. They rested in silence for hardly more than a few minutes, before he got up and said, "Let's go." They remounted and off they went.

After what felt like another hour or so, they came out of the forest. The sun was directly overhead so Isabel guessed it was noon. When do we stop for lunch? she thought. I could really go for a couple of Krystal hamburgers. She closed her eyes and imagined she could taste the sharp mustard and pickles. When she opened her eyes though, no Krystal. No Krystal, no McDonald's, no Arby's, no nothing. She wondered if she had come to this same place a thousand years in the future would there have been broad highways and frequent rest stops with a plethora of fast food selections. Instead of highways she saw vast green fields stretching out until they passed out of sight into rolling hills. Further in the distance there were more and higher hills.

Another creek rolled alongside the edge of the forest, and they stopped again to rest the horses. This time Alfred did pull food out of his pack. "Ummm," Isabel said with feigned enthusiasm, "dried beef. Just what I wanted." Alfred shrugged and looked at her quizzically, so she decided to let it drop.

They stopped longer this time, and by the time Alfred got up, Isabel had had enough of the silence and was ready to go. She was a little surprised when the horses took off at a run and was hard-pressed to hold on. She remembered that James had told her that if she relaxed and allowed her body to move with the horse, it was much easier. She did, and it was. They galloped up and down a couple of hills and it seemed the horses were enjoying it. They needed no urging at all. In fact, they resisted when Alfred stopped at the top of the third hill. Isabel pulled up beside him and gasped.

She was looking down a slope much steeper than any they had crossed. At the bottom was a broad river dancing and foaming as it rushed over rocks of every shape and size. Its uneven banks were steep in some places and shallow in others, and were decorated with clumps of trees alternating with lush lower growing foliage. The trees were changing to their fall colors and seemed to be pointing up, directing their eyes toward the incredibly blue sky. Meadows stretched out on either side, here and there dotted with grazing sheep and cattle. In the distance she could see scattered farmhouses. As she looked up the river, she could see what appeared to be a cluster of thatched houses gathered around a stone tower.

"The Romans built that tower," Alfred commented following her gaze. "A lot of what they built is still here. Now the people use the tower as a watch house and centerpiece for their village."

"That's a village?"

"Yes. That is Romsey." He paused. "We are going to follow the river for a while, but I would like to avoid the villages and towns as much as possible. The fewer people who see you the less likely we are to have to explain you."

"Explain what? I look like your humble servant."

"Yes, but you don't talk like a humble servant, and you don't sound like a man. As soon as you speak they'll know something is wrong."

Isabel didn't know whether to be flattered or offended, but Alfred did not offer to elaborate. He went on, "We'll be able to follow the road in areas where there aren't many travelers, but in other places we'll ride along its same direction from a distance." He looked out as though picturing what was beyond his sight. "We'll go as far as Stockbridge today and camp in the woods outside of the town on the other side of the river. Stockbridge has a good size market because it is where the north-south road and east-west road meet. Maybe I'll even get you some real food," he said looking at her sideways.

She was taken by surprise. Was that teasing? Did she see…could it be…a gleam in his eyes? A flash of humor? She couldn't be sure, because at that moment he took off down the slope, and his back was all she saw of him for a long time.

With the shorter days of the waning year, the sun was low in the sky by the time they got to the town. They passed without notice through the busy market place where many merchants were doing their last business of the day. Alfred tried to look casual as he led her past the busy crowds to a cluster of trees along the river bank.

"Stay here," Alfred said, satisfied that she was out of sight of any travelers. "If I am going to get food, I have to be quick. The merchants are closing their stalls." With that he was gone, leaving a breathless Isabel by herself in the darkening woods. Freawyn nuzzled her as though sensing her fear and trying to comfort her. "I'm not alone, am I, girl?" Isabel said, rubbing the horse's nose. "You're with me, aren't you?"

Isabel pulled a couple of rags and the comb Kathryn had given her from her pack and crouched on the river bank. The water was freezing, but it still felt good to wipe her face and hands. Looking around to make sure that she was, in fact, out of sight, she found a dry rock and sat down to begin the struggle between the comb and her wind-blown hair.

Isabel looked closely in the dim light at the wooden comb with its intricately carved handle. Funny, she thought, when there are fewer things to have it becomes more important to make even the simplest things beautiful. It's hard to think how much time it must have taken to do the decorations on this, and it's a simple comb. She felt very elegant and special to use something so beautiful on her regular old hair, and thought how it turned the whole common process into an event. She got so involved in it that she didn't even notice Alfred come back until he was almost right on top of her.

"I'll light a fire," he said, ignoring that he had startled her, "and then we'll eat." He kept the blaze small to avoid attracting attention, but she was so comforted by its warmth and light that it could have been a bonfire. Alfred laid out his bounty: a loaf of fresh bread, a large slab of cheese, two somethings that resembled pork chops, and several apples.

As Isabel began eating, she decided that it was time for conversation. "So tell me again where we are going?"

"To Mercia," Alfred said with a mouthful of pork chop.

"And what is in Mercia?"

He swallowed and looked away. "Trouble," he said. "A great deal of trouble." He sighed and took another bite.

"Define trouble for me, please," Isabel asked. It was like splitting hairs to get information from him.

"The Danes are battering Mercia's borders, forcing their way further and further west. The Mercian king is weak and his troops are ill-trained, so he wants us to come up there and take care of things."

"Us being?"

"Wessex. Ethelbald. Our army."

"And you are supposed to marry his daughter."

"Yes," Alfred replied shaking his head.

"And I am with you because?"

"Because I need to marry you instead of her. We have got to find a way to make that happen and still make the alliance with Mercia."

Isabel looked down and said quietly, "Do you want to marry me?"

Alfred stopped chewing and looked at her. "Yes," he said, "yes, I do. You are a much better choice for me than she is."

Isabel had to laugh at his matter-of-fact attitude. "Much better?"

"Yes. Much."

She was still amused. "Are you sure?"

He smirked. "Wait until you see Elswith."

"Bad, huh?"

Alfred shook his head. "She gets drunk on wine until she is sick and then continues the misbehavior while her servants clean her up. She smells sour all the time, except when she has fallen into a drunken stupor and her handmaidens can wash her in her sleep. She gives herself to any man she pleases, whenever she pleases, and wherever she pleases. She spends her days either sleeping or looking for trouble." He shook his head again. "Her father controls her no better than he does his soldiers."

"Yuck," Isabel said, making a face.

Alfred smiled. "That is a good word. Yuck. I like it. I see from your face that it sounds like what it means."

Isabel smiled back. "It means 'distasteful' or 'disgusting.' Even I have to admit I am better than that."

"Yes," agreed Alfred. "You are not 'yuck'."

She felt shy again as she asked, "Do you feel the same about me as you did before?"

"Before?"

"Before we came here. Before you and Merlin brought me here."

He sighed. "Isabel, it is complicated. There I had no responsibilities, no burdens. All I had to do was persuade you to come back here with me. That made it easy to focus only on you." He looked up at the sky. "Here it is so different. I have so many things to do, so much to accomplish. There are threats from every side, and I have to constantly be alert to fight. Some are obvious enemies, and some are not so obvious. I don't have time for softness. I can't let my guard down." He looked directly into her eyes. The pain she saw there silenced her. She wanted to comfort him, but she knew he wouldn't accept it.

Finally she said, "So we are a team?"

"Team?"

"People working toward a common goal."

"Another good word," he said with a small smile. "Yes, we are a team."

It wasn't what she'd hoped, but it was better than nothing. At least she felt like he wanted her with him and not that she was some albatross around his neck. Albatross, she thought, another allusion that no one will understand. Even the "Rime of the Ancient Mariner" is far in the future. She occupied herself trying to remember as much of the poem as she could until she finally drifted off to sleep.

Chapter 33

Alfred got her up at dawn and, after a quick meal, they set off again. They continued along the road by the river, seeing few travelers, avoiding the occasional farm or cluster of houses. After some time she could see a fork in the river ahead of them, and Alfred told her it was the joining of the Avon with the Test, the river they had been following. "There is a ferry in that town, Andefera," he told her. "It is the easiest way to get across the rivers. We'll take that and then turn west through the forests and onto the Great Plain."

"Is that the same plain that Stonehenge is on? We've come so far from there."

"It is the same, but you must understand how big it is. We will be far north of Stonehenge."

The ferry was a simple log raft with paddles. It seemed it could hold about four horses, or more people on foot. They dismounted and led their horses onto the raft, calming them with soothing words. The ride was uneventful, and Alfred seemed totally unimpressed, but for Isabel it was a new adventure. She remembered Tom Sawyer's Island at Disney World, and smiled to herself at the thought that this raft wasn't on a mechanical track under the water.

Once they were on the other side, Alfred didn't waste any time sightseeing. He was nervous whenever they were around people, nervous that someone would start talking to Isabel, and worse, that Isabel would start talking back. There hadn't been enough time to acclimate her so that she could converse comfortably without appearing strange. One sentence and they would know she wasn't a peasant or a man. A few simple questions and they would become curious to know more. The less people knew about her before she became his wife, the better.

They crossed through a small stand of woods, only half an hour all the way through, and came out to the great, open plain just as Alfred had described. It stretched ahead of them as far as she could see, a green ocean with wind-blown waves of grass. As before Alfred gave Rofan free rein, and Freawyn took off after him. They were running flat out but not racing. Isabel could feel their joyful spirits set free. They ran for much longer than Isabel would have thought possible, and then at their own will, slowed the pace to a walk. Alfred allowed Isabel to ride next to him. His posture had relaxed, and she sensed that he was easier here.

"We have a long way to go now," he said. "Tell me about this Tar-zan."

"What?"

"Tar-zan. And Jane. You said they were a story."

"Yes."

"Tell me the story."

"Do you know Africa?" she asked.

"I know of it from the writings of Julius Caesar. It is a great dark place, full of strange animals and people."

"That's right," Isabel took a deep breath and began. "Deep in the darkest jungle of Africa, a family of explorers plunged through the thick, lush underbrush. With them was their infant son. One night their camp was set upon by a pride of hungry lions. No one was spared but the infant who had been hidden by his mother. There he was found by a great ape, a gorilla, who found him familiar though hairless, and raised him as her own son...."

Isabel, having never read the original, had to make-up a great deal of the story, combining bits and pieces that she remembered from old Johnny Weismuller movies, the Ron Ely series, the movie Greystoke, the Disney version and even a little George of the Jungle. Alfred, of course, knew no different and found the whole story very entertaining. He hardly interrupted her at all except for an occasional question. She was surprised how much he knew about where Africa was, and that he had heard about jungles and wild animals on his travels with his father. He had even seen a lion during his stay in Rome.

She talked until she was hoarse. Finally she sighed and concluded, "When Tarzan went back to the jungle, Jane found that civilization no longer felt like home to her. She followed him to Africa, and they lived together as man and wife in Tarzan's house in the trees. The End."

Alfred rode along quietly for a while, his expression far away. Finally he said, "I think it would be better to be raised by gorillas than by Danes."

Isabel was surprised. "Why do you say that?"

"Because gorillas don't eat their own kind."

Isabel was horrified. "Danes eat people? I don't remember ever hearing that they were cannibals. You have seen this?"

"I have heard stories."

"Stories from whom?"

"From warriors come from battle."

"And they have seen this?"

"They have heard of it."

"But not seen it?"

"I don't know," Alfred said impatiently, "Why do you ask?"

"Don't you find the idea of people eating people abhorrent?"

"Of course I do. But I am civilized. They are savages."

"Of all the world history courses I have taken, I have never heard of any evidence that Europeans at this time were cannibals."

He looked as though she had spoken in tongues. "What?"

"I don't think that it's true."

"Why not? You don't know them."

"No, I don't. And I am sure they are terrifying and ferocious in battle. But it doesn't make sense. No species of any complexity eats its own except in a time of extreme starvations. You guys are making this up."

Alfred squinted at her. "Why do you care so much about this?"

"Because everybody has a story, Alfred, even your bitterest enemy. If you understand that story, then it makes your dealings with them more effective. Why are they coming over here? Are their people starving? Is their climate bad? Are they running out of room? Do they have bad leaders who are driving them out by denying them a decent quality of life? What is going on with them? Don't you have spies who can tell you about them?"

"Spies?"

"People who go to a place in secret to watch and listen without being seen."

"Yes. They come back and give us accounting of their men and weapons. They watch to see when an attack is coming, and then they come back as fast as they can to give us warning before the enemy arrives."

"Why don't you have someone try to find out why they are invading? If you know what they want, you can more accurately predict where they'll hit next. You may even be able to figure out a way to make peace with them."

Alfred looked thoughtful. "I'm not sure I want to know the enemy. It is much easier to kill him if I don't."

Isabel thought of the faceless storm troopers in *Star Wars*. She had often thought that George Lucas was clever to cover their faces so the audience felt no sympathy for them as they were plowed down like bowling pins. That, however, was the movies. This was real life.

"It seems to me," she said slowly, "and I admit I have very little knowledge of this situation, but it seems to me that you are not making much headway against these guys. You already said they have overrun—what was it?—North something."

"Northumbria."

"Right. Northumbria. Now they are moving in on Mercia. You seem to feel you—I'm sorry—'we'—we are next. Maybe it's time to change your tactics a bit."

"What would you have us do, invite them to feast?" he said sarcastically. "They are savage. They are evil. You have no idea how savagely they have slaughtered our innocents, how relentlessly they have plundered our towns and villages."

"No, of course not. And I am not a soldier, and I have no experience with war. I am trying to use common sense. You don't have to be friends with them, but it could be to your advantage to know about them. How do they live? Why are they here? If they are simply after wealth, then where are they likely to look for it? If they are looking for food or other natural resources, then what is it that they need? What in your country is most threatened? Are they taking slaves? If so, what are they doing with them? Knowing these things could help you find out their weaknesses and make strategies for fighting them. Maybe you could use your men better and save some of their lives."

Suddenly Isabel was struck by her own boldness and overwhelmed with guilt for what she had said. Foot in mouth again, she thought, covering her mouth with her hand. What did she know about what was going on here? "I am so sorry," she said emphatically. "I was way out of line. I don't know this situation at all, and I have no idea what I am talking about. I am really sorry."

Alfred looked at her, but she couldn't read his expression. She was afraid once again that he was sorry he had come for her.

Finally he said, "Don't apologize for a thoughtful opinion. I can't say that it will change anything, but I will think about it." His voice was sincere but otherwise without emotion.

They rode a little longer in silence until he stopped when he found a sheltered spot for them to spend the night. They unpacked and set up camp speaking only as was necessary. Isabel felt she was going to spend another cold night full of icy silence.

"I like your story of Tarzan and Jane," Alfred said. "Do you have more stories?"

She almost laughed out loud with relief. "Yes," she said keeping her voice even, "I know lots of stories."

Chapter 34

The new day started as the others, though the dawn was less bright through a cover of clouds. They pulled their cloaks more tightly about them against a colder wind, and plodded on miserably in the drizzling rain that started mid-morning. It was impossible to talk, but neither of them had anything to say anyway.

When the sky finally cleared and the sun came out, they crested a hill, and once again she gasped as she was met with a view of unspeakable beauty. This was not the large, deep, impressive valley of a great river, but instead a quaint cozy dip surrounded by gently rolling hills dressed in the deep reds and yellows of fall. A village of thatched wooden houses and well-trodden roads, of kitchen gardens and animal paddocks, was nestled in and about the trees. In the center of a perfectly cleared circle of low grasses was a tall stone cross.

Isabel wished that they might linger here a little while, get a bath, a hot meal and a change of clothes, and maybe even spend the night inside, but it was not to be. Alfred did take them through the center of the bustling town, and they did stop to get a meal at a wayside hostel, a place where travelers could get a meal and night's bed for a few coins or a decent trade. They had a delicious chicken pie and some apple wine, but though they praised the cook, they stayed to themselves, and Isabel's secret identity remained secure.

Before they left the town, called Marhlburhl, Alfred led the way to the stone cross. Up close, Isabel could see that it was beautifully carved with Bible stories that she could recognize.

Alfred dropped to his knees and bowed his head, for once unconcerned with who would see them. Isabel moved away from him with the horses to give him privacy and peace.

As they rode on, Isabel noticed that they were riding up higher hills, and the lands in-between were small valleys instead of broad plains. She was struck by the beauty all around her and finally understood why Alfred was unimpressed with all of the great buildings and machines in the twenty-first century. She could see that the true beauty lay in nature's original design. How presumptuous they were to think that they could improve upon that!

She was happily occupied looking all about her, when Alfred slowed so that he would once again be riding beside her. "I've thought on what you said, Isabel, and I believe it has some merit. There can certainly be no harm in knowing the enemy better and having the upper hand because of our extra knowledge." He paused. "You are good company. You tell entertaining stories, and you give thoughtful opinions. I like that very much."

Flattered, Isabel smiled. It wasn't exactly moonlight and roses, but it was certainly more like Alfred as she had known him in her time. "Thanks. I enjoy your company too." She paused, wanting to keep him talking, then said, "This time you tell me a story."

Alfred shook his head. "I am not a very good story teller."

"You told me Beowulf."

"I read you Beowulf."

"Tell me a story about you. I want to hear more about Rome. Did you go outside the city? What else did you see there? Tell more about the people you met."

Alfred looked closely at her face to be sure she really wanted to hear him talk about this trip again. She looked sincere enough, and so he began, "The country around Rome looks very different from here. For one thing it is much warmer and the trees and plants are very different." He talked on for some time, checking every now and then to make sure he wasn't boring her. Isabel would break in with an occasional question, but mostly she listened, closed her eyes and tried to imagine seeing what he had seen. The rest of the ride passed quickly and before she knew it, the sun was once again sinking off to her left.

The day had remained clear after Marhlburh and passed into a cloudless night. The pale moon had just started regaining its fullness, but there was little light to lessen the impact of a thousand sparkling stars against the black field of the night sky.

It seemed it was getting colder, even though it had only been four days since they had left. Isabel remembered that they were not only heading north, but they were climbing into higher elevations with naturally cooler temperatures. Too cold to stretch out, she leaned against a tree wrapped in two blankets, her knees pulled up to her chest to concentrate her body heat.

Alfred once again seemed oblivious to the discomfort of their situation. He was lying on one blanket with the other over him, staring up at the stars. Maybe chain mail kept a person warmer, she thought, or maybe it retains the heat of the sun from the day and acts like a little portable solar heater. Nonetheless it couldn't possibly be comfortable to sleep in. He was tougher than she was and more used to these uncomfortable conditions. "What are you looking at?" she asked.

"The stars," he answered simply.

She looked up. "They are beautiful. Do you know the constellations?"

"Do you mean the Greek constellations?"

"Yes."

"I know of them, but no, I do not know them." He paused and then, "I know a few. The ones that everyone knows." He pointed and said, "There is the Big Dipper. And we can use it to find the North Star over there." He looked at her in the dark. She saw his head turn, but could not see his eyes, "Of course, I know The Hunter. Every man does. He is easy to see with the three stars for his belt and his shoulders bent back to pull his bow. It's too early to see him. He's high in the sky in the winter months."

"You must spend a lot of time looking at the stars, as much as you sleep outside."

"Yes, but I see my own things. That group there looks like a lightning bolt. Over there I see a prancing horse. There is a huge bow and arrow. Those three I call the Three Sisters. And there, see that small group all together? That looks like a jeweled necklace, doesn't it?"

"Yes, it does." She nodded in agreement. "So are you able to use them to find where you are?"

"Yes. Anyone can recognize patterns and the changes in those patterns if they watch long enough. And of course, the North Star is always north. Knowing that alone you can find your way."

"If you know where you are going. I have no idea where we are going, so finding the North Star wouldn't help me much."

He chuckled. It was the first time he had laughed since they began their journey. "Yes, of course. You have to know where you are going. Surely you have realized that we are going north."

"Yes, but we're twisting and turning. Where *are* we going?"

"Worcester."

"Worcester. I don't know if Worcester is northeast or northwest."

"It's to the northwest, in the mountains. But I am going to take you east in the morning."

"Why?"

"Near Swindon there is a great drawing of a running horse made out of chalk on the side of one of the hills. It is remarkable. No one knows when it was done or how." He looked back at the stars, "There are so many mysterious things around. You can't help but be amazed and wonder how they got there."

"Like Stonehenge."

"Yes, such as Stonehenge. There are other stone circles, but that one is the most remarkable."

Isabel sighed comfortably. Her body was warm in her blankets, and her soul was being warmed by their camaraderie. She felt herself starting to doze off. "I'm going to sleep now, Alfred. Good night." Her last thought before she dozed off was how nice it would be to have Alfred in the blankets with her, but then she remembered the chain mail and decided it would be pretty hard to cuddle up to. Maybe another time.

Isabel had adjusted to their schedule, and actually woke up first the next morning. Alfred was not far behind, however, and was still the first one on his feet. They packed up quickly and headed on.

We are heading east, thought Isabel. We've turned more toward the rising sun. She was proud of herself. She felt like some kind of frontier woman, sleeping under the stars, guiding her way by the path of the sun. She took a deep breath and sighed. With that deep breath she got a whiff of herself. Five days without a shower. She needed a bath. She hustled Freawyn up so that she was riding next to Alfred. "Alfred," she said, "can we stop somewhere tonight where I can get cleaned up?"

"It's too cold to bathe, Isabel."

She became more insistent. "I can smell myself."

He leaned over and sniffed. "I don't smell anything. You seem fine to me."

"Alfred, look," she said unwilling to yield her point, "I think I am doing pretty well considering where I have come from. I'm putting up with a lot. But I am used to bathing every day. I don't think once a week is a lot to ask for."

Alfred would not concede. "The water is too cold out here, and we cannot stop for such a thing. It would draw attention to you, not to mention making it impossible to hide the fact that you are not a man. After this is over, you can do what you want. As a princess you will be able to make all the demands of others that you want. But now, here, we can't." He considered the subject closed.

Isabel, disgruntled, dropped back behind him. Did he ever lose an argument? She decided to leave him alone about it for the moment, but the conversation was not over. She didn't know much about being a ninth century woman, but in the twenty-first century men did not deny women the right to bathe.

Swindon was another cluster of thatched houses that Alfred avoided by taking them off the main road. He swung around to one side and followed up a different, less traveled road. It wasn't long before she saw the great white horse in the distance. "Holy cow! When you said huge, you weren't kidding!"

Alfred smiled, "Isn't it something? Perhaps the same giants that built Stonehenge drew this, too. There are more of them to the south but this one is more or less on our way."

"Can we get closer to it?"

"Yes," he said, pleased with her enthusiasm. "We'll stop there to eat."

Up close, the overall picture was lost but she could still see the chalk lines. Like the pyramids, she thought, ancient peoples could do so many things that we would find difficult even with our technology.

After they ate, Alfred rode beside her again. "Let's have another story."

She was ready. "It just so happens I was expecting you to ask," she smiled. "In the distant future, during my other lifetime, your entire island is one country, united under one queen. Her government has a force of men and women, like your troops, who are trained to travel all over the world, find evil people and stop them from doing bad stuff. The best of these people, called secret agents, is a man named Bond, James Bond. He is handsome and charming, and his leaders give him lots of remarkable weapons to use." She couldn't really remember the plot of any of the James Bond movies, but she had spent a good bit of her quiet riding time making up one of her own. She didn't think Ian Fleming would mind. As she expected, Alfred was mesmerized with her descriptions of the gadgets, and since he had seen cars, he was able to visualize the really fast one she described which could turn into a submarine. He hardly interrupted at all, until finally, once again, she was nearly hoarse from talking.

His eyes were big and his expression was full of wonder. "What a magnificent story! This James Bond would be of great help. Too bad he doesn't live now."

"He doesn't live then either. It's just a story."

"But a wonderful story, Isabel, and well told."

"Thanks." She blushed at his praise.

The sun was setting to their left as they came upon another wood. Alfred pulled in front and led them in, sure where he was going even though there was no path that Isabel could see. They rode only far enough to be hidden, because Alfred didn't want to travel through the forest at night. Isabel heard rushing water and so was not surprised when they came to a small river, but she was surprised when Alfred rode through it to the opposite side and stopped at the edge of a small pool, separate from the river.

"The water in the pool is warm, so you can bathe yourself. You'll still need to be careful though because it will be cold when you get out. I'll build a fire, and go first to make sure it is safe." After the fire was going, Isabel sat close to it with her back to the pool to allow Alfred his privacy. The Speedo in the gym had left little to the imagination, but when someone was bathing, it was a very different matter. He was not gone long when he came back dressed, his clothes sticking to him where he was still wet, chain mail shirt in his hand. He grabbed a blanket from his horse and wrapped himself in it. "You may go now," he said. When she hesitated and looked embarrassed, he said, "Don't worry. I won't look."

Isabel walked over to the pool, looked back to see that he was in fact sitting with his back to her, then slid behind a bush just to be sure. It seemed to take forever to get all of her layers of clothing off, and she dreaded putting them back on. She slid into the pool and immediately forgot all her concerns about what else might be in there. The warm water was worth whatever risk she was taking. She swam and floated longer that Alfred had, but then he was not so used to bathing as she was. She realized it was getting dark, so she hurried to get out and put her clothes on. She had always hated getting dressed when she was wet, so she skipped a few steps and put on her pants and white shirt without the tedious undergarments. Hearing her return, Alfred stood up and held up a blanket to wrap her in.

This is a situation, Isabel thought playfully, a situation to try and bring him back around. While half her brain was screaming that he couldn't possibly want this, the other half had her step up close to him face to face, instead of turning her back to him. In this way, he had to reach around her to cover her with the blanket instead of draping it over her shoulders.

Alfred knew exactly what she was doing. He held her blanket open and looked at the clothes clinging to her wet body, her shirt open at the top where she had not tied it. The deep rise and fall of her chest gave away her thoughts. He reached out and traced the open neckline of her shirt. She closed her eyes to focus on his touch. He moved his finger up to trace over the shape of her lips, then leaned down to kiss her.

His touch was light but not hesitant. They had already been down this road, already done love's first kiss. As their kisses deepened, they drifted into a world that was not his or hers but theirs, a place where only they could be, of no light and no sound, only their two bodies pressed together, touching everywhere they were able. Moving closer to the fire, he drew her down with him. She felt the muscles in his arms flexed and tight, holding her close. Through her clothes she could feel the steady beating of his heart. He wrapped the blankets around them, creating a cocoon against the cold night air.

He looked down at her and saw her eyes sparkling in the firelight. "I love you, Isabel," he said, his voice barely above a whisper.

Chapter 35

Isabel woke with the first rays of the sun shining through the trees, her head cradled against Alfred's shoulder. She lay for a moment breathing deeply of him, wishing she didn't have to give up her warm spot. He stirred and tightened his embrace. "Good morning," he said hoarsely.

"Good morning," she replied.

Alfred took a deep breath and sat up reluctantly. "We've got to go."

"I know," she said also sitting up. Stretching she stepped behind the bush to pull on the rest of her clothes. When she stepped out, he had on his mail shirt again and was loading their camping gear back into the horse's packs. She thought with some disappointment that it was going to be as if the night had never happened, until he came over to help her mount her horse. That in itself was unusual, as he had left her to her own devices for nearly a week. She tensed with anticipation. Even so, she was not ready when he wrapped her in his arms and kissed her soundly. She was still a little stunned when he bent over and linked his fingers to make a step for her. She put her foot in his hands, and he pushed her up onto Freawyn.

From Rofan's back, Alfred turned toward her, indicating she should pull up next to him. "I want to give Gloucester a wide berth," he said. "There will be a lot of people going back and forth between there and Worcester. We are close now, and we have to be especially careful." He led them directly north away from the town, determined to make a sharper turn to the west when they were clear of Gloucester and its common road with Worcester.

As they rode, Isabel could see Alfred's proud shoulders slumping forward ever so slightly as though someone were piling rocks on his back. He surprised her when he spoke. "I need a story," he said. "Something exciting to take away my worries for a time."

"Hmmm," she said thinking, "exciting. Give me a minute." What would he find exciting? Oh, yes, of course. "Once there was this archaeologist…"

"Archaeologist?"

"Someone who goes to the site of ancient civilizations and digs around trying to learn about them."

"Hmm," he said thoughtfully, "go on."

"Anyway, there was this archaeologist named Indiana Jones who went searching for the Ark of the Covenant, the chest that was supposed to hold the stone tablets with the original Ten Commandments. It was said that the army that had this chest would be invincible. A horrible, evil leader of a dreadful, deadly army was searching for it to make his army the most powerful ever seen. With it he could take over the entire world. Indiana had to find it before they did and save all the free peoples of the Earth."

Alfred was enthralled with the story and stopped her frequently to ask questions. She didn't mind. *Raiders of the Lost Ark* was one of her favorite movies.

When she was finished she looked at Alfred and was surprised to see that he looked a little haggard. She wondered if he was getting sick. "Alfred, are you all right?" she asked, concerned.

He looked at her with a sad smile. "Yes," he said. "Thank you for another wonderful story. I wish it had not ended."

"You don't look right. What's the matter?"

"We are only one day's ride away, and I still have no idea how to prevent this disaster."

"We'll be there tomorrow?"

"Yes, but we'll stop outside the city to sleep and go in rested the next day. I am sure they are wondering where I am. It doesn't usually take me this long to get there. Going on a more direct route by myself, I can make the journey in three days. We've been on the road a week. Messengers may have traveled back and forth in that time so that I will have to answer for my delay to both Burhred and Ethelbald."

Isabel felt guilty. She was the reason he had taken so long. "I'm sorry, Alfred," she said, "I'm sorry I slowed you down."

He pulled close to her and pulled her reins to stop Freawyn. He tipped her chin up to look directly into her eyes. "Do not be sorry," he said emphatically. He put his hand on her shoulder and lowered his voice as though there was someone else around to hear. "To have you close to me as you were last night I will answer a thousand inquisitions and tell a thousand lies." Holding her gaze for a moment to make sure she believed him, he sat up straight on Rofan and sighed, "It is just as that poem you read to me on that first day we spent together. I fear we have 'miles to go' before we rest."

Isabel nodded her understanding, rendered speechless by the strength of his feelings. They rode in silence another hour and stopped for the night. The passion of the night before gave way to Alfred's worry, so they simply lay together through the night, arms and legs entwined, dozing fitfully.

The next day's ride into Worcester was gray and wet, the weather reflecting their mood. The beauty of the Malvern Hills was lost on them, though Isabel remarked that under other circumstances it would take her breath away.

As Alfred had said, they stayed outside the city that night. Looking as odd and dirty as they did, Isabel was not surprised when they were turned away from a local monastery. The abbot directed them to a nearby cottage, however, where they would find shelter and a good meal.

The woman at the cottage greeted them warmly, as though she had been expecting them. "I've prepared a little meal for you and then you can go right to bed. Your room is all ready."

"How is that possible? How could you have known we were coming?" Alfred asked suspiciously.

"Prince Alfred," she replied kindly, "Merlin is my good friend. He told me you would be here, though he didn't know exactly when. He asked me to take care of you and your lady."

"You've seen him? When?" Alfred asked urgently.

"Not tonight, young prince. Tomorrow is soon enough."

Isabel woke in the morning thinking she must have died and gone to heaven. She was inside, in a bed, and there were wonderful smells coming from the front part of the house. Thank you, God, she thought. Suddenly she remembered Alfred, and she was out of the bed in a flash.

She expelled her breath in relief to see him sitting at a small table by the fire, finishing a plate of food. He looked even more haggard than the day before, and she guessed he had not slept well. She went over and sat on the floor at his feet.

The old woman walked in with a basket of eggs and smiled when she saw them sitting there. "It does an old heart good to see young love," she said. "You will find a way to be with her, Prince Alfred, I know that you will."

They both looked at her in surprise. "Who are you, and what do you know of this?"

"Only what Merlin has told me. I told you that he is my friend. My name is Morgan."

"When was he here? I must see him at once. Is he long gone?" Alfred fired off the questions like the round of a machine gun.

She laughed, but it was a kind laugh with no malice or mischief. "Calm down. He's been here just two days ago and said you'd be coming. He is waiting for you in Worcester. He loves you both mightily, yes he does."

Isabel's tears rolled down her cheeks. Merlin was safe, and he was near, and he was going to help them. She felt Alfred's mood change from dread to hope as though she was receiving telepathic signals from him. He turned to her, sparkling enthusiasm replacing the dull exhaustion in his eyes. "I'm going. You stay here. We will be back for you as soon as we can." He started to run out the door, and then stopped and turned back. He pulled Isabel into a bear hug and kissed her soundly. "I will be back. I love you."

"I love you, too," she called after him though he was already out the door.

She looked at the old woman and thought how remarkable that they felt so easy around her. "Who are you to Merlin?" Isabel asked.

"Just a friend, little one. Just a friend. A very dear, old friend." She walked over and put her arm around Isabel's shoulder. "Why don't you get dressed, and I'll make you some breakfast? Then we can chat."

Isabel returned to the bedroom to dress. Finally she could wear the fine clothes Kathryn had packed for her. She could hardly believe it, but it was true. Somehow, some way, she was going to be the wife of a prince.

Chapter 36

Rofan was already in motion when Alfred ran out of the cottage and jumped on. The horse felt the energy and urgency of its rider and once Alfred was on, he set out at full speed with no urging from his rider. It took them thirty minutes to make the five mile ride.

In the shadow of the castle gate, Alfred dismounted. As he composed himself, he stepped around to stroke the horse's nose and scratch him between the ears. "Thank you," he said gently.

He turned to lead the horse through the gate and struggled once again to control his emotions. There, standing in the arch, with people coming and going around him unaware, stood Merlin. Alfred walked briskly to his side and held out his hand, resisting the impulse to throw his arms around him. "Hello, old friend," he said warmly. "I feared we'd seen the last of you."

Merlin smiled. "I had doubts myself there for a while," he replied channeling his feelings into the firm strength of their handshake. "But now I am none the worse for wear."

"And Malcolm?"

Merlin's face clouded. "Malcolm lives and is healed. But his loss has cost him dearly. Those he serves no longer trust him, and so the bridges are closed to him for a while. I don't know how long. He is cunning and will no doubt find a way to get out. For now, however, he is not a problem for us."

"That's good," said Alfred. "I despair that we will never find a way make this happen."

"Before I arrived, I too had little hope that we could put Isabel in her rightful place," replied Merlin thoughtfully, "but something is going on here that we don't know."

"What do you mean?"

"Burhred is very nervous. When he received me yesterday, he would not look me in the eye, and he trembles like a man who has been frightened near to death. He is completely resolute that you will marry his daughter, but he is hiding something important."

"Maybe there will be a way out of this yet," Alfred said hopefully. "Let's pay the king a visit."

They took Rofan to the stable and proceeded into the castle. Burhred's servant announced them, and the king received them right away. Alfred found Burhred extremely anxious and closed off exactly as Merlin had described him. He was not a young man anyway, but it seemed as though he had aged years since the last time Alfred had seen him. His face was deeply creased with lines of worry, and his eyes had the dark circles of a man who hadn't slept in days. His hands shook with involuntary spasms, and he clenched the arms of his chair with white-knuckled grip to calm them. He was obviously a man who had suffered some great calamity.

"Alfred," Burhred said, making a weak attempt at sarcasm, "I see you have finally arrived. Did you decide to linger along the way for your leisure? Did you hunt? Did you find places of rest?"

"Your tone belies your need for me, my lord king. You know I did not dally without reason. There are those who would do anything to prevent this union, so I thought it best to travel in an unexpected way."

The king did not believe what he heard and so for one brief instant looked directly into Alfred's face to catch him in the lie. He immediately looked away before Alfred could unnerve him into revealing more than he should, but it was too late. That quick glance laid bare the king's shame and fear. "Whatever the circumstances, it is of no importance," he said, waving his hand in dismissal. "You are here now. The marriage has been delayed long enough. The Danes are at our door and as the husband of my daughter you will defend us."

"Yes," Alfred replied suspiciously, "I will do my duty."

"The marriage is tomorrow. I suggest you go and ready your troops to fight."

Alfred's heart felt like a large, heavy rock in his chest. How was he going to get out of this?

Merlin met him at the door. "Now what?" asked Alfred. "Whether Burhred's behavior is suspicious or not, Ethelbald does not care. This alliance is essential to the protection of our borders. It will take place; there is no doubt."

"I know," replied Merlin. "but I am confident a solution will present itself. Let's go find the state of your men."

They gathered their horses at the stable and rode to the garrison outside the castle wall. Since Alfred had been gone, the men had built barracks and set up an archery range. At some point they had been practicing their battle skills in a nearby field where the grass had been beaten down by battling feet. He saw no one on the practice fields at this time. In fact he saw no one at all. He went to the doorway of the barracks and called out. A man slightly older than himself hurried to the door.

"Prince Alfred," he cried enthusiastically, falling to his knees at his commander's feet. "Praise God that you have returned to us!"

"What is happening here?" asked Alfred with authority. "Where are the rest of the men?"

"The men have grown tired of waiting, my lord. They spend all their days in the town seeking strong drink and willing women. I'm afraid we are not as you left us."

Alfred was disgusted. "I don't blame the men, whom I would not have expected to have self-control. I blame Burhred for not maintaining the army that we brought here to protect him." He turned to Merlin, his anger seething. "Perhaps this is why he cannot look us in the eyes. He has ruined us for the fight."

He turned back to the man at the door. "Are you here alone?"

"No, my lord, there are a few others."

"Take them and go. Call back all the men. We will begin immediately to bring them back to strength. Tell them I am back, and I will withstand no insolence. If they do not want to fight, then they can go home in shame. We will keep an accounting of all who come here, and those who are not on the list will get no pay."

In spite of Alfred's angry tone, the man seemed overcome with happiness. "Yes, my lord. We are ready to fight for you again." He called to the others, and they ran eagerly to recall their missing comrades.

As soon as word got out that their commander was back, the men came streaming out of the town and back to the garrison like ants spilling out of an anthill. They collected in a large group in front of him, and he mounted his horse so that all could see and hear him.

"You are not the fighting men I left," he said disapprovingly. "You could have fought off any siege then. Now you could not hold back a herd of sheep. You will start now to train again and will not rest until you are as you were." He looked out across the crowd and picked out several men. "You are my lieutenants. Divide the men into groups and work them until they drop from exhaustion. You," he said pointing at one, "you take a group to the archery field. Each man will shoot until he can hit the target three times in a row. You," he said to another, "go to the battle field. As each man finishes his archery, he will come to you and fight with poles until he regains his quickness and balance. You," he said to the third, "you will have them run. They will run until their legs will not hold them for exhaustion, and their breath will not fill their bodies. You others," he said pointing to the ones who were left, "form groups to take through the rotation. When they are not doing these things, they are to be making more weapons and attending to the ones we have. You are nothing now, but when I am done you will once again be the most fearsome fighting force in all of Britannia. Now go, and do not let me see one man at rest."

For several hours Alfred watched as his troops moved awkwardly through their paces. Some had lost little of their stamina and skill, while others seemed to never have held a weapon or exerted more effort than it took to raise a glass. He was so filled with disdain for their condition that he forgot for a time the other matter pressing on his mind.

As the day wore on, he stopped to look over the list of those who had come back. The count was exactly as it was when he had left. In fact it appeared he had picked up a few extras. Mercians, no doubt, men who wanted to defend their country but had no faith in their king. He noticed a young man, hardly more than a boy, approaching with his head bowed. He walked up and knelt down. "What is it?" Alfred said gruffly.

"I would speak with you, my lord," the boy said, his voice shaking.

"What then?" he replied impatiently.

"I hear in the town of your marriage to the king's daughter, Lady Elswith."

He was irritated by the memory of his predicament. "Yes," he said sternly, "What about it?"

"Sir, I thought you should know. The other night I was in town, enjoying the company of a young lady, if you know what I mean," he looked up with a twinkle in his eye, then looked back down when he saw his commander's humorless expression. "Anyway, I was set to come back after dark, and I noticed these people coming out of the castle, one of them screaming and thrashing about. I was curious like any man would be, so I hid myself and got close to see. It was a woman, screaming and hollering like a pig set to be stuffed. Some of the king's men was holding her arms and legs, forcing her in a wagon and tying her down. The wagon took off like the horse was spooked, that woman fighting those ties and shrieking foul language until they were clear out of sight."

Alfred was still stern. "What has this to do with me?"

"It was the Lady Elswith, I am sure of it. I seen her in the marketplace one day and another hanging herself out the window shouting down at the folks around. I think she'd been drinking that day. She weren't shy about her pleasures, if you know what I mean."

Alfred's hard expression changed to shocked surprise. "Are you sure?"

"Oh yes sir, yes sir. I wouldn't trouble you if I wasn't."

"You may have done me a great service here. If I find you have spoken the truth, I will send you home a hero."

The man looked up at Alfred in wonder, as though he was seeing an angel of God. "If you don't mind, sir, though I'd thank you for that, I'd just as soon stay. I been ready to fight them savages for months. We can beat 'em, sir, if you're with us."

Alfred looked down at the man kneeling before him, no longer just one more faceless soldier on a field of battle. This soldier was a simple man with simple needs who wanted to defend the country and the people he loved, and therein lay his true nobility.

He turned his gaze to the field and the hundreds of men following his orders, struggling to become the fighting force they had been only a few months before. But things had changed. He had changed. He was as great a leader and strategist as he had ever been, but when he looked at his men, he saw something he had never seen before. As though a veil had been lifted from his eyes, he saw fathers and brothers and sons, many of whom would never go home again, trusting that he would make them strong and lead them well.

He took a deep breath, turning the overwhelming sense of awe into an overwhelming sense of duty and resolve. He would train them to be ready to face the enemy. They would strike fear into the hearts of all who opposed them.

His thoughts turned to Isabel. She had been right. They may be poor, and they may be illiterate, but they are our people. Our people. They needed her wisdom as they needed his strength. They needed a woman who would understand them when they came for help and would speak for them in his ear

Alfred did not reveal depth of his emotion to the boy in front of him. "Go then, back to your troop. Hone your skills to protect yourself. I will find another way to reward you if what you say is true."

"Yes, m'lord, thank you, m'lord." The boy bowed out, then turned and ran back to continue his training.

Merlin had been standing by them the whole time. He watched the clouds of emotion play across the younger man's face. After a moment Alfred turned and faced him, his expression eager. "We must find her, Merlin. We must find what is going on here. Maybe this is the answer we've been looking for. Will you go and find out what you can?"

"Yes. Of course," Merlin said, turning his horse and rushing back to the castle.

It seemed an eternity before Merlin returned. When he saw him coming, Alfred did not wait but rode out to meet him. "What did you find?"

"It was Elswith," he said, pointing to the west. "She has been taken to a nunnery just beyond that hill."

"We'll go there now." Alfred called to the man who had first met him at the barracks. "You are in charge. See that these men are fed and rested tonight. I will have them up at sunrise to begin again.

"Yes, m'lord," he replied, bowing, but Alfred was already gone.

Chapter 37

Merlin and Alfred found the nunnery without difficulty, but their reception was hardly warm. "It is late," the abbess greeted them, not caring who they were or what their purpose was. "You should come at a decent hour."

"Time is pressing on us, woman," Alfred replied. "You can let us in, or we will use force. Either way, we will be admitted."

Reluctantly she moved aside. "What is it that you want here?" she asked, her tone suggesting that she knew the answer to her own question.

Alfred's face was stone. "A woman was brought here, a screaming woman carried from the castle in the middle of the night. Where is that woman?"

She cowered at Alfred's powerful presence, but would not yield. "I don't know what you are talking about."

"I think that you do. Shall we search or are you going to show us?"

She looked as though she would make objection, then simply sighed and hung her head. "Follow me." She led the way to a hidden door. They followed her up a dark stairway to a dark, hidden alcove with only one door. She pulled out a key and unlocked door.

The stench made their eyes water and their stomachs heave, but it paled in comparison to the horrific sight. The bedding had been shredded and was scattered all over the room. Excrement clung to the walls where it had been thrown. Food, too, had been thrown against the walls, and broken pieces of plates and cups were littered among the ruins of the bed. Clumps of hair were visible in the debris. Clumps of human hair.

A sudden movement from the shadows drew their attention to the creature crouching there. It had the figure of a woman, though long, dirty hair hid most of her face. There were huge bald spots where she had pulled out the hair that now littered the floor. Her clothes were made of rich material, but they were dirty and torn beyond recognition.

When she moved her hair aside to peer at them, they got a good look at her dirty face. Alfred gasped. It was Elswith. Though he despised her, he would never have wished such a condition on his most terrible enemy. Her eyes were dead, all recognition driven from them by madness. Slowly she stood up and made as though to come over to them. With a maniacal laugh she ripped what was left of her clothing and jumped at Alfred to drag him into her lair. He side-stepped so that she missed him and hit the floor hard, so hard that they heard her bones crack; but instead writhing on the floor in pain, she crawled back to grab his leg and pull it toward her mouth so she could bite him.

Alfred stomach lurched and refused to be subdued. He pushed his way out of the room and dashed down the stairs. What he had seen was more shocking than the aftermath of any battle, and more appalling than any sin he had ever seen committed. Merlin and the abbess followed and found him standing outside breathing deeply of the cool, clean night air.

"What happened to her?" Alfred asked between gasps.

"God has punished her for her evil, immoral ways," the nun replied sadly.

"What? How? What will happen to her?"

"That is in God's hands, of course. But we have seen this before. She will get worse and worse until one day we will find her dead."

"Can't you at least clean her up?"

"She will not let us near her. She attacks anyone who tries to help her. We have no choice but to leave her to her own end. We put food and water inside the door. Whether she eats or drinks before she thrusts it upon the walls, I cannot say."

The night air was clearing Alfred's head and restoring his calm. Rage replaced horror. He turned to Merlin. "Burhred expects me to marry her anyway? How did he intend to bring her to the wedding? Did he think I wouldn't notice that she was so changed?"

He turned his attention to the abbess, who had lost her advantage and once again cowered before his anger. "How? How did they intend to do it?"

"I do not know, my lord," she said in a small voice. "I am merely a servant of God and the king."

Fire blazed in his eyes when he turned on Merlin. "Let's go."

He took three great strides to where he had left Rofan waiting and sped off without looking to see if Merlin was following.

Alfred burst into the Burhred's bedroom to find his bed empty. Slowly the door behind him began to swing shut and revealed the old king, hiding with his sword drawn. When he saw that it was Alfred, he pushed the door closed and stepped out, sword down. "What has brought you to my bedchambers in the middle of the night?" he asked, trying to sound imperious.

"What trick are you playing at, old man?" Alfred raged. "Did you think I wouldn't notice that my bride has gone mad? Did you intend to use witchcraft to thrust her upon me?"

"What do you think?" Burhred replied, overwhelmed by his grief now that his secret was out. "Do you not think my daughter's condition brings me enough misery on its own? What was I to do?"

"Speaking honestly would have been a start." Alfred was unmoved by Burhred's pain.

"Had I told you the truth, would you have married her then?"

"I did not want to marry her in the first place."

"I know that. But you were willing to do your duty. Are you still?"

"Are you mad? I hope I never lay eyes on that creature again. If you still want our alliance we must find another way." Walking away was not an option. Ethelbald wouldn't care if Elswith was mad or not. Alfred's happiness was of no consequence in the plan for this marriage.

"I will not simply give my kingdom over to you. You are a great soldier and leader of men, Alfred, but I am the king. If I give you leave to do what you wish, I will soon find myself without a throne."

"Why do you think that? I have no desire to be king."

"No? Ethelbald does." Burhred drew himself up with resolve. "I will not yield. You must have reason to owe me unconditional allegiance, or there will be no alliance."

Alfred was defeated. He looked back at Merlin, who was lost in thought. Finally Merlin said, "Burhred, if Alfred married another of your daughters, would that be enough?"

Burhred looked suspicious. He did not trust the manipulations of the wizard. "I have no other children. You know that."

Merlin nodded. "That is true. But you could adopt another child, a worthy woman, as your daughter and make her your heir."

Alfred wanted to laugh out loud. Merlin was brilliant.

Burhred still wasn't buying it. "What do you mean? What trick is this?"

"Let us bring you a woman, a woman of intelligence and compassion. She would do you great honor as your daughter. And she is of high moral character. If she says so, you can trust that she will take your interests to heart."

"And what of Elswith?"

"She is beyond our help now. But you can still make a wise decision that will save your kingdom."

"Bring her to me and I will consider what you say," the king replied wearily.

Chapter 38

It was odd, really. Odd that she had this feeling that they were coming. Morgan said that she could feel it too. The old woman busied herself making breakfast, while Isabel sat outside watching and waiting.

Soon enough they came riding up and Isabel, overjoyed to see Merlin, sprung from her seat as though she had been sitting on a catapult. "Merlin!" she cried rushing to embrace him. "I was so afraid for you. Are you totally ok?"

"Yes," Merlin said with a smile, returning her embrace. "I am fine now. I am glad to see you, too." Alfred did not appear so happy. Merlin thought it was time to leave them alone. He lifted his face and sniffed. "Mmmm. Do I smell bacon?" He left them and went inside.

Alfred walked up to Isabel and stared for a moment into her face, before enveloping her in his arms. Isabel was alarmed. This was not a simple hug of greeting, nor was it full of sexuality and suggestion. It was filled with sadness and need. She pulled away to see his face. His eyes glistened with unshed tears. "What is it?" she asked. "What has happened?"

Alfred shook his head, his guard down with the woman he loved. "It's Elswith. She's gone completely mad. She's savage and dirty, worse than a wild animal. It was the most horrific sight I have ever seen. Worse than the most terrible battle." He looked directly into Isabel's eyes, and she saw the threatening tears. "I didn't want to marry her, didn't approve of the way she lived, but I would never wish this on anyone. The wrath of God is mighty, more mighty than I ever imagined."

Isabel didn't quite know what to say, so she said nothing. She let him lean on her, drawing his strength from her. Finally he pulled away and smiled a sad smile.

Inside, they found that Merlin had started without them. He was sitting at the table by the fire, his plate heaped with bacon, eggs and bread. "I'm starving," he said with humor. "One of the things I miss most when I am gone from being human is the food." He looked over at the old woman and shook a piece of bacon in her direction. "Morgan is the best cook for miles around," he said with appreciation. "I would make this trip for the delights of her food alone."

Alfred sat down, and Morgan put a plate in front of him as full as Merlin's. He looked at it as though he was going to be sick. "I don't think I can eat," he said weakly.

Merlin squinted at him. "Alfred, let go of the horror. What has happened to Elswith is appalling, I'll give you that. She is paying a terrible price for what she has done. But there is no one for her to blame but herself."

"What happened to her?" asked Isabel.

"I don't know. Somehow it is tied in with her immoral behavior, though, I feel certain," Alfred answered.

"More directly than you think," said Merlin. "I can't be sure, of course, but I believe she is in the final stages of some sort of venereal disease."

"STD's don't cause this," Isabel said emphatically.

"They don't in your time because they are easily treated," said Merlin, shaking his head. "Now, however, in the ninth century, they are the mysterious wrath of God. There is nothing anyone can do but wait for her to die."

Merlin turned back to Alfred. "Put it out of your mind, boy, and eat your food. God did not make her sick; she did that herself. However God can make use of the tragedy to get things done, and so can we."

Though Merlin's attitude seemed a little cruel, Alfred had to admit he made sense. He started picking at his food and found his appetite quickly enough. "Tell Isabel about your plan," he said through a mouthful.

"It's very simple really," said Merlin. "I have suggested that Burhred adopt you and name you as his heir. We'll have your name legally changed to Elswith. Ethelbald and Judith will never know the difference. All they care about is getting control up here, and they will have it. All Burhred cares about is keeping his honor, and he will have that. Mercia and Wessex will have their alliance, and Alfred can get busy driving back the invaders. Everyone wins."

"Everyone but Elswith," Isabel said feeling guilty.

Merlin's expression grew serious. Looking from one to the other, he said, "I told you, Elswith has made her own bed. We would never do this to her on purpose." He rose up as if he had been struck by lightning. "That's not it, is it? You don't think I did this to her?"

"I don't know what you can do," admitted Alfred. "I know how badly you wanted us to be together, and now I know that at least some of your reasons were your own."

Merlin looked indignant. "Boy, drive that thought from your mind. I use magic, for lack of a better term, when I see fit. But I would never intentionally do that to anyone. I didn't need to. She did it to herself." He looked back at Isabel. "I am not pleased about what has happened, no matter how it seems. But in this situation, the most helpful thing we can do is solve Burhred's problem as well as our own."

"He agreed to this?" asked Isabel, suspicious.

"Not exactly," Merlin admitted, "but he agreed to consider it. He wants to meet you and evaluate your worth as a daughter."

"I don't know, Merlin," Isabel replied, shaking her head. "I've just found my real parents. I don't know that I want to give you up."

"In truth, child, you will always be ours. Nothing, not even a distance of a thousand years could change that," he said tenderly, touching her face. "But it is also true that we bear no relationship to you physically. Your body is not the one originally intended to house your essence, but it is the body you have. And in our time, that body has no parents."

Isabel was struck by the insensitivity of the statement, and then surrendered to its veracity. She wondered if they were even asking for her agreement. It seemed the only solution, and, in spite of the terrible thing that had happened to Elswith, it was the solution they had been looking for. "So now we do what?"

"We eat, and we rest. Alfred and I have been up all night, and we need to be clear-headed if we are going to pull this off. Later today you will put on your finest, and we will go together to meet the king. Then we will trust in God and your charming personality," he said with a smile.

Isabel smiled back. Her finest. She only had one nice dress. She looked to Morgan who gave her a nod of confidence.

When Alfred and Merlin woke up from their rest, they found a princess standing before them. Morgan had given her another blouse, one with golden thread woven through the white fabric which not only made it look richer, but also caught the sunlight and made her seem to sparkle. It was beautiful under the pale blue gown she had brought from Kathryn. Morgan had tamed her hair and pulled it back with a matching blue ribbon so that it was off her face but still hung loose down her back. She had also given her a more formal-looking cloak to replace the old, dusty, worn-out one she had from Kathryn's son.

Isabel even felt beautiful, though she believed it was an illusion. Her confidence made her stand straighter and hold her chin up a bit so that she naturally looked more regal.

"I believe we are ready," said Merlin.

"Yes," replied Alfred, mesmerized by the vision of Isabel. "We are ready."

They left Morgan with hugs and thanks and rode to the castle. They had to go more slowly, as Isabel was not accustomed to riding in a skirt. Sidesaddle was uncomfortable for her, and she never got beyond the feeling that she was about to topple off.

Freawyn was patient, however, and set the pace for the other two, more restless horses.

The three of them found Burhred in his great hall, surrounded by advisors whose advice was useless to him. He was obviously a man in great despair, and those around him were dejected over his unwillingness to make decisions or act. Alfred and Merlin arrived, and he dismissed everyone else. "I will speak with these people alone," he commanded..

When the room was clear, he said, "So, this is the woman you would have be my daughter."

"Yes, my lord," Merlin replied.

"Come here, child," Burhred said holding out his hand. "Let me see you better." He squinted to look at her, and Isabel thought he probably needed glasses, except that they hadn't been invented yet. He grabbed her arm and stopped her when she came into focus. "Hmmm," he said, "you are not so beautiful as my Elswith, but you are not displeasing either. Perhaps you would rather be my wife than my daughter."

This was so unexpected that Alfred almost lunged at the king, Isabel gasped and even Merlin swayed a bit. Merlin came to his wits first. "That would not solve the problem of your alliance with Wessex," he said taking a deep breath.

The king looked disappointed. "That is true. It's a shame though. Sometimes it's the plain ones that please a man most."

Alfred clinched his fists and bit his bottom lip. Isabel smiled at him to let him know she was all right. She could handle this. He relaxed a little, but still looked as if he would like to thrash the old man, who had obviously learned nothing from his daughter's tragedy.

"So what do you have to offer me as a daughter?" Burhred asked.

"What do you mean, sir?" Isabel asked, not sure of what he wanted.

"If I make you my daughter and use this lie to make an alliance with Wessex, will you see to the interests of your adopted country? Or will you immerse yourself in the frivolity of life at court and forget us entirely?"

Isabel considered this. She knew nothing about his country and its people. How could she serve their interests if she didn't know what those needs were? What exactly would her responsibilities be? They were all silent, giving her a chance to ponder the question. Merlin and Alfred tensely awaited her response, and Burhred was pleased with himself at being smart enough to catch her off guard.

"I don't know much about your country," she said thoughtfully, "but I know that Alfred holds it in high regard. I believe it would serve both you and him if I spent time learning about its history and its people. Then, yes, I could represent Mercian interests to Wessex. That is if Wessex is willing to listen to my opinion." She smiled at Alfred slyly, and he visibly relaxed.

Burhred was impressed. "And what of me? How will you honor me as your father?"

"It seems to me that the best way to do you honor is by being the best person that I can." She added, "And of course, I should always revere you as the absolute king of Mercia. Alfred and I would always defer to your wishes in matters of importance."

Burhred was flattered, but not entirely convinced. "Let me look more closely at your eyes. Your words are the right ones, but are they true?"

He pulled her face right down to his. He was unshaven and his breath smelled of old garlic and decay. Isabel wasn't sure she could stand it, but she tried hard to breathe through her mouth and hold his gaze.

He released her and looked at Merlin. "I see no deception in her, wizard. Is that some trick of yours?"

"I have done nothing," Merlin replied holding up his hands as though showing they had nothing to hide. "She is as she is with no interference from me."

Next Burhred turned to Alfred. "You have been quiet back there. Are you hiding something?"

Alfred moved forward. "I am not. It is no secret that I did not favor your daughter, but I was prepared to do my duty. This woman, however, has touched me with her honesty and her wisdom. She will serve us both well."

"What of your parents, child?" he asked Isabel.

"I have none," she said. I'm not really lying, she thought. My physical parents will not be born for a thousand years.

"Where do you come from then?"

Isabel looked at Merlin, unsure how to answer.

"She lived long with no family, growing up alone," Merlin said without hesitation. "Lady Kathryn of Eastlea took her in and is as a mother to her. She has no right nor any inclination to contest an adoption."

The king sighed and appeared to be thinking deeply, looking at each of them in turn, and trying to detect any deceit or malice. "What shall be the nature of this adoption?"

"Your paper can state simply that you are adopting this woman as your daughter and making her your heir. I suggest that we officially change her name to Elswith, so that the king of Wessex will have no reason to question the sudden appearance of another child. This will also protect the dignity of your daughter, so that no one will try to find out what happened to her and discover her state."

This last statement saddened the old king, and Isabel moved to rest her hand on his shoulder. "I am sorry about your daughter," she said kindly.

Burhred patted her hand, touched by her sincerity. He called in his secretary to draw up the paper of adoption. "Say this," he said so all could here, "On this day, Burhred, king of all Mercia, commands that henceforth Isabel of Eastlea shall be known as Elswith of Mercia. The king adopts this woman as his child and heir from this time forth and forever more." The secretary wrote slowly then offered the paper to the king for his signature and wax seal. The paper passed to Isabel. "You must sign it, too," he said, "so that none other may claim this adoption to be his or her own."

"Yes, sir," Isabel said, obediently, "Which name do I sign?"

"Both, one right under the other," the king replied, "so that anyone who sees this will have no doubt that Isabel of Eastlea and Elswith of Mercia are the same person."

Isabel did as she was told. Overwhelmed by the suddenness and importance of what had happened, she swayed unsteadily and was relieved when Alfred stepped up behind her so that she could lean against him.

"Now," the king sighed addressing his secretary. "Take that paper and make a copy which we can also sign, then hide them away, one at the monastery and one at the abbey." The acquisition of another child had no effect on him. "Now let us take care of this marriage and put this matter behind us. I'll call for the bishop right now."

Everyone was surprised when Alfred spoke up. "I do not want to be married here, Burhred," he said with a commanding tone. "You are getting what you want from us, but I also want something. I will take her to the monastery. We can do this there as easily as here. The abbot there can marry us in the view of your magnificent mountains."

In spite the commanding tone of Alfred's statement, Burhred was proud of the beauty of Mercian countryside. "Agreed. We will go to the monastery." He looked down at the secretary who had finished the second copy. "We will sign this while you send a boy to fetch my horse."

"Yes, lord," said the secretary bowing out.

The four of them rode to the beautiful monastery in the mountains. Isabel realized that anxiety and exhaustion had prevented her from appreciating them the first time around. Now they were aglow with the setting sun, the trees in their fall colors shining red, gold, orange, purple, brown and evergreen against the darkening but perfect blue sky.

The abbot dashed out from his dinner, flustered at their unexpected arrival and even more so by their demand to be married immediately. He rushed to get his book of prayers and ceremonies and met them outside where he could barely read in the light of the setting sun. When he pulled Alfred and Isabel to stand before him, and rested his hand on theirs joined together, he became calm, and smiled. "God is smiling on you, children. I can feel the power of His love in your union." He took a breath and began, "We are here to celebrate the marriage of this man, Alfred of Wessex, and this woman, Elswith of Mercia." He paused for a moment, realizing that this was not the Elswith he knew, but a look from King Burhred told him to say nothing and continue. "Marriage is a holy state, a joining made by God Himself, which can be set asunder by no man. Alfred, do you understand this?"

Alfred answered, "I do."

"Elswith, do you understand this?"

"I do."

"Do you Alfred, accept this woman, Elswith, to be your wife? Do you grant her all the rights and privileges that go with that station? Do you agree to provide for her living, to care for her illness, and to share with her the bounty of your success? Do you promise to keep yourself only for her as long as you both live?"

Alfred smiled and looked down at Isabel, "I do."

"Do you, Elswith, accept this man, Alfred, to be your husband? Do you promise to care for him and serve him in whatever way he requires? Do you promise to be wise with his wealth and protect the bounty of his success? Do you promise to keep yourself only unto him for as long as you both live?"

Isabel, returning Alfred's gaze, answered, "I do."

"Let it now be known that from this moment forward to the end of their lives, Alfred of Wessex and Elswith of Mercia are husband and wife. May God bless their holy union. Amen."

Alfred pushed the hair off Isabel's face and cupped it in his hands. "I love you," he said and kissed her softly.

Tears spilled out of Isabel's eyes and her heart swelled to bursting in her chest. "I love you," she whispered and closed her eyes as her husband leaned in to kiss her again.

Beth Warstadt

Beginning Again

Alfred's room in the castle was barely recognizable from three months before. True, his armor was still piled in the corner. His desk still sat to one side of the fireplace, and it was still covered with papers and pens and jars of color paste.

Now, however, the cold, bare walls were hung with tapestries. Chairs were gathered around the fireplace, and a large red rug covered the earthen floor. The rug warmed the room considerably and served as a sleeping mat for two large dogs. The dogs were curled up together in the early morning gathering the last bit of heat from embers that had been a roaring fire the night before. A basket filled with canvases and brightly colored yarn rested on the floor by the chair closest to the desk.

The monk's cot had been replaced with a bed large enough for two, newlyweds who were waking from a sound night's sleep. Their bodies were so completely entwined it seemed as though only one person huddled under the abundant bed clothing.

Alfred nuzzled the back of Isabel's neck, causing her to settle more deeply against him. "Good morning," he whispered into her hair.

"Mmmmm. Good morning." She idly stroked the arm that he had thrown over her. As she became more wakeful, she realized what day it was and sighed. "Do you have to leave today?"

Alfred lifted her hand and examined it, measuring its smallness against his larger one, weaving their fingers together. "You know that I do."

She squirmed suggestively and said in a teasing voice, "Isn't there anything I can do to make you stay?"

"Stop," he choked out, embracing her more tightly to hold her still. "You have your father's magic in you, and you are trying to work it on me. You are trying to make me forget my duty."

"And this is a bad thing?"

"Isabel," he said in a pleading tone.

"I know. I'm teasing." She knew what had to be done, but that didn't mean she liked it. "How long do you think you will be gone?"

Relaxing since she had let up on her seduction, Alfred started playing their fingers together again. "I'm not sure," he said honestly. "There's a lot to do up there."

"Take me with you. I don't have to be on the battlefield. I can stay in the castle with the king, and you can come there whenever you get the chance. I promised Burhred I would get to know his country. This would be a good opportunity."

He pulled her over to face him. "No, I want you here. You are safer here."

She smirked. "Are you sure about that?"

He sighed. "I know. Judith hasn't exactly welcomed you."

"I'm telling you," Isabel said, "that Judith is a real piece of work. And she hates me. She must have wanted you bad. It's a good thing she can't shoot lasers out of her eyes or you would be a widower."

"Lasers?"

"Never mind. Let's say that if looks could kill, I'd be dead."

"You have to stay out of her way."

"I know. I'm going to spend as much time as I can with Kathryn. I don't think Judith or Ethelbald will mind very much if I am gone."

"That's a good idea. Brother Cuthbert has already agreed to go down there with you and help you with your reading and writing."

"Reading and writing," Isabel said, trailing off.

"What?"

"I am a college graduate. Now I am learning to read and write again."

"You're learning fast. Soon you'll be the teacher instead of the student."

"I know, and I do enjoy it, it's only that…my life is so odd."

Alfred chuckled. "What do you mean?" he asked though he already knew the answer.

"Three months ago I was a mousy little librarian with no life and bad hair. A thousand year old man—a gorgeous thousand year old man," she kissed him lightly, "walks in, takes my breath away and persuades me to time travel…get that, time travel…with him and be his wife. I find out that my real father is a wizard, an alien from another universe, and then I'm almost killed by another wizard who hates me even though I'd never seen him before in my life. I'm adopted by a king, married to a prince and…voilá…I'm a princess, passionately in love, huddling under the covers with her handsome prince in a medieval English castle." She gave a little laugh and shook her head, "Go figure."

He pulled her to him and tucked her head under his chin. She had almost dozed off again, when he said, "Now it seems like none of that happened, doesn't it? Like it was all some kind of dream. Like we went straight from being born to being here, as it was supposed to be. I can hardly remember what it was like to be without you. It is as if someone merely told me about it."

She nodded against his chest. "I know. It's hard to think of who I was before, or even *that* I was before. It seems as though I simply began again, and everything that happened before I met you has been wiped away. There is no past, only now, only the future." She opened her eyes and pulled back to look up at him. "We do have the future, hear me? Be careful when you are out there on the battlefield. We have things to do."

"I'll be careful," he promised, "more careful than I ever was before." He pulled her back into a tight embrace, "Now I have a reason to come home.

Beth Warstadt has a life-long love of reading and writing. When she discovered there was actually a college major for that, her path was set. She got her BA and MA degrees in English at Emory University, and then worked fourteen years selling college textbooks. On her fortieth birthday she decided that if she was going to have a writing career she had better get on with it, and the result of that journey is the publication of Soul Lost and Megan's Christmas Knight, both available through amazon.com. She has two grown sons and lives in Suwanee, Georgia, with her husband, Steve, who is an optometrist. When she is not writing or reading, she enjoys movies, television, and cooking.

Visit Beth at her blog http://bethwarstadt.com/ or on Facebook at https://www.facebook.com/bethwarstadtauthor/ .

Also from Beth Warstadt

At her lowest, after making a devastating social blunder, Megan stands on the edge of the cliffs that offer her a final solution to her humiliation. She is shocked when a handsome stranger on a magnificent white horse whisks her back from the brink like a damsel in distress.

Nick helps and rescues people, but always holds himself apart, guarding his mysterious past. Things change when he meets Megan. Could she be the one to challenge his commitment to a lifetime alone?

Available in print and on Kindle from amazon.com.

Made in the USA
Columbia, SC
17 September 2023

23009448R00146